Susan Pleydell was the *nom de plume* of Isabel Senior, née Syme. She was born in 1907 into a well-to-do farming family at Milnathort, near Kinross. They moved to Dollar when she was in her teens, and later to another farm near Rumbling Bridge. She had great musical ability, inherited from her mother, and after a local education was sent to the Royal College of Music to study the piano. Later she taught at a girls' school in Bexhill at which time she was introduced to Murray Senior, then head of History at Shrewsbury School. They married in 1935. He had two headmasterships in the 1950s, one of a grammar school near Manchester until 1956, the other in South Wales. She taught the piano at Shrewsbury and for some years afterwards.

She had always been well read and having long had an urge to write began in earnest in the mid 1950s. It took a lot of effort to reach publication, but the first novel, *Summer Term*, eventually appeared in 1959. It makes full use of her experience in schools, as does its sequel, *A Young Man's Fancy* (1962). Her other eight novels, the last published in 1977, benefit from her experience in music, her Scottish background – and, of course, her own imagination, sympathy and powers of observation.

She died in 1986.

By the same author

Summer Term
A Festival for Gilbert
A Young Man's Fancy
The Glenvarroch Gathering
Good Red Herring
Griselda
Jethro's Mill
Brighouse Hotel
Pung of Dragons

THE ROAD
TO THE HARBOUR

SUSAN PLEYDELL

Greyladies

Published by
Greyladies
an imprint of The Old Children's Bookshelf

© Susan Pleydell 1966

This edition first published 2015
Design and layout © Shirley Neilson 2015

ISBN   978-1-907503-46-7

Set in Sylfaen / Perpetua
Printed and bound by the CPI Group (UK) Ltd,
Croydon CR0 4YY

THE ROAD
TO THE HARBOUR

CHAPTER 1

IN THE old days of leisure and lavish hospitality a surprising
number of distinguished people visited Balgarvie. The place
was remote, the journey from London long and arduous,
and the attractions, apart from some fine scenery, were of a
purely specialist kind. Balgarvie House was very large, very
cold and very ugly; the roads were bad; there was no neigh-
bouring society and the Garvie family owned and nurtured
one of the most famous sporting estates in Scotland and had
no ideas beyond it. But "sport" was the operative word.
The gentlemen—with or without their wives and daughters
according to the docility of these ladies—came for the
shooting, the fishing and the stalking, and it was one of
the things they liked about Balgarvie, they told each other,
that there was never any nonsense. No tennis or croquet
distracted the young men during the day, no dancing or flir-
tation kept them up late and sent them out in the morning
with heavy eyes and wavering guns.

Two world wars and social upheaval left the place
outwardly little changed, for the Garvies were a practical
race and adapted themselves and their property to the times.
The same or similar sportsmen still came but they now paid
a stiff price for the privilege. The House was more comfortable as a hotel run by an experienced manager than it had
ever been as a private dwelling, and the reigning laird,
Colonel Hector Garvie, lived in a small convenient
house nearby and saw to it that the game was there.
The permanent and local staff, indoor and out, was aug-
mented for the season by recruits from the universities and
public schools, and some of the gaiety—and nonsense—
lacking in the pre-commercial era came with them. But
it never disturbed the guests. Season after season they

1

returned, secure in the knowledge that everything would be as usual.

Both Colonel Garvie and Mr. Saunders the manager were a good deal startled to receive in the month of June—a very late date for booking—a request for accommodation from a single lady: A. Logan (Miss). Plenty of women are keen on sport—fishing most commonly—but a woman sufficiently strong-minded or dedicated to come to Balgarvie alone was unprecedented. Mr. Saunders, who carried a considerable mental picture gallery, looked inward, and nervousness at the thought of any spinster, young or old, floundering about the calm Balgarvie pool caused him to make a mistake.

"Perhaps," he suggested, "I'd better just tell her we're fully booked. We were till poor Mr. Prendergast passed away."

Colonel Garvie saw no pictures, not being given to it. He was puzzled, even a little uneasy, as he searched his memory for Logans, but he hated fibs. "We have a room," he said testily, "and this is a hotel. What harm can the woman do, poor thing?"

Mr. Saunders compressed his lips. As a rule the Colonel was happy to forget that he was not a host entertaining friends as his father and grandfather had done before him; but when he did fall into one of his rare inn-keeper moods it was no good arguing. One of the least desirable rooms, high up and remote, was reserved for Miss Logan, and she, all unconscious of her singularity, came.

She came on a Monday, a hot day towards the end of August, driving a smart newish convertible. Since the country was a sparsely populated area of mountains and moors, the narrow, unfenced road carried little traffic and any strange vehicle was an event. This one was memorable, and from Land-Rover and estate-wagon, beat-up jalopy and trades-man's van astonished faces stared at the cream-coloured car and the young woman driving it. The turnout was not exactly bizarre but it bore no imaginable relation to sport, agriculture, the hydroelectric or the fish trade, and the girl would have caught the eye in any setting.

As the car climbed the long winding pass which brought her within sight of her journey's end she was sitting up straight, even leaning forward a little, and at the top she rolled in to the side and switching off her engine got out. Balgarvie, the whole district, lay before and below her and she stood still beside the car looking at it for a moment before she strolled away on to the moor. She was a fairly tall, long-limbed girl with a figure which wore slacks and pullover with perfect decency and success, and in the August sunshine her colouring was spectacular. Her hair, though it was predominantly dark, had a generous proportion of gold, her eyes were gold-flecked hazel, and after days of driving an open car her skin had a smooth golden tan. Anthea Logan as a young girl had been a gawky creature with a face which was too individual—too intelligent, perhaps, and too humorous—for prettiness, but at twenty-eight she had grown-up to the long limbs and distinctive face and was beautiful. But though she knew she had become beautiful and was pleased about it, her interest in her looks was limited. She liked good clothes, but the first requisite was comfort and wearability so that once on they could be forgotten; and her grace of movement was a gift of God: she never thought about it.

Standing on the moor now with her hands in her pockets nothing was farther from her thoughts than her own appearance in such a setting. Her whole self was absorbed in the setting itself. Behind her and to her left, which was the north, were the high peaks and forests, a soft intense blue and a dramatic skyline. All round was the heather of the moors and in front of her, five or six miles away, was the sea. The silence of the empty hill country was more than

3

the absence of noise, it had a positive quality which small natural sounds—bees in the heather or the cry of a grouse—enhanced. And there was the indescribable highland smell . . . heather, honey, hills; fresh water not far away and a faint tingle from the sea.

The human population was confined almost entirely to two groups of buildings in front of her to the east: Balgarvie House, boldly turreted and baronial, with out-buildings and a spatter of cottages, and, a mile or so beyond it on the coast, Balgarvie village. From this distance the village was a compact little grey unit dominated by its church steeple, as simple and complete as a toy. The land here fell down to the sea in steep grassy slopes coloured with bracken and a scattering of heather, and to the right, perhaps a quarter of a mile from the village, a small solitary red roof was just visible over the hill. To this tiny red spot Anthea's eyes kept returning with a narrowed long-distance stare, intent and serious, and finally she sat down on a patch of dry grass—of the same pale honey colour as her corduroy slacks —and lit a cigarette. She was not ready to arrive at Balgarvie.

Now that it was so close she was, in fact, dreading her arrival. There is danger in meeting a friend—even more a lover—after a lapse of time, and there is the same danger in returning to a beloved place: danger of disillusionment, of finding oneself unwelcome. Eight years ago she had spent some weeks at Balgarvie, and though at the time she had only known that it had taken hold of her and she loved it as she had not imagined one could love a place, they had, as it happened, been her last weeks of young, unclouded happiness. In the hard years that followed, Balgarvie had been her strength, her guarantee that there were still nice things in the world, but with the end of the long road in sight she sat on the grass, knees up and arms resting on them, wondering if she had been a fool. What, after all, did she

4

know of Balgarvie? She knew that it was a plain little village surrounded by beautiful country and it had hidden treasure in the shape of a harbour and a fishing fleet—literally hidden: you couldn't see it till you were there. How much had she idealised it? And was there anything real—solid—in her belief that it was the place where she could recover from the hard years, learn to see them in proportion and begin again? Rehabilitation was the word. She was twenty-eight years old and alone, bereft of parents, brother and lover, without even close friends. But she had talent and—it had been well proved—guts, and she was free. . . .

Anthea ground her cigarette out carefully and got up. *She* had no doubts: Balgarvie was where she wanted to be, to live and work for the next stage and establish herself as a person. What was still unknown was whether Balgarvie was willing, and it was time to call up faith and courage and find out.

She went back to her car and drove on, downhill now, passing the gates of the House without a glance. As she approached the village there was nothing to suggest that it was in any way different from a hundred other Scottish villages. There was the grey street, which in the morning smelled deliciously of new bread: there were the church, the modest primary school, two dull pubs, six or eight shops and the solid houses of the Minister, the doctor and the vet. Anthea parked her car at the end of the street farthest from the church and glancing along its uneventful length felt a remembered thrill of glee and delight. It kept its secret so well!

One road, for the use of vans and fuel tankers, approached the harbour sideways. The direct approach for able-bodied pedestrians was one or other of the wynds— narrow paths, so steep that they had to become staircases now and then, between the houses. Even from the top of the Water Wynd little could be seen except a huddle of roofs and the open sea, but from all directions boats were coming and Anthea ran down quickly, past front doors and gable ends, and took a deep breath of the salty, fishy smell of the quay.

Balgarvie Bay was a shallow semicircle. From the northern tip an ancient stone pier with a light on the end of it pointed south, and breakwaters, more modern structures, sheltered the inner basin. The sea this afternoon was calm and blue, the houses crowding up the steep hillside were white, pink or grey, old red tiles glowing on many of the roofs and by contrast giving colour to the commoner purple-grey slates. On the quay and the breakwaters heaps of pastel-coloured net lay about, and the fishermen, working with neat economy of movement, wore oilskins of bright yellow or pale blue, or windcheaters of lovely faded red. In the foreground were great fuel tanks and an ugly functional building which was the fish-market, constituting what has been called a refreshing eyesore and demonstrating Balgarvie's indifference to the picturesque.

Anthea added another and a foreign note of colour, but nobody, apparently, saw her. There was no hostility, no feeling that she was being deliberately ignored, only a rather comfortable sensation of invisibility. She stood for a while beside the fish-market to watch *Ocean Harvester* and *Sea-Farer* unloading, *Embrace* and *Crimond* backing and sidling to their moorings, and *Lea-Rig* coming quietly in through the gap between the breakwaters, its crew in pale blue and a gull riding on the mast. Then she walked along to the old pier where she could look back on the whole scene.

Nothing had changed. The boats and their names were familial, and the unexpected richness of colour. And the sounds were the same. There was hardly a human voice to be heard, but the winches on the boats unloading clanked as they brought the catch up from the holds, the boxes of ice-packed fish banged down on the stones and were dragged or wheeled, scraping or rattling, into position in the market, and gulls screamed as they circled and dived. Small boys scrambled about the boats to hitch a ride across the harbour and a baby staggered to meet an oil-skinned man who picked it up and carried it away, a string of fish dangling from his free hand. She looked for and found the tiny bakery which made ambrosial gingerbread with nuts in it, and a general store which she connected with bulls'-eyes of uncommon power: then, to her left, her eyes followed a path which wound away up a steep grassy slope to the house whose roof she had just been able to see when she stopped the car at the top of the hill. It was an old croft, whitewashed, with a modest byre and shed built on, which looked as if it had grown out of the hill-side. She could see almost nothing of the house itself, but she saw her memory of it clearly: a dilapidated cottage, waiting, surely, to be bought or rented for a song and gradually, lovingly restored—like herself, in fact, rehabilitated.

Anthea smiled, amused and relieved. Her imagination had not deceived her, memory had not exaggerated. Balgarvie was her destination, peculiarly her own place, and to-morrow she would come back to the harbour and begin the process of taking root. Now she must go and check in at the hotel. As she turned, still smiling, and walked back along the pier, a tall elderly man with tidy grey hair came towards her, strolling with hands clasped behind him. Their eyes met with the friendly interest of strangers who recognise in each other a common enthusiasm, and as they passed they nodded and murmured a greeting.

When Mr. Saunders received Miss Logan the uneasiness he had felt about her all along was confirmed. She was too young, too striking—she looked disturbing. She was not the Balgarvie type and it was clear from her manner that she did not know about Balgarvie House. She thought it was an ordinary hotel. And what could conceivably have brought her here without gun or rod or even golf clubs? He smiled, as was his duty, with a discreet display of teeth and the hope that she would find everything satisfactory, giving thanks as he did so that his managerial instinct had prompted him to allot to her that undesirable room and with a vindictive little thought for Colonel Garvie. This would teach the Colonel a lesson and, with luck, put an end to the inn-keeper.

The remote room, in fact, delighted Anthea. One of the turrets bulging out from a corner afforded views of both sea and hills, and she did not mind the stairs. Though Colonel Garvie and the House itself had been equally resistant to modernisation two things had been forced upon them: visitors who paid demanded interior springs, and they were not content, as visitors used to be, to queue for baths. Even this least desirable room boasted a modern bed and a bathroom—a vast, oddly shaped apartment which made Anthea giggle. Over heavy, old-fashioned furniture and faded carpet, outraged ghosts of bedroom china and hot-water cans shrouded in flannel seemed to hover, and a small maid in a black frock and white apron appeared like an apparition from the past. Blushing she announced herself as Peggy the chambermaid and inquired in a soft whispering voice if Miss Logan would be wanting anything. Well—aim—if she did want anything she would mebbe give the bell a ring. . . . With a bashful glance she withdrew, carrying with her, for the edification of her colleagues, an accurate and detailed picture of the new guest and all her visible belongings.

Anthea whistled as she unpacked and bathed. The lovely day, the boats coming in just when she was there to see, and now this comic but so comfortable old house and the promise of a good dinner for which she was very ready—surely the omens were good. When she was dressed she looked at herself in the mirror, approving her green frock as a very nice piece of understatement, and then, catching sight of her pleased, expectant face, she laughed aloud. "Ass!" she said and scowled warningly at the reflection. "Just don't get carried away. You're not home and dry yet—not quite. But now for the flesh-pots. I wonder where the bar is. . . ."

Picking up her handbag she set out on the journey to the hotel's public rooms. It was a long one. Downstairs, two long flights; turn right into a dark passage which stretched before her like a tunnel. She was half-way along, in the darkest part, when she heard quick footsteps behind her.

"Hey!" hissed a voice in a curious kind of muted shout. "What do you think you're doing? You're late—*Gotcha!*" Hands grasped her by the shoulders, twirled her round and a kiss, hearty rather than impassioned, landed squarely on her mouth.

Anthea's emotions did not naturally explode into sound. The instant of sheer astonishment was silent, and then it was her assailant who exclaimed.

"*God!*" He dropped his hands and backed weakly against the wall. "Oh God! I say, I'm most frightfully sorry! I thought—I don't know how to apologise—I thought you were someone else, you see—I'm most frightfully sorry. . . ."

He was a very young man—a boy, thought Anthea: nineteen or twenty, dark, slight and horrified. It was perfectly obvious that he had thought she was someone else, and she broke into his stammering. "It's all right," she said. "There isn't much light."

"No, but—" he peered at her anxiously, "—I mean I was absolutely certain you were—the other person. You're not a bit like her in *front*, but from behind you were exactly—"

She laughed and said she thought any thinnish female back would look exactly like any other in this tunnel. "But don't worry. It wasn't such a terrible experience. Rather a nice kiss, really."

9

The young man, who had been quite pale with dismay, blushed. "Well—I'm glad of that," he said and grinned faintly. The mists and dizziness began to clear and he looked at her with amazement. Who could she be? His eyes went to her left hand. Nobody's wife. Somebody's gorgeous daughter? But whose . . .? "If you're not joining up with your friends immediately," he ventured, "would you have a drink with me? To restore our shaken nerves . . .?"

Anthea said cheerfully that she had no friends to join up with and would be delighted. They emerged from the passage into the hall. It was very lofty and very large with a profusion of bays, nooks and lobbies, and from the walls, heads of dead animals and portraits of dead Garvies stared with glassy detachment. "It's really magnificent, isn't it— in its way?" said Anthea. "So confident . . ." and the boy, with a quick glance at her amused face, agreed. He was recovering his poise. In a manner which she heartily approved he made no more apologies, and dismissing any lingering embarrassment proceeded as if their acquaintance had begun—rather promisingly—in the conventional way. His name was Lawrence Vine, he told her as they made their way towards the bar at the far end of the hall near the dining-room, and when she said, "Anthea Logan" in response to a polite, unspoken inquiry he looked surprised and then amused.

"Oh you're Miss *Logan*," he said. He gave an involuntary laugh and explained. The Vines, his parents and himself, were Balgarvie regulars and the Laird had confided to them his mystification about Miss Logan. "We dreamed up a sort of picture of a mighty huntress—you know, the kind who goes off into the jungle accompanied only by a handful of loyal natives." A sidelong glance commented cautiously on the inappropriateness of the picture. "Are you, in fact, a keen sportswoman?"

"No," said Anthea. "I couldn't be less keen on sport—or on loyal natives, for that matter." He appeared to be a little nonplussed and she added, "It isn't a condition of entry, I hope?"

"Oh—there's no rule. But of course there isn't much else. . . . What will you drink?" They had reached the bar and with a comprehensive gesture he presented the array of bottles and the white-coated barman. "This is Morgan—everybody's pal. Miss Logan has just arrived, Morgan, and I nearly knocked her out in the tunnel. She needs a stiff pick-me-up."

"Och Lawrence! Will you never learn to look where you're going?" responded the barman unexpectedly. He fixed eloquent, rather plaintive eyes on Anthea. "How do you do, Miss Logan. I'm sorry you had such a rough welcome to Balgarvie. What can I get you? Sherry? Or would it need to be something stronger—more medicinal? Lawrence is a toothpick of a boy but you're not so massive yourself."

Anthea looked at him. He was a hefty young man with a lot of vigorous hair and a consciously irresistible look, but Laurence seemed to be taking the personal tone as a matter of course and the brashness could be accidental. She said pleasantly that the encounter had not been so violent as to call for restoratives, and chose a dry sherry.

Though Morgan would clearly have been delighted to continue the conversation à trois, Lawrence picked up the drinks and moved at once to a table some distance away. "Cigarette?" he said, and when they had lit up and were settled he resumed the development of the acquaintanceship. "Do you sketch?"

"Sketch? Oh. . . ." She laughed. "No, I'm afraid I'm non-sketch too. I'm sorry if it worries you."

"Oh it doesn't worry *me*." He made a gesture with his cigarette, signifying broad-mindedness. "But the Laird will be concerned. He won't feel you're getting your money's

11

worth unless you're actively engaged in something he can put a name to. Nobody ever does come, you see, except for the sport."

He added the explanation apologetically, in case he had sounded as if he were probing, and she smiled. "I know all about the sport," she said. "I've been to Balgarvie before. But I really don't want to do anything but walk about and look at the harbour."

"Ah!" The exclamation was one of satisfaction and the lively dark eyes looked at her with pleasure. "You're One of Us," said Lawrence.

She said, "I'm delighted. One of who?" and he made his spacious gesture again and relaxed. A tricky corner had been turned.

"Balgarvie just gets some people," he said. "Every year about Christmas I think I'll give it a miss this time—there are other places—and by March I'm sending agitated telegrams to my parents urging them to make sure of the bookings. I've an uneasy suspicion that I'll come every year of my life. It isn't enterprising."

"But then—don't you come to shoot or fish or something?"

"Yes, I do shoot and fish and get a stalk if I'm lucky, but I wouldn't much mind missing that. It is the place—the harbour." He glanced at her shrewdly. "Don't worry. I won't stop and call your attention to crow-stepped gables and out-size cod. But we're a minority group, you know. Nobody will believe you."

"I know," said Anthea. "I'm surprised you do. I don't mind though. I'm not applying for club membership."

"Still, it's always a pity to be labelled a nut-case," Lawrence thought. "Saves trouble if you can think up a plausible story." He considered. "Pity you don't sketch. Bird-watching? In the last resort you could say you're here for a bet, like the man who went for a walk in America."

12

His voice changed. "But—if you've been here before, why is the Laird suffering from bafflement?"

"I didn't stay in the hotel. I stayed at the Manse. The Minister's family—" she explained, "the McNaughtons—are sort of cousins."

"O-oh!" said Lawrence, a long sound of comprehension. "*That's* it! Senility hasn't set in after all." He looked at her with eyes full of mirth. "I thought you were Ness, you see."

"Ness?" Anthea stared at his pleased face. Behind him she saw the improbable hall of Balgarvie House and groups of drinkers, almost all men and most of them well past their first youth. Superimposed, somewhat incongruously, were the McNaughton children, Ness and Ian: a skinny, restless little girl and a smaller boy, square and placid. Of course they had grown up, but she had never really taken it in. "You thought I was Ness?" she said. "But that's ridiculous!"

"I assure you," Lawrence retorted gleefully, "you were exactly like Ness walking along that passage. Blood will out."

"But blood hardly comes in. We're such distant cousins. I don't know what kind we are."

"Can't help it. Your backs are alike—the way you walk and hold your heads." He went on looking at her, delighted that he had some excuse for his gaffe and delighted too, because her bewilderment brought her a little nearer to his own level.

"How do *you* know Ness?" she asked with a touch of asperity for his triumph.

"Why, she's here," he said, surprised. "She's one of the waitresses."

Anthea collected her wits. Ness would be about twenty. She was at one of the universities—Edinburgh, was it, or St. Andrews? Naturally she would have a job at the hotel.

"Ian's here too," Lawrence was saying. "He's a ghillie. But didn't they know you were coming? They haven't said anything about it."

"I expect they know," she said, "but it wouldn't be anything to talk about. They'll hardly remember me and I don't suppose I'd recognise them." She stopped and raised her eyebrows at Lawrence, who seemed to be struggling with inward laughter.

"I suppose," he said, "I ought to beg pardon again—a secondary apology—because it was your distant cousin I thought I was grabbing." Anthea said that was between him and her distant cousin and he laughed outright. "I don't know if it makes it better or worse, but the attack was not in the least amorous. When we were kids I used to pull her hair—while she hacked my shins—and now I kiss her because it annoys her more. She's very severe, is Ness, and she rises like a rocket. At least," he added rather regretfully, "she used to but this year her line is Christian fortitude. I merely get chid—chidden? Not chided, surely. . . ." He got to his feet as the door leading to the dining-room opened and a girl in a neat black and white uniform came through. "Here she is. Ness in person." And in the same muted shout with which he had hailed Anthea in the passage he hissed, "Hey! Ness!"

Ness McNaughton did resemble her distant cousin Anthea Logan in build and in the texture of hair and skin, but there the resemblance stopped. Her colouring was fairer, and her hair, in contrast to Anthea's, which had been cut by a master hand, was scraped up into a ruthless bun. The face below it was, as Lawrence had said, severe, and scorned even the modest weakness of a touch of powder, but the hair was not perfectly amenable to restraint, and as she turned in response to Lawrence's hail and saw Anthea she lit up with a smile which made it understandable that she got kissed in passages—and not solely for the purpose of annoying her. She passed a paper across the bar to Morgan, adding a more personal warmth to the smile as she did so, and came quickly towards them.

14

"Hul-*lo*, Anthea," she said in a voice muted like Lawrence's shouts. "Nice to see you again. When did you get here? I meant to ask about you but I haven't had a minute."

She was cordial but it was rather a dutiful cordiality and she did not come quite close, as if to repel any idea of a cousinly demonstration. Anthea, taking her cue, sat still as she replied that she had only arrived an hour or so ago.

"And the first thing that happened to her," Lawrence put in, "was that I grabbed her in the tunnel thinking she was you."

"Oh no! Poor Anthea!" Ness laughed, a silent laugh showing beautiful teeth. "Lawrence almost always is the first thing that happens to people in this place," she said to Anthea, and then to Lawrence, "but you *couldn't* have thought she was me. We're not a bit alike."

Lawrence said that if he hadn't thought so he wouldn't have grabbed. "From the back," he said obstinately, "you are alike. Not—alas, poor Ness!—from the front."

Miss McNaughton gave this piece of impertinence the treatment it deserved. She said, "Of course not," very coldly, and with heightened colour turned back to Anthea and asked if she had been to the Manse yet.

She hadn't had time, Anthea replied. "But I thought I'd go down after dinner—if that would be all right."

"Oh yes," Ness said. "Mummy's looking forward to see-ing you. She was half expecting you for supper, as a matter of fact, but I suppose as you're paying for meals here you may as well eat them. I won't be in myself, I'm afraid, and I shouldn't think Ian will be. You haven't seen Ian? You probably won't know him—he's huge—but you'll see him about outside. He's one of the ghillies."

Anthea was vividly reminded of what a pest her cousin Ness had been at the age of twelve. At that time a fervent patriot, her main topic of conversation with the English vis-itor was criticism of everything English, and it seemed doubtful if she had acquired much tact in the intervening years. Resisting the impulse to make excuses for not having gone to the Manse for supper she remarked amiably that the hotel must be a godsend and asked about the job. "Do they work you very hard? When do you finish in the evening?"

There was a perceptible stiffening. "Well, it depends. We take turns on the late shift," said Ness, and then, being scrupulously honest, added, "Actually, I'm not on late tonight. I'm going to listen to some music."

"Me too. Run you down if you like," said Lawrence and was struck by the idea that Miss Logan—Anthea—for whom he was falling in a big way, might like to listen to music too. She could go to the Manse any time. "Couldn't Miss—" he began, but the idea was promptly killed.

"She's going to the Manse," Ness said flatly. "I've got my bike, thanks. Look—I must fly. They're beginning to go in. I hope you'll be comfortable, Anthea. Are you staying long?"

"I'm not sure," said Anthea.

"Oh. Well—see you, I expect. . . ." There was another smile, brief and mechanical, and she hurried away.

Anthea looked after the erect black-and-white figure. Was this just Scotch brusqueness? Or had she been snubbed?

"It's all right," said the voice of Lawrence Vine, English and apologetic, "you haven't got halitosis." And he added with slightly reluctant justice, "As a matter of fact, if you had she'd be sweet to you."

CHAPTER 2

IF Anthea had cherished any social ambitions with regard to Balgarvie House she would have recognised in young Lawrence Vine an invaluable acquaintance. He combined the comprehensive information of an observant child living in grown-up company—which was very much the position he occupied in the hotel—with considerable social *nous*, and he was not without influence. His father, Sir Francis, was the head of an ancient family banking firm, of the exotic kind that has nothing to do with cashing cheques for the public, and the Vines were very well established.

There were about thirty guests in the hotel, most of them regulars, and they, along with Mr. Saunders, who knew his job, and Colonel Garvie, functioning by instinct, maintained the tone somewhere between that of an Edwardian house-party and a very exclusive club. Like Mr. Saunders, Lawrence perceived that Miss Logan had blundered in expecting to find herself in an ordinary, or fairly ordinary, hotel, and he was astute enough to know that however detached she might feel she would have a smoother ride if she knew her way about. To this end he devoted the few minutes after Ness left them, placing his gifts along with his heart at her feet.

To Anthea the company looked wonderfully dull. The bishop without his mitre, the judge without his wig were indistinguishable from the politicians or the surgeon, soldiers or big business. The ladies were merely a small flock of wives. But as Lawrence talked, casually and entertainingly putting her wise, individuals began to emerge. First the foreigners: every year they got a few of those. He invited her to observe the French gentlemen near the bar. All three were reputed to be millionaires, but they could neither speak English nor shoot very well and their bag to-day had been described as "the whole two children snip".

"*What?*" Anthea ejaculated. "Oh—snipe! But why have they come if they can't shoot? Don't tell me *they're* drawn by the harbour."

"Oh no," said Lawrence. "They don't know it's there. Hardly anybody does, fortunately." And he went on to tell her, with an ineffable air of grandeur, that she didn't appreciate the status value of Balgarvie. It was worth quite a push—and some suffering. The Americans were doing better. He led her eyes to a large important man who was talking steadily to everyone within reach. That was Senator Simpson Cleever, a notorious foot-and-mouth type and a prize bore but he could shoot. The two younger chaps with him were aides—bodyguards or secretaries or something. The other youngish character—not the scornful one, the keen, perfectly tailored type—was in the Foreign Office, name of Peachey. He was a Balgarvie regular and always very conscientious about foreigners. Nobody else took any notice of them.

"Only one Scot in the whole boiling," said Lawrence. "There. . . ." He pointed discreetly and Anthea saw the tall old man who had been at the harbour. Catching sight of her he gave her a polite little bow with his pleasant lightening of expression, and she explained, "We met on the pier."

"Oh yes—he's One of Us. He's often down there and he knows everybody. His father was the Minister here about a hundred years ago and he was born in the Manse. Sir Andrew Gibb. He used to govern bits of the Empire. He's a sportsman too—a wonderful shot. A dear old boy."

It was at this point that a relaxed, alert-looking man and a dark-eyed woman came towards them and Lawrence got up, summoning them with a peremptory wave, and introduced her to his parents. A moment later Colonel Garvie found her. It had dawned on the Laird of Balgarvie early in his commercial career that the flexible hour or so before dinner was a good time to mingle with his clients. Pleasantly tired and relaxed after hot baths they were ready to talk about to-day's sport and plan to-morrow, and whisky flowed freely in every sense of the word. And the habit of courteous hospitality, which would never leave him till the end of his life, led him to welcome personally each new-comer to his House.

He approached, an upright, capable, limited man in a faded kilt, and Anthea turned smiling to meet his bow and outstretched hand. "Miss Logan?"

"How do you do, Colonel Garvie," she said. "You won't remember me but I remember you very well. My cousin, Mr. McNaughton, brought me to the House once, years ago."

"Oh indeed? You're a cousin of McNaughton's?" Enlightenment and the satisfaction felt by every Scot in discovering that a new acquaintance is related to somebody brightened the Colonel's eyes and were followed by visible astonishment that any relation of the Minister had enough money to stay in Balgarvie House. He apologised for having failed to remember her, though he had some excuse, he said gallantly, for if it was years ago she couldn't have been very big. "But I'm surprised McNaughton didn't speak of it."

"When did the Minister last have a chance to speak to you?" asked Sir Francis Vine.

"Well, not just lately, it's true," he confessed. "When the season's coming on, you know, Miss Logan, I'm not so regular at the church as I should be. Now—we can give you some sport, I hope. What's it to be? Fishing? McNaughton's a great man with a rod. . . ." But he was less disconcerted to hear that she was no sportswoman than he would have been five minutes earlier. He could not have explained why it was so, but though the local Minister was as ardent and expert a fisherman as the visiting bishop it was unlikely that any of his female relatives—even an unsuspected one with money—would be sporting women: which reminded him that he must tell Saunders. Nice thing if they had turned away the Minister's cousin. He tried golf. They had made a little nine-hole course, he said. Some of the ladies liked it.

"Me for one," Lady Vine said cheerfully, "when I can find anyone to play with. Any hope, Miss Logan?"

Anthea admitted that she did play and felt a little regret that she had not thought of bringing her clubs.

"Oh we'll find you some clubs," said Colonel Garvie, looking round as if he expected to put his hand on them there and then. "Morgan or Alec or one of them will see to it."

"Well, that's something," murmured Lawrence as they went towards the dining-room. "Not *good*, of course, but golf and the Minister should see you through."

"A low pass," said Anthea.

Mr. Saunders knew that it doesn't do to keep ravenous sportsmen waiting for their food and the Balgarvie dining-room was always amply staffed. Besides the head waiter and an experienced woman who was his permanent lieutenant, there were three girls in the smart black-and-white uniform and two young men. Morgan, who came in and out, combined his duties as barman with those of runner to the wine-waiter.

Anthea, watching everything as she ate hare soup, local prawns and delicate hill mutton, thought how well the students did their job. They were efficient and quick to respond. If guests liked silent impersonal service they got it, if they enjoyed respectful friendliness they got that, and the whole room was made pleasant by their young good looks and manners. She saw Lady Vine smile at Ness and include her in the conversation and heard the dark, urbane young man who waited on the French party make them laugh with a French joke. Mr. Peachey of the Foreign Office, who had the sheen of polished steel, sat with his scornful friend and was discreetly jocular with a tall, very pretty blonde. The appetising little brunette who waited on Anthea herself was smiling and chatty, and, with the fair youth who talked to her in a gentle murmur about wine, prevented the feeling of being an outcast which is apt to assail the solitary diner. With what seemed rather excessive professional decorum Ness avoided looking at her; Morgan, coming and going, looked at her too often, but she was inclined to be envious of Lawrence, who was as much at home backstairs as he was in the front of the house. They must, she thought, have a lot of fun.

She would have been delighted if she had known what joy she had brought them. Though the jobs were good, Balgarvie House was uneventful. The clients were, on the whole, dull and the young staff were accustomed to making the most of even the slightest excitement. Miss Logan was by far the most hopeful material the season had so far offered.

"She really is quite gorgeous," said the tall blonde, sailing in to the servery. "And it's really very noble of me to admit it, considering the blow she is to my hopes. I hate to think what may happen to my confidence."

"Never mind, Louisa," said the fair youth. "You're not so plain yourself, and Mr. Peachey may prefer blondes." A kind of romantic serial was currently running, concerning Louisa's search for a rich husband, and she remarked sadly that Mr. Peachey's eyes kept straying in Miss Logan's direction.

"So do mine," said the dark young man on his way out. "So do Lawrence's. Old Morgan's are permanently fixed."

"Morgan'll get a rocket if he doesn't watch it," Louisa said with some satisfaction. Abandoning romance she began assembling her tray. "Is that hair dyed, Biddy?"

Anthea's brunette didn't know. "You're the expert."

"But I haven't got close enough to see. What's she doing *here*? Does she think it's Gleneagles?"

21

"Don't know. Ask Ness." Biddy picked up the tray with Anthea's mutton on it and added as Ness came in, "Louisa wants to know if Miss Logan dyes her hair."

Ness, without looking at anybody, said flatly that she didn't think so. "It's the same colour it used to be."

"How do you know? Has she been here before?"

"She's a cousin of sorts."

"A *cousin*? Of yours? Oh no!" Louisa's shriek was muffled but it carried a full content of glee and there were smiles on other faces. "But how lovely for you, Ness dear. Yes? No?"

"You get more Peachey every day," retorted Ness. "It doesn't make any difference to me." She turned to the hatch through which the chef's face peered grinning. "Lady Vine wants a small, Robbie. No fat."

"Will Miss Logan appreciate Morgan, do you think?" inquired Louisa of the company generally.

"Och, whisht, Louisa," said somebody as Ness coloured angrily.

"Gairls!" A sharp voice came from the door and the spectacles and grey perm of the lieutenant appeared. "Get *on*. It's you and not the guests that's supposed to be waiting, kindly remember. Louisa!"

"Okay, Ma. On my way," said Louisa and she sailed away, gracefully and smiling, bearing mutton for Mr. Peachey and his scornful friend.

Anthea did not wait for coffee. She fetched a coat and set out in search of the side door which led to the yard and garages.

It would have been quicker in the end to go out by the main door and round. Her room was in the east wing, the yard was on the west of the house and she found herself in a confused area of passages, stone-floored, dark and menacing: and once more she was overtaken by a gentleman, but not, this time, seized and kissed.

"For the side door," said a light resonant voice as she hesitated at a cross-roads, "the turning to the *left*. If an architect designed this mansion, which is hardly conceivable, he would, one feels, have given the psychologists food for thought. A tortuous mind, to put it mildly. I myself support the school which attributes the offence to some determined but bibulous Garvie doing it himself—But here we are. . . ." The door was reached and opened. Emerging into the light she saw sleek, colourless hair, a colourless face, and pale but far from vapid, eyes looking at her through well-polished spectacles. The steely charm of Mr. Peachey hit her. "My name," he said modestly, "is Peachey—Desmond Peachey. And you are Miss Logan. I know, because—" he made his confession with a laughing boyish glance, "I'm afraid I asked."

"How do you do," said Anthea.

"You can't imagine," he went on as they crossed the yard, "—yours is the white car, isn't it? I'm afraid you'll find the roads quite primitive. I keep an ancient jeep for these excursions. Can I drive you—? Ah—just to the village. I'm going in that direction too. A friend of mine—one of the writing tribe—has a place—As I was saying, you can't imagine how excited we all are about you."

"I heard that I had mystified poor Colonel Garvie," said Anthea. "But didn't you know the excitement is over? After all I'm no Diana—not even an international spy," she added, remembering the Foreign Office. "I'm just a relation of the Minister."

Mr. Peachey crowed delightedly. "Ha ha ha ha ha! Splendid! I'm so glad you're not a Diana—they do frighten me so badly—or a spy. That would have been a beautiful thrill for us, of course, but I fear Balgarvie would have proved a singularly unrewarding field."

He escorted her to her car and with swift flourishing gestures opened the door, throwing out as he did so a swarm

23

of baited hooks. He hoped the Manse wouldn't claim too much of her time: she mustn't think Balgarvie was dedicated to slaughter: did she know the country well? He ventured to say that he did—he adored it actually—and he would be delighted—his jeep was capable of anything short of rock-climbing. Had he heard something about golf . . .?

Anthea could only allow herself to be ushered into the driving seat, and, smiling weakly, murmur noncommittal responses. He hovered, scintillating, while she found the head-scarf which lived in the car and put it on, and she drove away at last feeling battered. She was out of practice in this sort of thing—slow on her returns.

Mr. Peachey's jeep followed her to the village, not too closely—he was far too efficient for that—but closely enough to keep her aware of him, and as she reached the street and turned left, he accelerated and saluted her with a playful fanfare on his horn as he turned right. Where, wondered Anthea, could a member of the writing tribe, sufficiently great to be a friend of Mr. Peachey, have found a "place" in Balgarvie?

A minute or two later she was being kissed by Mrs. McNaughton, who was Cousin Maud: a thin, bright-eyed woman rather worn down by perpetual conflict between a ruthless conscience and a warm, tolerant heart. The Manse, like the harbour, was unchanged. Anthea, smelling its individual blend of polish and soap with overtones of mothballs and church, had decided eight years ago that this was the odour of sanctity, and smelling it again now she had a vivid revival of her Manse feelings. Plain living and high thinking are admirable in themselves, but at the age of twenty she had felt vaguely guilty all the time she stayed in the Manse and she could very easily feel guilty again.

"I'm so glad," Cousin Maud was saying as she took her arm and led her to the drawing-room, "to have you to myself for a little. At least," she added scrupulously, "I would have liked the children to be here to welcome you, but we really see very little of them just now. Walter is visiting down at the harbour."

"Balgarvie must have widened its scope," said Anthea, referring to the absence of Ness and Ian. "I seem to remember that a film once a week was the extent of its night life."

"I don't think it has changed much," Mrs. McNaughton said doubtfully. "It hasn't even got the film now. But there are all these students at the hotel. They seem to find a lot to amuse them in the evenings."

"More than the guests, perhaps?"

Mrs. McNaughton had no views about the guests, but the children's absence was evidently a source of disquiet. It seemed a pity, she said, that they were not more content to stay quietly at home. "Cousin Walter thinks they waste so much time, but perhaps it's natural. Rather a pleasant man has come to—well, he isn't here all the time but I suppose one can say he lives here. He's very hospitable. They go there a lot. He has a wonderful collection of gramophone records, I believe."

There couldn't be two, thought Anthea and asked, "Is he a writer?"

"Yes," said Mrs. McNaughton, a little surprised, "he is a writer. But he's really very nice, I think. Do you remember that lonely little house with the red roof—the Tully? He bought—"

"*The Tully?*" To Anthea herself the involuntary exclamation sounded—and felt—like a shriek. Mrs. McNaughton apparently heard only the mild astonishment she might have anticipated.

"It is strange to think of anybody like that living there, isn't it?" she said. "It was such a miserable little place and it had been empty for a while. I don't think he paid more than

25

a hundred pounds for it, but they say he has made it very nice." Finished with the subject of the Tully she went straight on. "You've grown very pretty, Anthea dear. Let me look at you. . . ."

Anthea met kind, anxious eyes and forced a smile. "Art helps, Cousin Maud."

"Oh—" the eyes scrutinised her more closely, "but you don't look *made up* at all. I was just thinking you're too pale, dear. Come and sit here—by the window, I remember you liked our view—and tell me about your mother and—and everything."

There was a curious tension. Anthea sat down where she could see the view; a steeply sloping garden, a few hunched and oddly beautiful roofs and the sea. Mrs. McNaughton fussed about as though nervously reluctant to bring preliminaries to an end.

"I thought we'd wait and have coffee when Walter comes in—he won't be long. . . . Do you smoke, dear? I think Walter . . ." she opened a box with a college crest and peered in. "Yes. I hope they're all right. He only smokes a pipe, of course. . . ."

Anthea helped herself to one of three brownish, speckled cigarettes and Mrs. McNaughton replaced the box and sat down with an air of resolution.

"I was so glad you thought of coming to Balgarvie, Anthea dear, but I wish you were staying with us."

"It's so kind of you, Cousin Maud," said Anthea who was ready for this one, "but I thought if I stayed at the hotel I could see you without making extra work for you. And," she added with some firmness, "I wanted to be independent."

"Well," Cousin Maud admitted, "it is more of a rest, perhaps, *not* staying with friends, but I'm afraid the hotel is terribly expensive. You did ask?"

Anthea laughed. "Yes, I did, and it's certainly pretty steep. But it isn't for long."

"Of course you girls with professions are really very well off now, and I suppose your mother left you a little. But," Mrs. McNaughton was apologetic but she persisted, "it is a pity to waste . . . I could have got you a room at the post-office. . . ." She looked at Anthea's face, and her heart triumphed. "Still," she said more warmly, "perhaps it will do you good to be really comfortable—luxurious—for a little. Oh Anthea—I thought of you so much when your mother died! And of both of you when Randal and your father . . . I longed to come to you—both times. But it's so far to the south of England and Walter said—we both felt—what could we have done?"

"Mother was very tired of being alive, you know," Anthea said quietly.

Mrs. McNaughton looked at her for a moment in silence. "Yes," she said, "I expect she was." There was another pause. Tears trickled slowly over her thin cheeks and Anthea stared out of the window. "But," she went on, "it's over and you're young, darling. Your life is before you and you must look forward, not back."

Anthea turned quickly. The kind voice broke through the defensive reserve which had grown to be a part of her and which had been stiffened, first by Ness's curious antagonism and then by the disapproval of her staying in the hotel. "Cousin Maud," she said, "I'd like to tell you—" She stopped. Firm footsteps were crossing the tiled hall.

"Here is Cousin Walter," said Mrs. McNaughton and dried her eyes as the door opened and the Minister came into the room.

He was a spare stern man with a humourless face and nothing of his wife's air of being a battleground. "How are you, Anthea?" he said and gave her a hand-shake which she

27

remembered—painful but without warmth. "It's a long time since we have seen you."

"It's a long way, Cousin Walter," she replied. "But it's very nice to come back."

Mr. McNaughton said she was looking well and sat down.

"I'll get the coffee," said his wife. "No, Anthea, it's all ready to heat up. You sit still and talk to Cousin Walter."

Talking to Cousin Walter was easier said than done. Taking a pipe from his pocket he proceeded to fill it, slowly and in silence. Anthea took out her cigarettes and he glanced up.

"Match?"

"I have a lighter, thank you."

"M'h'm." His grunt and his expression as he returned to the pipe seemed to say that it was just as he had feared. "So you're at the House," he remarked after a moment. "That will cost you a bonny penny. It's very luxurious, no doubt. That will be your car outside, I suppose."

"Yes," said Anthea. Leaving aside the matter of luxury she agreed that the House was expensive. "But if I'd gone abroad I'd probably have spent a good deal more."

The pipe was filled and he reached for his matches. "Well, it would depend how you did it. Sixty-five guineas a week they tell me the hotel charges. Of course that includes the sport, which won't be of much interest to you. You could go a long way and see a lot for that."

"Of course you could, if you wanted to," said Anthea. "I wanted to come here."

He applied a match to the tobacco and, squinting at it, spoke between puffs. "The place is well enough—quiet—good change, I dare say." He blew the match out. "But I wouldn't have thought the House was the thing for you."

There was a silence, chilly and inharmonious. In the dull room, furnished with random pieces from old homes, the two figures were sharply exaggerated: Anthea's beauty invested with something of the extravagant artificiality which the Minister saw in her, while he was all black, dry and unsympathetic. He smoked his pipe, staring at nothing in particular. She looked at her cigarette and chafed, searching for some impersonal topic which would get her out of this improvident-young-relative box. A bridge . . . she had driven over the Forth road bridge the day before, and she had lifted her head to offer it up when a rattling of wheels was heard and Cousin Maud came in pushing a trolley.

"I was just saying to Anthea, Walter," she said with determined brightness, "that after all I believe it was a good idea going to the House. A few days of real luxury will do her good." She trundled the trolley into position and sat down, smiling at Anthea. "And then, dear, why not come to us for a while? You will still have some weeks, won't you, before you go back to your school?"

There was no escape for the improvident young relative. "As a matter of fact," Anthea said reluctantly, "I'm not going back."

The rest of the evening was meaningless: a matter of sitting in the Manse drawing-room till the time came when she could suitably leave. Conversation moved uneasily over the surface of family affairs with the curious awkward half-intimacy of relatives who know the facts but do not know each other well enough to understand them. Anthea did not really expect that her cousins Maud and Walter would ever approve whole-heartedly of what she was or what she did—though at all times Cousin Maud would do her best with extenuating circumstances—and she had known that both her stay in Balgarvie House and her recklessness in giving up her job would meet with disapproval. Anything that savoured of self-indulgence was anathema to the Mc-

Naughtons and compared to the Manse the hotel was almost Babylonian: and departure from regular, recognisable employment was rebellion against discipline, dangerous to body and soul.

Even without the additional barrier of disapproval it would have been difficult to talk enough about the profession of writer which she hoped to follow to convince them that it imposes its own discipline—and often hardship: and talking about the last seven years was almost impossible with anybody. Driving slowly back to the hotel the recollection of the one barren little exchange made her frown.

"Your brother, I understand, left the country as soon as he was free?"

"Yes, he went almost immediately."

"Have you heard from him?"

"No. I won't hear from him."

"Well—under the circumstances, perhaps, it is for the best."

Under the circumstances, thought Anthea, it was, perhaps, for the best that nothing more should be said, but the one moment when Cousin Maud cried and told her she must look forward, not back, had been upsetting: she hadn't known how much she wanted someone to talk to her like that. And there was the blow about the Tully. . . .

The garage arrangements at Balgarvie House were as primitive as the roads leading to it. In the yard was a row of sheds. If you felt strongly about having your car under cover you put it in one of them, but the doors were never locked and most vehicles stood outside wherever they happened to come to rest. Anthea put hers under cover and coming out of the shed lingered for a little, in no hurry to go in. A dog was yipping amiably in the kennels, woken up by her arrival but not resenting it unduly, and the peace of the night and the yard itself, which had something of the same accidental beauty as the harbour, brought back equanimity. The

McNaughtons disapproved of her and the Tully was not for her, but Balgarvie was still her place, her home. She indulged in a brief hatred of the man who had stolen the Tully, that lovely squalid little croft which by every right of love, long dreams and plans was hers. He had stuffed it with a wonderful collection of gramophone records—culture. Without doubt he had tarted it up to contemporary quaintness. Mr. Peachey felt at home in it. . . . Still, there might be other cottages, and it was, perhaps, salutary, a safeguard, to meet disappointment at the outset. To make do with less than perfection is, after all, the human lot.

Having cheered herself up successfully Anthea was walking across the cobbles to the side door when she heard another car approaching. She hastened her steps—she had no desire to encounter Mr. Peachey's charm again that night—but it was an estate car which rolled into the yard with Lawrence at the wheel. It could hardly be said to be parked when it stopped and disgorged a surprising number of bodies. Some of them, tall and generally lanky young figures, walked away from the house to the ghillies' quarters beyond the kennels. Lawrence and four of the dining-room staff came towards her and she paused sociably.

"Hullo," she said. "Have you heard some good music?"

They said they had, smiling at her with particular warmth and interest, and then the four, her own brunette and the fair-haired wine waiter, the blonde Louisa and the dark young man, melted away to the staff entrance at the back of the house while Lawrence opened the side door. He was—indeed they were all—extremely cheerful, and he turned to her as if he were bursting with exciting news.

"I say," he began, "do you know about this place where we go to listen to records? The Tully?"

"I know it," said Anthea.

"Oh. Well, the chap who owns it is a writer—"

"So I heard."

Her tone did not match his enthusiasm and her face was repressive but they were walking along an ill-lit passage and Lawrence did not notice. Triumphantly he produced his news. "He's a friend of yours."

Anthea stopped and looked at him. His lively face was full of cordial congratulation and she stared at it dumbly, a premonitory chill making the flesh creep on her bones.

"Want to guess?" cried Lawrence gaily. "But you never would. He says you haven't seen each other for years and of course hardly anybody knows he lives here—I mean the public doesn't. It's John Gregorson."

CHAPTER 3

AT Lady Vine's suggestion Anthea went out with her after breakfast next morning to watch what she called the take-off. Leaning restfully on a gate they looked on at a scene of bustle in the yard. Men with guns; men with fishing rods, their hats bristling with flies and tendrils of fine gut. Keepers, authoritative and unhurried, and tall boys in disreputable jeans or flannels carrying lunches and game-bags: Land-Rovers and estate cars throbbing; dogs—and Colonel Garvie—everywhere.

"There's Ian McNaughton wondering whether to approach or not to approach," said Lady Vine, and Anthea, seeing one of the boys looking at her doubtfully, smiled and went to meet him. He was very large, as Ness had said, and not unlike her, but he lacked her confident efficiency. His youthful face was pink with shyness and he was greatly hampered by the antics of an excited young dog on a lead.

"Hullo, Ian," said Anthea, remembering the lesson of the night before and keeping her distance.

"Oh hullo—er, Cousin Anthea," responded a soft voice which had still not decided where it would eventually settle.

"Not *Cousin* Anthea," she protested with a horrid vision of herself on a shelf between Cousin Maud and Cousin Walter.

"No? Well, I wasn't sure." The pink deepened but embarrassment was dispelled by the dog. Eyes and teeth gleaming with enthusiasm it flung itself at a departing car and the whispering voice became a roar. "Bracken! Get *down*, ya fool. *Sit.*"

Bracken, hauled forcibly back to heel with one black ear inside out, dashed at Anthea with an air of such undaunted gaiety that she laughed aloud. "He's rather nice," she said, "but does he always go on like this?"

33

"Always," said Ian. "I don't think he's ever going to learn but he's a nice beast," and the conversation continued, the whisper and the roar alternating. "Sit *down*. . . . Are you staying long—er, Anthea?"

She said, "No—about a week," and returned the ball. Had he left school? How did he like this job . . .?

He had one more year at school and the job was all right, he said, stooping to unwind the leash which was being woven round his legs. Better than doing nothing all the holidays, and the money came in handy. "Bracken!"

"Ian! Where's Ian?" shouted an organising voice and he gave Anthea an apologetic smile.

"Have to go, I'm afraid," he said. "Be seeing you again, though. Come on, you silly brute," and he departed, towed by his irrepressible charge.

"Boy with dog," remarked Lady Vine when Anthea rejoined her at the gate. "Poor Ian! Too much to have to cope with a lady and that foolish animal at the same time."

"I thought Bracken was a help rather than a hindrance," said Anthea. "It gave him something to do with his hands. He's a nice boy."

"He's a pet," Lady Vine agreed. "The only restful Mc-Naughton," she added with an amused glance at Anthea and waved farewell to her husband and son as they drove away in an estate car with Ian adjusting a stranglehold on Bracken in the back. "They're going to the far beat to-day," she said.

She leant against the gate smoking her cigarette and talking in a light, charming voice: knowing everybody, interested with a kind of amused affection in everything. The perfect woman of the world, Anthea thought. Entertaining, agreeable and undemanding, friendly within limits which protected her from becoming involved. She broke off to greet people—a word of encouragement for the Frenchman, congratulatory to the Americans, the great man and his older secretary who were both shooting well—and brought the conversation back with small comments. "How cosmopolitan we are. . . . I don't know what the young secretary does all day—he doesn't have much fun. . . ."

They had been coming to Balgarvie for so long, she said, that it was like home without the chores. "I adore it." A wave of her cigarette embraced the whole district. "It's the perfect holiday. Francis and Lawrence are happy and I can do exactly as I like. I can hardly bear it when it's time to go away."

"But could you bear to stay?" Anthea asked.

"Ah well—I've often wondered. I'm *afraid*"—the light voice was regretful, not perhaps very sincerely—"that glad as one is to 'get away from it all,' ordinary life would have a pretty strong pull by, say, the middle of November. What about you?"

Her look was curious but not too much. People were as a rule only too prone to confide, and the affairs of others are boring more often than not: but apart from the relationship to the McNaughtons the young woman beside her, decorative, attractive and apparently well enough endowed with worldly goods, had offered no information at all.

She did not offer any now.

"I think," Anthea said lightly, "I'd last longer than November—not that I mean to try. I expect it depends a good deal on how strong the pull is."

"To look at you I should imagine many pulls—strong ones."

"Oh," said Anthea, "out of sight, out of mind."

Lady Vine glanced at her again but her face was only amused and the charming mouth smiled as Mr. Peachey bustled towards them, gun in hand.

"Slackers!" he cried. "Have you no shame?"

"No," said the ladies with one voice.

Brightly he deplored their spirit of non-partake, adjuring them to emulate the examples of gallant British womanhood they saw before them—the bishop's wife was packing herself into a car with rods and lunch baskets and a small elderly woman with a hat pulled well down handed a gun to one of the tall schoolboys.

Lady Vine turned her shoulder deliberately. "Don't think for a moment that I am moved by Desmond," she said to Anthea, "but if you would care for a game of golf . . .?"

"Oh, thank you, but—" Anthea began hastily and broke off with a laugh. "How rude I sound! Really, I'd like very much to play another time, but to-day—I just want to mooch about."

"Most reasonable," said Lady Vine. "Another time by all means."

She and Mr. Peachey watched the girl walk away back to the house, slim, graceful and unhurried. Lady Vine approved of and priced the corduroy slacks and the thin jersey with pushed-up sleeves. Mr. Peachey thought Miss Logan was clever about colours. That soft honey colour, whatever they called it, was admirable with her curiously attractive hair and golden skin. And her figure was really—

"Eye-catching, isn't she," Lady Vine remarked amiably.

"Very," he agreed at once. "And the air of mystery adds something—or does one merely imagine it?"

"We now know she is related to the Minister."

"True. But would that in itself be sufficient to bring her to Balgarvie? I haven't the pleasure of being acquainted with the Minister."

Lady Vine, who was acquainted with the Minister, smiled. "Hardly, perhaps. But she's fond of the place. She's a harbour fan, Lawrence says."

"Ah," said Mr. Peachey without conviction.

She looked round at him. "Foreign Office," she said. "You really must guard against the habit of suspicion. It's most insidious."

"My dear Lady V.," he made one of his quick gestures, "you know my insatiable curiosity. I gazed and speculated from my pram. In the Office it's so often better *not* to see, that I have to give it its head in private life. And it is intriguing, do admit. Nothing like Miss Anthea Logan has ever happened before in the history of Balgarvie House. Saunders is in quite a twitter."

"How silly!" said Lady Vine. "We must have new faces from time to time—why shouldn't we have a pretty one? She's a charming young woman and she seems contented— she won't clamour to be entertained. Lawrence likes her —Yes, I know, he's only twenty and she's quite lovely, but he isn't a fool. He isn't even very susceptible."

"No indeed," Mr. Peachey agreed cordially. "His resistance to the so obvious Louisa is evidence enough. But, Lady V.— I must solve Miss Logan. Shall we agree to pool our findings? Quite kindly. I couldn't be more amiably disposed."

Lady Vine hesitated. There had been something different about the girl this morning—a slight blankness about the eyes—and she felt an unexpected pang of compunction at the thought of exposing it to Mr. Peachey's curiosity, however amiable. "Well," she said doubtfully, "if there are any findings. . . ."

"That's just it, isn't it?" said Mr. Peachey.

As Anthea walked away from Lady Vine and Mr. Peachey she forgot about them instantly. She was going to pick up her lunch and disappear—literally take to the hills. Her first day at Balgarvie had been fully and lovingly planned. There was a particular walk, a long loop to the south among hills and glens, well away from the grouse moors, which, taken at a reasonable pace, would bring her via the Tully to the harbour latish in the afternoon. This walk had taken on an almost ritualistic flavour. It was an approach, deliberate and ceremonious, as a prince approaching his kingdom, or a pilgrim his Mecca, might elect to complete his journey on foot as a gesture of respect and a sign that he was in no unseemly hurry to snatch the good things awaiting him. Balgarvie was neither a kingdom nor a Mecca to Anthea. She had merely wanted to live there, and since she was not now going to live there, there was nothing, strictly speaking, to approach. But she was going through with her plan. In the last seven years she had learned that she could put up with anything if she had to, and the object of the operation now was to look squarely at the collapse of her house of cards and once more come to terms with reality. At least she could congratulate herself on having kept quiet about her little plan. Nobody need ever know why she had come to Balgarvie, or guess that, not once but twice, John Gregorson had come as a wrecker into her life.

She went up the steps into the House and in the hall the young barman, Morgan, came forward as if he had been waiting for her.

"Good morning," he said with the smile she had found brash the evening before. "The Colonel told me you would be wanting golf clubs."

"Oh yes, he spoke of it," said Anthea. "I shall want them I expect, but not to-day."

She did not think she had been short, but the smile faded and the eyes gazing down at her became plaintive again. "If you wouldn't mind just having a look," he begged. "You see the Colonel is—well, one mustn't say fussy, but he's sure to ask, and if you've seen the clubs and said they're all right then it's arranged and he'll be satisfied."

"Very well," she said, resigned. "Where are they?"

"You're not annoyed?" Morgan asked anxiously. "I don't want to be a nuisance. It's only—it isn't always easy to get things right. I'm not too good at it, I'm afraid, and Colonel Garvie—well, he's particular."

"It's perfectly all right," said Anthea, irritatedly aware that unnatural affability would be required if wounded feelings were to be avoided, and Morgan's face cleared.

"This way," he said and led her back to the wilderness of the west wing where she had been lost the night before. It revealed itself in daylight as a rabbit-warren area mainly consisting of gun-rooms. There were glimpses of racks with rifles and shot guns, racks of fishing rods, rows of waders on floors and game-bags on hooks. "Here," said Morgan, and opening one of the few closed doors displayed a tidily stored assortment of games equipment.

There was quite a long row of golf bags, some of smartish leather, well-furnished, some humble canvas affairs far gone in decay. "Who on earth do all these belong to?" exclaimed Anthea.

Morgan was happy to tell her—so far as he could. He didn't, he said apologetically, know all of them, but he went conscientiously along the line. These were Lady Vine's, Lawrence's, the Bishop's—he didn't play often. This was Mr. Peachey's bag: he didn't play much either but he kept this bag at Balgarvie. "These," he pulled one out at last, "are the ones the Colonel thought would suit you. They belong to his daughter." He glanced at her for size. "They should be all right and they're not in bad condition."

Anthea agreed that they would suit her and had, for the moment, finished with them. But Morgan was sliding each club out, examining it knowledgeably, and there were his feelings. Lady Vine, she felt, would smoothly detach herself at this point: she weakly asked the expected question. "Do you play yourself?"

"Me?" He looked up and smiled. "Yes—when I can." His eyes dropped again to the club he was holding and his hand moved caressingly along the shaft. "Matter of fact I've played quite a bit. I love it, actually." Some people, he went on to say modestly, thought he was rather good, but he simply had to tell them he couldn't afford to take it seriously.

"You don't play here?"

"Oh no. It isn't much of a course and—well, it's for guests, you see."

Anthea saw. "Well, thank you," she said, turning to the door. "I'll know where to find these when I want them."

"If you wouldn't mind," Morgan said earnestly, "it would be better if you let me get them for you. I mean, I'm responsible, you see. But I'm always about and of course any time—don't feel the slightest hesitation."

"Oh very well," said Anthea and almost decided to cut out golf; but though she walked briskly away along the passage she had not yet cut out Morgan, who shut the door and hurried after her.

"I believe," he said socially, "that you are Ness's cousin." He fell into step and went on in a lower tone, "Ness is—rather a wonderful person."

Anthea said that they seemed to be a very nice crowd altogether.

He agreed. Oh yes, they were a marvellous crowd. He had seen her talking to Lawrence again this morning. Lawrence was a dear chap. They had rather a lot in common, actually, and of course he—Lawrence—was just like one of themselves.

Anthea said, "Well, he is one of yourselves, I suppose—except that he isn't doing a job here and now like the rest of you."

"Ah," said Morgan deeply. "I knew that's how *you* would see it. But some of the guests don't quite realise that we're not exactly ordinary skivvies, and even among the staff—well, it would surprise you how much some of them think of money and status. Not Ness, of course. Actually, it was through Ness I came here." The voice dropped again. "She has understanding. A sense of the real values."

They were back in the hall and Ness's cousin looked up at the handsome-young-animal face now full of soul. "Well, that's good," she said briskly. "Thanks, Morgan." She nodded a good-natured but final dismissal and in a moment was away, walking fast down the drive.

In the afternoon, having covered a good ten miles, she came, a little weary but strictly on schedule, to the Tully. There was a right of way past the croft, by right of use if nothing else, for she remembered the citizens of Balgarvie climbing the path in best suits and bowler hats for the Sunday walk. Then it had been a working croft but poorly managed and hopeless looking, with scruffy hens, a melancholy cow tethered on the hillside and a tramp-like woman in a sacking apron and a man's cap who dashed out, however cautiously you approached, and held you in shrill relentless talk. But the Tully now was as far from the squalid croft she had known as the quaint contemporary nook of her angry imagining the evening before. Nothing fancy had been done to it, it was simply in good condition—the whitewash fresh and the red roof sound: and there was a small well-stocked garden where the hens used to scratch. The new owner had, as she would have expected of him, done exactly as she would have done herself.

A black-and-white collie, large and amiable, got up from the porch as she approached and after a brief, scrutinising glance came to meet her, smiling welcomingly and waving a fine plume of a tail.

"Oh lord, yes!" said Anthea. "You're a detail I'd overlooked, but of course I'd have had to have you. Did you go with the property, or did he cleverly find you . . .?"

Delighted to have company he came close and held his head invitingly. She fondled it, gathering from indications given that what he liked best was having his ears gently pulled and the spot under his chin scratched. For a curiously suspended, silent moment the Tully ceased to be the cottage that should have been hers—everything ceased and she stood in a kind of vacuum, looking at John Gregorson's house with her hand on his dog.

Since she had not obeyed her first impulse and bolted like a frightened rabbit when she heard he was here, she was going to meet him again, and it had seemed a good idea to get it over quickly and without an audience: but it was, after all, a relief that the Tully was empty. She walked on and the dog came too, padding companionably beside her down the path and along the quay.

She was making for a bench on the old pier and as she reached the end of the quay she—and the dog—paused to look at a group of small motor-boats moored in the angle between the quay and the pier. Automatically she noted their names: *Wild Rose, Jessie, Mary Brown, Skua* . . .

"Hallo," said a voice. "You've made friends with Dan, have you?" and she looked up to see Ness leaning her bicycle against a wall.

"Oh it's Dan, is it?" she said. "He escorted me down the path. He's a darling."

"Too much of a darling to be much use," said Ness with an inflection of scorn for agreeable uselessness and English soppiness. "Still, he's a nice beast," she added, relenting slightly. "He belongs to the man who has the Tully now. Where are you off to?"

"Well, I've been, really," Anthea said and gave a brief description of her walk. "Now I'm going to sit and look at the harbour for a bit."

"I remember you used to be nutty about the harbour," said Ness. She gave a kind of nod, terminating the conversation. "I've got to give somebody a message."

Anthea was about to walk on, as she was clearly expected

to do, but before Ness could deliver any message a fisherman who had come briskly along the pier got in first.

"Hey, Greg!" he yelled. "Are ye awa' tae yer bed?"

From *Skua*'s tiny cabin a tow-coloured head and a mass of freckles looked out and reported back. "It's Ecky. He says are ye awa' tae yer bed."

There was a laugh. "Not bloody likely," shouted a deep voice. "I'm having hell with a fangled line. These damned hooks! I'm bleeding to death. So's Willie."

Anthea stood still. The voice coming from a little boat in Balgarvie harbour, in familiar converse with a fisherman, was surprising enough: it was what is known as Englified, educated and unashamed. Ness and Ecky were both grinning, but not at its novelty and with no sign of the contempt which might have been expected.

"Dae ye nae herm tae let a pickle blood," was Ecky's heartless response. "Did ye get onything? I seen ye got fangled."

"Couple of boxes," said the voice. "What sort of shot did you have?"

"No bad. Thirty-twa boxes o' flats. Ye're richt, then, are ye? Cheerio—sune be Setterday."

"If we live to see it."

The fisherman grinned and with a sideways nod to the ladies walked away. Ness inflated her lungs.

"Hey, Greg!"

The freckles looked out again. "It's Ness and anither wumman."

"Go away, Ness," shouted *Skua*'s skipper. "I'm not receiving."

"I've a *message*," Ness retorted and delivered it at the top of her voice. "The Laird says can you take a party to the Black Loch to-morrow and why the flaming hell don't you answer the phone."

"Damnation!" snapped the skipper and came out of the cabin. He was, when unfolded, a big man, with black hair and a face so tanned that it looked like brown leather. He wore filthy flannel trousers and one of the faded red windcheaters, and in his bleeding hands was a wicked tangle of line and hooks. In a tone of strong complaint he began, "I thought he was all fixed—" and then broke off to say in a different voice, "Hallo, Anthea."

The fisherman's hail, "Hey, Greg!" had brought Anthea to a stand-still. However long she anticipated it, wherever it had happened, the meeting would have been a shock. The remembered sound of his voice took her breath away. She could not have moved if she had wanted to, and as he climbed up from his boat to stand beside her on the pier all her will-power and sheer physical strength went into the effort needed to control the bonelessness of her legs and keep her teeth from chattering: to smile and respond.

"Jock," she said, "have you turned pirate? Of all the unlikely places to find you popping up!"

The dark face changed as he returned her smile. "Think so? You don't look so improbable standing on Balgarvie pier." He glanced at the dog which was still in the party. "Did Dan—"

"*Good gracious!*" Ness, who had been staring openmouthed from one to the other, found her voice. "Do you *know* each other?" She turned indignantly to Anthea. "Why didn't you *say?*"

Anthea was surprised. "But," she said confusedly, "I thought—didn't you know? You were at the Tully last night, weren't you? I only heard the name of the man with all the records from Lawrence Vine afterwards."

"You and Morgan must have gone before the matter came up," John Gregorson told Ness and added to Anthea, "Lawrence surprised *me* by telling me you're related to the McNaughtons. I'd no idea you even knew them."

"She's a cousin," Ness said huffily. She seemed to feel the whole thing as a personal affront. "Lawrence might have

44

mentioned it to me while he was running about surprising everybody."

"Probably forgot you weren't there when we were talking about it," said John Gregorson. He was looking at Anthea with eyes which were more intent than those of a chance-met acquaintance but he expressed no amazement and contributed no exclamations. "You look very good," he said easily. "I was coming up to the House to call on you this evening."

"I tried to call on you a few minutes ago," said Anthea.

"Look," said Ness, remembering what she had come for, "I've got to go. What am I to tell the Laird, Greg?"

Behind the commonplace exchanges, Anthea's declaration of ignorance of his identity, his or her connection with the McNaughtons, were undercurrents hidden from a third person—or at any rate from Ness—and he had forgotten the message which had brought her to the harbour.

"The Laird?" he said carelessly, and with the patience of a governess recalling the wandering attention of a child she repeated the message.

"Can you or can you not take a party to fish the Black Loch to-morrow?"

"I expect so, but I'll ring him later—oh damn! My phone's out of order. I'll ring him from the pub."

"There's no need to go to the pub. I'll be seeing him anyway."

Mr. Gregorson at last gave her his attention, but though her tone was severe he was not intimidated. "Hop it," he said disrespectfully. "I'll ring him *from the pub*—where I'll be anyway. Tell him that if it makes you happy."

"Oh all right," grumbled Ness. "You need something on those hands. They're a mess. Cheerio."

She turned away but Anthea said, "I'll come with you," and she turned back.

"But you said you were going to sit and look at the harbour."

There was an involuntary flash of laughter between grey eyes and hazel, and before Anthea could speak John Gregorson said, "Do sit and look at the harbour, Anthea. I'll just dispose of this"—the tangle of line and hooks—"and get the worst of the dirt off, and then we'll have a yarn and catch up."

"It looks as if she'll have a good long time to wait," observed Ness.

"She won't mind," he said.

Ness turned to walk away. "I've got the bike anyway," she concluded inconsequently.

CHAPTER 4

NESS went away, John Gregorson swung himself down into his boat and Anthea walked along to her chosen bench and very thankfully sat down.

Since the harbour was there in front of her she might be said to be looking at it, but the familiar scene was confused and out of focus—the clean lines of masts vague and shimmering, everything half dissolved like an impressionist painting. She herself felt half-dissolved, as if supreme effort, mental and physical, was required to keep her in one piece, and for a moment the sensation was actually alarming. But she could not afford the luxury of reaction. She stirred, and lighting a cigarette set about collecting herself.

How she had got away from Lawrence the night before she hardly knew. All the way along that interminable passage, across the hall, along her own east-wing tunnel, he had been talking with the happy volubility of hero-worship. To him it was a joyous coincidence that his old admired friend Greg and his new friend Anthea, whom he was ready to adore, were already friends of each other, and it left him—fortunately—less observant than usual. Somehow Anthea had responded, somehow, at the end of the tunnel, she had shaken him off, and then she was in her bedroom shivering: cold with shock, hot with resentment.

Last time she had seen Jock Gregorson she thought she was engaged to him. Next day she found she wasn't. His decision—it hadn't, she knew, been an easy one—she had learned to accept: indeed she understood and sympathised with the instinct which put so strong a talent first and refused to stifle it with the responsibilities of marriage. But though she did not grudge him his free, creative life it was too much, the final irony, that he had chosen to live it in

Balgarvie. The harbour—the Tully . . . they were not, after all, hers, they were his. And how, in all the world, had it come about?

Her cigarette was finished before she saw him, cleaner and empty-handed, walking along the pier. He was a man of thirty-three or –four who had worked very hard and achieved success of a kind to which there is no easy road and which depends entirely on individual ability and effort. He had needed to be tough and he was tough, both in body and mind—and, if it can be separated, in spirit. But it was the toughness of well-seasoned oak. The struggle, the effort, had not warped him, and Anthea, as she watched him coming towards her, thought with a stir of amusement that success had left him singularly unaffected. He was at the moment perhaps the most highly regarded of the younger English writers, much talked of, much written about, but there could not be a less "successful" face. In the windcheater and the disgusting trousers, stained with blood and oil and fish, he was magnificent. With that appearance, his ability and reputation, he could lord it in the world if he chose. It didn't surprise her that he didn't choose, that living in the Tully suited him better: and it was not, after all, surprising that he should have done so exactly what she had planned to do. Resentment, she reflected ruefully, was an unreliable weapon. In the actual presence of the man it folded up. . . .

But she had a job to do, a part to play, and she looked at him as he came up to her, his dog at his heels, wondering again how he came to be here. He met the look with one equally searching and sat down beside her.

"Well, Anthea?" he said. "This is strange, isn't it?"

"Very strange," she said. "The last place in the world I'd have expected to meet you."

"Is it? It was you who told me about Balgarvie, remember."

She made an involuntary movement and, annoyed with herself, turned it into reaching for her cigarettes. "Here you are," he said. He lit one for her and turned away to light his own. Anthea inhaled smoke and mustered her forces, her eyes on a boat which was coming in through the gap. It was—appropriately—*Guiding Light*.

"I suppose I talked a lot about Balgarvie," she said. "I took a great shine to it."

"But you've never been back?"

"No, there never seemed to be an opportunity. But it's a curious place for you to make your home, isn't it? Or is it just your summer resort?"

He said, "No, it's home," and she looked at the white croft on the hill, the work-scarred little *Skua*, and the man, work-scarred too, with lines of thought on his face and grey hairs among the black.

"Your books—" she turned to him with sudden, natural warmth, "you've had a wonderful success and so thoroughly deserved. It's very good, Jock, to be able to tell you how glad I am about that, and how very much I like all you've written. It's so satisfactory—" she laughed at the adjective, "satisfying?—and so rare—to find yourself reading something that clearly has lasting value."

"Thank you," he said. "It's very good indeed to hear that from you." But his face held pain rather than pleasure, and she turned away again and took the conversation back.

"But with such success—you're famous, surely *well off* if you're not rich—Balgarvie is an unexpected setting for you."

"Well . . ." He put cigarettes and lighter back into his pocket and, seeing that he had left another smear of blood on the windcheater, dabbed his hand carelessly with a greyish, all-purpose handkerchief as he talked. "When I came up here I was far from famous *or* well off. I knew—but you know about this—that if I was to do any good I had to get away from regular salaried jobs. I can't write books as a side-line. On the other hand, if you set out to do what you feel you have to do, write the books you want to write, you have to face the fact that nobody's going to pay you for your hard work and good intentions. It's your own gamble."

"So you came up here to put your shirt on it?"

"I came with about tuppence—just enough to buy a very leaky cottage which no one in their senses would look at. And wrote and fished and grew lettuces—and ate the fish and the lettuces—and did all kinds of odd jobs and gradually tidied up the Tully."

"Single-handed?"

"No." He turned to look at her. "I think everybody in the place gave me a hand in one way or another. I have reason to be grateful to you, Anthea, for giving me Balgarvie. And I am grateful."

"Well—it's a healthier place to starve than an attic in London," she said after a moment. "I'm very glad it—worked out. And you mean to stay—renouncing the world, the flesh and the devil? What about the rewards of fame?"

"I think," said Jock, "that success, as commonly under-stood, is more stifling than the harness of a salaried journalist —and a hell of a lot more boring. I do mean to stay. I'm not here all the time—I'm fond of sin and far from renouncing the world—but this is where I live and work. And you needn't imagine in your superior, urban way that the rewards of fame are lacking in Balgarvie. You should see my mod. cons. I'm all-electric and they come from far and wide to admire the plumbing. What about you?"

She was smiling at the plumbing, and, at the sudden question, held on to the smile. "Oh, there's nothing very in-teresting about me."

His eyes glanced at the casual, expensive clothes and lin-gered on the glinting hair. "You've still got your lock," he said. His hand moved as if tweaking the lock, which fell determinedly over her left eyebrow, would be the natural thing to do, but he restrained it and said instead, "You're more beautiful than you were. And you look prosperous, I'm glad to see."

"Mustn't grumble," said Anthea.

"How do you like the hotel? Shall I come and ghillie for you—help you hook a salmon?"

She exclaimed regretfully. "Oh dear! What a perfect arrangement—if only I'd known. . . . But I'm pledged to complete non-sport. I can't go back on it now."

"Ah," said Jock, "that must have taken courage. You must make friends with Lawrence Vine and old Sir Andrew Gibb. You can hardly hope to be universally popular, but they'll support you. Have you been writing? If so it must be under a pseudonym, but I was sure—a lot of people thought you would."

Though she had been amused she had not relaxed and she was ready—as far as she could be. She hadn't been writing, she said, till just lately. "Now I've made a beginning—I hope." She held up crossed fingers. "But it's as you say—impossible to do much if you're in a job and tied."

"Published?"

"No—but accepted."

He said, "Good," and asked what sort of book, what publisher and what, if any, pseudonym: but she shook her head. She had a superstition, she said. She wasn't going to count or talk about her chicken before it was hatched.

"H'm," he said and eyed her speculatively. "Refined pornography? Paying, of course, but no—I don't see it. Smear-sneer—not in character. Flowery romance . . .?"

A laugh escaped Anthea but she refused to be drawn and he moved, leaning back and crossing his legs with an air of great patience. "If I ever have occasion," he said conversa-

51

tionally, "to describe the emotions of a man trying to open up a battleship with a tin-opener I shall be able to make a very convincing thing of it. Experience is never wasted. Very well. Let literature pass for the moment. I'm glad you've made a beginning—though I don't think your business sense is going to carry you far. So you have a job. . . ." There was a pause and then he turned to her, his face and voice serious and urgent. "Anthea, did you have to disappear so completely?" She did not reply and he went on, "You know I was abroad. When I got back you'd vanished. Nobody knew where you were. Even in the *Trumpeter* office I couldn't pick up the beginning of a trail, though you had some good friends there."

She asked, "Why should you want to?"

"You know very well why I should want to." He spoke sharply, refusing to be brushed aside. "You may feel—you have reason to feel—that I behaved badly to you seven years ago, but you can't imagine—you *know* that it wasn't done lightly. Let alone that it was trifling."

"I know that, Jock. But—"

"Then you know, too, that I thought about you and cared about you very much. I wanted to know how things were with you and when I heard you'd gone, packed in your job, I was—I wanted to know where you were, what you were doing. I came up here to look for you. I never thought of the McNaughtons, of course; you'd never mentioned having relations here. I just asked around. But nothing came up and I began to feel I couldn't go any further. I had no right."

Anthea stirred. So that was how he had come to Balgarvie. A further irony. "I don't think you behaved badly," she said. "I never thought so. But it's over and dead—why dig it up? It wasn't only because of you that I left the *Trumpeter*. I did want to—do something different, but there were family reasons too. I don't want to talk about it."

There was a silence. She felt herself shivering and after a moment he put out a hand and gave her a quick reassuring pat. "Well, you don't have to talk about it," he said. "But we've met again and we can't pretend the past didn't happen—unless we're enemies. Are we enemies?"

"No, we're not enemies," said Anthea. But she knew she had made a tactical error. When he asked her why she had disappeared she should have been ready with an easy, convincing reply. Plausible untruths, however, never came readily to hand; she had hesitated and now they were in deep water, in danger not of being enemies but of being again too great friends. Jock was cleverer and stronger than she was, and a difficult person to deceive: the more difficult because it would be so easy to respond to his concern, to open up and tell him all that had happened to her in those seven years. But she wasn't going to do that and she had to recover her ground.

"Really, there isn't much to tell," she said. "I was needed at home. My father died and my mother's health broke down, so I got a job where I could be with her. It all worked out very well."

There was a pause and then Jock said, "I see. It seems a pity—you'd made such a good start with the *Trumpeter*—but there are other, perhaps better, ways of using a talent for writing than working for a newspaper. Your mother . . .?"

"She died last winter." There was silence again. Wondering why he had relaxed the pressure, what he knew or guessed of her story, Anthea glanced at him from under her eyelashes. She had never suspected him of lack of feeling, but she was startled by the expression on the dark face. "It's over, you know, Jock," she said quickly. "There's no need to think any more about it."

"Anthea," he said, "there have been times—many times when I would have given everything to have that letter unwritten."

"There was no need. You have nothing to reproach your-self with—or regret."

Their eyes met in a look which was completely un-guarded and honest, but very briefly: Anthea turned away at once. Jock said quietly, "You're generous—but you were always generous," and went on looking at her, seeing both Anthea now, sitting beside him on the old pier in her honey-coloured slacks, the sun catching the gold in her hair, and the young girl Anthea he had known in London. "At the time," he said, "it seemed the only decision." His voice was still quiet, serious and factual. "Marriage—with how-ever much love and happiness—and the work I'd been aim-ing for all my life, just didn't go together. But it wasn't easy."

"It would have been lunacy to marry," said Anthea. "And it was only a temporary brain-storm. We got on well and had fun and one day it blew up on us—inevitably, but it hadn't gone far enough to do much harm. Of course you were right. Your work is proof of that." She lightened her voice. "Actually, I can never understand why men marry young. It's surprising, in a way, that they do it at all. One sees the advantages for a woman."

He gave a sudden laugh with a note of delighted recog-nition in it. "There are reasons—quite powerful reasons, I assure you. And advantages, besides the obvious one, for a man too. There's something to be said for home comforts."

"Maybe," she said, "but the ball and chain is a hell of a handicap. Forget it, Jock." She turned to pick up the satchel in which she carried her lunch and oddments. "Seven years is a long time. Long enough to forget most things and change everything."

She was getting up, bringing the meeting to an end, and he made no attempt to prolong it. He rose too and stood looking down at her. "That sounds a little bit slick," he said. "I know I haven't changed—*basically*—and I don't believe you have."

Anthea began to walk back along the pier. "It's difficult not to sound slick if you want to avoid long-windedness. I dare say one doesn't change much *basically*, but what's basic? Seven years of people and places and work and thoughts make quite a lot of difference, you must allow."

"Very true," he agreed politely and asked with slight ironic emphasis, "How long are you staying at Balgarvie House? Will you honour me by visiting my poor dwelling?" He pointed. "The Tully. You know it, do you?"

"I know it well," she said. "When I heard it had been bought and done up by some blasted writer I cursed him heartily."

"Cursed him, did you? Why?"

"Oh—I had a fancy for the Tully myself at one time."

"Did you? Well—you can have it."

"What?" She stopped and turned, startled and half indignant. Then she laughed. "Ass! What's your price with all the mod. cons?"

"I won't sell it, but if you want it, it's yours."

"Just like that? Like a chop on a plate?"

"If that's the way you like to put it. Yours and no strings."

They were walking on again slowly and she was not looking at him but she saw the tall figure in the faded red windcheater vividly enough; the hard tanned face and hands, the air of being thoroughly at home, an integral part of Balgarvie. "I believe you really mean it," she said, "but—"

"You know I mean it."

"But I wasn't serious, you know," she went on as if he hadn't spoken. "I think of the Tully along with Peter Rabbit's house and Pooh Corner—cosy and delicious but not real." An echo came to her of Lady Vine talking that morning. "Balgarvie—it's lovely, but it isn't everybody who could bear to live here. For me it's an occasional place; peaceful and beautiful when you want to get away from real life for a bit."

"Is it?" said Jock.

"I'm grateful, you know. Really grateful."

"Nothing to be grateful for," he said a little abruptly and stopped beside his boat. "I ought to finish tidying up here. . . . Come and listen to some records one evening, Anthea, will you?"

"I'd like to. And see the house and admire the plumbing."

"We'll fix it then," he said. "And Anthea—I mean this. If you ever need it—or want it—to use for a time, or live in altogether, the Tully's yours."

Willie, the 14-year-old crew, had gone home to his tea. Jock Gregorson, alone on *Skua*, watched Anthea cross the road and disappear, climbing rather wearily up the steps of the Water Wynd. He began automatically to work at the tidying that remained to be done, but his mind was far away and he did not notice when he gave up working and sat still. This in itself was not unusual. Everybody about the harbour was used to seeing Greg working silently or just sitting with a far-away look on his face, and they knew he was making up his books. But now he was thinking about discrepancies.

Anthea Logan at twenty-one had been an exuberant creature whose liveliness was undimmed either by reserve or discretion. Everything in her head was liable to come boiling out and the *Trumpeter* laughed at her a good deal —but not too much. She was no fool, and expert opinion said she was a girl to be watched: she could be going places. Jock had found her most glorious fun. Her zest and joviality, her sheer enjoyment of life, were as exhilarating as a sea breeze, and as their first effervescent companionship grew more intimate it revealed something far beyond fun: a sympathy, a kinship of mind which remained unique in his experience. Then—they had gone to the Festival Hall and the Bach Double Concerto pulled the trigger—they found they were in love. It had been their habit to talk volubly and end-lessly when they were together, never having time for all they had to say, but then they were silent. When they left the hall they walked about London. At her door, when they eventually got there, he kissed her for quite a long time and then, still without having exchanged coherent speech, he left her. He had never seen her again till this afternoon when he ducked out of *Skua*'s cabin and there she was, looking down at him from the pier.

Two things had happened when he got back to his flat. First, the realisation, as he came out of his daze, of the choice that confronted him: then the urgent, unexpected assignment which sent him abroad. He had three alterna-tives. He could refuse to go to Moscow: but aspiring foreign correspondents go where they're sent, when they're sent. He could rush round to Anthea and tell her he'd be back in about a year. Or he could write and say good-bye. He had made his choice, a desperate choice, feeling that in deciding to keep his freedom he was resisting a temptation. He had talent. His first duty, his obligation, was to use it —more, he knew he must use it or be less than half himself. He must use it, develop it as far as it would go, and there could be no half measures. Any remnant, any indefinite waiting or hope for the future would be worse than immediate marriage. It had to be a clean break, with the hope and belief that as their love had been so sudden and so brief a thing it would pass. In a way it had—the agony had passed, but time had only confirmed that it was no fleeting fancy. He had loved Anthea as he had never loved another woman, and, as he had told her, there had been times when he would have given all his talent and half his life for the chance to choose again.

But only times. He could not regret that he had done the work for which nature had shaped him. Even when he heard that she had vanished from the *Trumpeter* world, and rushed up to Balgarvie to look for her, he had not been sure whether he wanted to find her for his own sake, beyond putting his mind at rest about her. It was still a case of living single and doing what he wanted to do or marrying and abandoning it for the bread-winner's harness. Now, of course, it was different. He could support a wife and family without altering his way of life, and as an artist he was disciplined and mature: no longer groping.

Jock crawled out from the cramping shelter of the cabin. The climax of the day was approaching and the harbour was busy. Most of the boats were in, the rest following quickly. The winches groaned and shrieked, boxes banged and scraped. Vans came rattling down the road bringing buyers and transport for the catch, and the brassy tenor of the auctioneer could be heard tearing through every other sound in preliminary conversational exchanges. The incoming tide and the movements of the bigger boats made *Skua* bobble and fidget, but he noticed nothing.

How much had he done to change the eager out-going girl into this beautiful young woman, so composed and so implacable in her reserve? He knew he was not wholly responsible. Though his search for her had failed, it had not been difficult to discover why she had gone: she had indeed been needed at home and he was not surprised that she would not talk about it. It must have meant total disruption and, according to his information, poverty: but she was elegant and expensive, living at the rate of sixty-five guineas a week at Balgarvie House. She had cursed the unknown writer who owned the Tully, yet Balgarvie to her, she said, was no more than a place for an occasional holiday. He looked at the harbour, seeing it again, and heard the young Anthea in a London pub describing to him the scene when the boats went out at night. "The most beautiful thing I ever saw," said the young voice. "I would like to see that when I'm dying. . . ."

He shook his head, as if he dismissed emotion, and frowned. The House, damn it. . . . If she wanted an expensive hotel holiday, why Balgarvie, the dullest of its kind? If she wanted Balgarvie, why the hotel? And if the past was forgotten, dead and buried, how was it that in one brief look they had shared such sorrow?

Anthea, dragging herself up the steep wynd, longed for her bed. Bed: warm, and secure, where nobody could get at you, where control might relax and where, as the hot bottle and blankets did their work, it was possible to pretend that everything was different. She reached the top of the wynd and walked on, fending off distress and the consciousness of disaster which were pressing so insistently, and bracing her tired muscles for the effort of slogging along the mile of road which stretched before her. But she was hardly out of the village before she heard a motor horn performing a vaguely familiar fanfare and Mr. Peachey's jeep drew up beside her.

"A hitch?" he cried, leaping out gallantly and hastening round to open the passenger's door. "Did I discern a slight lagging in the footsteps?"

She admitted, smiling, that he did, and climbed in. The relief, though fine for her body, was less restful for the mind but it would soon be over and she adjusted herself to the new effort. "I'm ashamed," she said ruefully. "I've been lolling in the car too much and I'm whacked—nearly—by a ten-mile walk."

"That dangerous first enthusiasm," said Mr. Peachey getting in beside her. "But—ten miles? One is allowed to be tired by ten miles of this country. Where have you been?" For the second time Anthea described her route and he clucked regretfully. "If I had only been a few minutes earlier I might have picked you up at the Tully—extraordinary name, isn't it? Nobody has been able to explain it to me: one feels it ought to mean something, but if it ever did it doesn't now. I went to look for John Gregorson, who lives there, but I didn't find him."

"He's in his boat," said Anthea, "disentangling a horrid mess of fish hooks."

"Oh *is* he?" Mr. Peachey's head turned, swift and inquisitive. "Do you know him then? I didn't think . . ."

"I used to know him. I haven't seen him for years."

"A surprising encounter, was it?"

"Very."

"Yes." He was looking ahead again. "Extraordinary place to find him, really. Still—he likes it and it certainly seems to suit him so far as his work is concerned. I think he's surprised everybody, there. I suppose you knew him in his *Trumpeter* days. Did you know him well?"

Anthea said, "Pretty well for a short time. You know how people come and go"—and cursed herself when, inevitably, he pounced.

"Ah! That sounds as if you were in that rackety world too."

"I did embark," she said, "and got as far as brewing the tea in the *Trumpeter* office."

"But you didn't persist? No. . . . It's an unsettled sort of life, I suppose, though I only observe from the fringe. Do you—presumably you had the usual ambition which leads one into the racket—do you, in fact, write?"

"Well," she said reluctantly, "nothing to speak of."

He laughed archly. "Ha, ha! I suspect you! But you keep it dark? *Nom de plume* and things?"

"Yes." This time there was no hesitation and he smiled.

"I suppose it's a tiresome thing to carry about with you," he observed unexpectedly. "Gregorson lurks in Balgarvie and you muffle yourself in anonymity." She said that there was no pressure whatever to penetrate her anonymity, and there was another swift glance. "And apparently I am not to be allowed to judge whether there should be. Oh well, I shall do a course of the women writers and see if I can deduce. You're not Agatha Christie, for a start."

They were coming to the hotel gates and he slowed for the turn and changed the subject as he changed gear. "I went to see if I could persuade Gregorson to put a tie on and come and drink with our American V.I.P. this evening. Simpson Cleever, do you know? He's a very good shot, but I think he's finding Balgarvie House just a trifle stark—or stagnant, perhaps."

"Simpson Cleever?" Anthea wrinkled her brows: she was not much interested in political personages. "Ought I to know about him? I don't—except that Lawrence Vine described him as a foot-and-mouth type."

"Ssssss!" Mr. Peachey drew in a hissing scandalised breath and, as the drive was straight and the car moving slowly, risked a brief closing of the eyes.

Anthea apologised. "Sorry. Do I mean emissary?"

"Emissary or observer," he said loudly and then dropped his voice to a conspiratorial mutter. "*Off the record*, Lawrence is right—an acute case, I'm afraid." His voice rose again, hopefully. "But quite clean about the house. Will you help to make my little gathering joyous for him by joining us before dinner?"

He had stopped and was getting out as he spoke, and when he opened the door and held out a hand, Anthea moved rather stiffly. "Thank you," she said. "I'd like to come, but—"

"By jove!" he exclaimed with concern. "You are tired, aren't you. Overdone it. . . ." He put a steadying hand under her arm. "I know what you want: an immediate bath and tea in your room."

"It sounds heaven," said Anthea, "but it's miles. Do they do it?"

"Of course they do it—it's what they're for," declared Mr. Peachey stoutly. "You go straight up and I'll tell them. You're all right, are you?"

She laughed. "Yes, of course I am. This is ridiculous. Thank you so much, Mr. Peachey."

"Not at all." He bowed. "I adore being knightly. The name is Desmond. Do join us later, won't you?"

Last lap, thought Anthea, climbing the stairs, and when she reached her room she went straight to an armchair and collapsed.

She was still sitting there with closed eyes when her tea arrived. "Come in," she called and opened them to see Morgan with a loaded tray.

"Your tea, Miss Logan," he announced correctly. "Mr. Peachey's orders. I hope it's all right?"

"M'm," said Anthea. "Thank you."

He was bright and chatty. "Where will you have it? It's been a marvellous day for your walk, hasn't it? At least it's looked marvellous, what I've seen of it." There was a pause for a wistful smile. "Actually I haven't been out at all

to-day—there hasn't been a minute. Tired? You look weary—a teeny bit fragile. Don't move—let me—where shall we—" He poised the tray over the obvious table. "Here, I think, don't you?"

"Just put it down, will you?" said Anthea.

The noise stopped and she shut her eyes again.

CHAPTER 5

WHEN Jock Gregorson arrived at Balgarvie and expended most of his capital on the Tully—at that time in a far from waterproof condition—the misdeeds of his youth unexpectedly proved themselves assets. For years while his parents were abroad he had spent the school holidays with his grandfather, a solitary, long-widowed minister whose parish lay between the moors of Galloway and the sea. Since there was nothing to amuse a boy in the manse, Jock went out and fell into low company from whom he learned how to handle a boat, a great deal about game, and most of what there is to know about poaching. This companionship partly explained the ease with which Balgarvie took him to its heart, and he had been for a time a member of *Lea-Rig*'s crew, while the poaching paid off in as many days as he liked to put in during the season as an auxiliary keeper and ghillie on the Balgarvie estate. Though two pounds a day and tips were no longer an object the jobs had been there when he needed them, means of subsistence exacting little in the way of thought or responsibility and so no distraction to his real job, and when he was at home he was still available if the estate or one of the boats was short-handed. He went to tea with the keepers and occasionally to dinner with the Laird and Mrs. Garvie; he drank with the fishermen at the Sun Tavern and went into the hotel for a meal or a drink from time to time. The young people of the village and the migratory flocks of students looked upon the Tully as a club and used it freely.

Mr. Peachey, finding nobody at home, went in—everybody went in—and left a note. He was laying on a little party to cheer Cleever, it said. "He needs relaxation and is eyeing Louisa with a speculative gaze. We have acquired, to the astonishment of all, a mysterious beauty named Anthea Logan, at once more glamorous and no doubt stronger in defence than Louisa, and I propose to recruit her. Come and meet her and, for once, do your stuff. Seriously, I do think people ought to take more uplift about visiting brass. The Establishment here, being off duty, simply dodges and it creates such a bad impression. To-night, by the way, 6:45-ish. D.P."

Jock smiled sourly when he read it and threw the note away. Then he picked it up again and tore it into small pieces. He was not much stirred by the neglect of visiting brass, nor concerned about Louisa, whose defences Mr. Peachey probably underestimated: and he had very little desire to see Anthea putting on a glamorous-beauty act either for Cleever or Peachey. But why mysterious? He turned on the bath, thinking about it. A young woman, alone, attractive and un-sporting, was certainly a novelty at Balgarvie House, but—mysterious? He stripped off the windcheater and disreputable slacks and made lavish use of his electrically heated bath water; and when he was clean he went to the cupboard which sheltered his wardrobe and took out a respectable suit.

Preparations for a cocktail party at Balgarvie House were not elaborate. They consisted of laying it on with Mr. Saunders, who detailed a student to the task of waiting on it. The host, when the time came, established himself in a corner, his chosen friends joined him, and the cost was later added to his bill. It was all very unobtrusive and those who were invited, *vis-à-vis* those who were not, could easily pretend it was not taking place.

In addition to the Americans, Mr. Peachey, doing good all round, had invited the Frenchmen; and in the English contingent, besides Anthea and Jock, were his scornful friend, whose name was Carruthers and who had been joined in the course of the day by an equally scornful wife, and the Vines.

Anthea had had a bad time upstairs when reaction could no longer be staved off and stirred-up memories asserted themselves, and she was a little late. But she had got herself well in hand again, she was prepared for the sight of Jock's black head towering above the rest of the party, and she had confidence in her frock. It was a slim, straight dress, creamy-white and severely plain, and Mr. Peachey's eyebrows and spectacles endorsed her own opinion of it as he hurried to meet her.

"Better?" he murmured confidentially. "Splendid! You look—to put it with all possible restraint—restored." He took her lightly by the elbow. "Now let's get all the bore of introductions over in one, may we? But here's Stewart—" he scooped the gentle wine-waiter forward, "let him give you a fortifier. . . ."

The introductions were performed with characteristic flourish. "Senator Cleever, I don't think you've met Miss Logan—let me present you. . . ." The other Americans—Mr. Scudamore, Mr. Hart. The French gentlemen, names clearly pronounced but unregistered. "And I want you to meet Vida and Bryce Carruthers, Anthea." The Americans said "Miss Logan" and bowed, the Frenchmen said "M'selle" and bowed. The scornful Carruthers, male and female, stared and said "Hallo," there were friendly nods from the Vines, and she had reached Jock Gregorson in his tidy suit.

Mr. Peachey, wishing uneasily that he could remember exactly what he had said in the note he left at the Tully, said brightly, "I know I don't have to introduce you two," and the gentlemanly figure before her, in contrast to the pirate she had been talking to in the afternoon and as a culmination of a somewhat absurd ceremony, widened Anthea's social smile to a grin. "Hi, Jock," she said, raising her glass, and met a well-remembered gleam of response as he returned her salute.

He and Sir Francis Vine were engaged in conversation with the Frenchmen, who looked as if they were wondering why they had been asked to this party, and Anthea was addressed by Lawrence in a voice tinged with reproach.

"I hear you and Greg met at the harbour." He was a little disgruntled. Having revealed the two principals to each other he had felt that he had a right to preside over their reunion—that, in a manner of speaking, it belonged to him. Instead it was Ness, with no benign feeling towards it all, who had been the witness, and it had led to the most disagreeable scene in the history of a relationship which, from the age of ten, had never risen much higher than armed neutrality. To call it a rocket was an understatement. "She was really angry," he said.

"Did she go for your shins?" asked Anthea.

"No, I wish she had. If I'd had a nicer nature I suppose I'd have made sure she knew, but I sort of took it for granted. Or rather," confessed Lawrence honestly, "I never gave her a thought. Everybody else knew."

"Well, I dare say it was a bit galling to be the last to hear," Anthea said on Ness's behalf. "*If*, as you imply, it's of general interest."

Lawrence gave her a be-your-age glance. "Nobody—in the pantry, I mean—has talked about anything else all day," he said.

Ness's manner that afternoon, though it had been overlaid at the time, had lingered somewhere in Anthea's memory: a rather painful little suspicion. If Ness was in love with Jock, as she easily might be, it would be natural enough that she should resent her, Anthea, in the part of his old friend. But that did not explain the earlier coldness, the unmistakable avoidance of contact.

"Why *didn't* she hear, if everybody's been talking about it?" she asked Lawrence.

"Oh well," he said, "Ness and Morgan are the ones who never stoop to idle chatter. They *don't* hear almost everything." Anthea laughed and he smiled at her, his brief rufflement over.

It was his ardent desire to have a good talk with her about Greg's books. Like many of his class—young, intelligent and perceptive—he had an admiration almost amounting to veneration for John Gregorson's work, which had the bite his class demanded and was yet, more unusually, constructive: and Anthea, enchanting in her own right, had additional enchantment in having known Greg—pretty well, his observation told him—before he was famous. Mr. Peachey, however, intervened. Miss Logan was not here to waste her time on Lawrence.

It was true that Balgarvie had been a disappointment to Senator Cleever in some respects. He was a good shot, there were plenty of birds, and as far as sport went the place lived up to its reputation and he had no fault to find with it: but socially, or rather in mixing, it had so far fallen short. Senator Cleever liked mixing. He liked decorously convivial men and would have been glad to have more opportunity of exchanging views with those, representing as they did a wide variety of interests, who were his fellow guests: and he liked decorative, attentive women listening to what he said. He was enjoying this civilised pleasure with Lady Vine, a charming, well-informed woman, and now here was this Miss Logan. Mr. Peachey offered up Anthea and Lady Vine stepped back.

"This is a beautiful country, Miss Logan." Senator Cleever, a tall, heavy man, carefully balanced on large feet, had forgotten the snags and spoke with enthusiasm. "For a man privileged to hold a position such as my country has done me the honour to confer upon me, a sanctuary like this, far removed from the stresses of our times, is a boon. A necessary refreshment. My life is one of well-nigh ceaseless travel; a continual, if I may humbly put it so, giving out . . ."

Anthea was uneasily aware of her ignorance. Apart from a few authors, living and dead, the President of the United States was the only one of its citizens she could be sure about—even he might grow a little hazy towards the middle of his term of office—and she had no idea how her new friend rated or what his particular line might be. All she had to do, however, was listen or appear to listen. She looked decorative and attentive and nodded respectfully from time to time and the Senator, encouraged and prompted by Mr. Scudamore, poured forth extracts from his speech which had worn a groove so deep that it was difficult for him to jump it.

She didn't dislike the Senator. He was a bore but an undemanding bore and his self-importance was of the simplest possible kind. He loved being important and sincerely believed that, in fact, he was. Mr. Scudamore, who was the senior of the two secretaries—or bodyguards—was neither simple nor a bore, and aroused her admiration by the skill with which he leavened the senatorial lump. Never for an instant did he poach or steal the show. If there was flattery in his manner to his chief it was highly acceptable to the flatteree; and his interjections contrived to make the pompous, reiterative flow not only bearable but nearly admirable. Looking at the Senator's solemn, honest face and his secretary's keen one, Anthea wondered a little why the clever man was content to play feed so assiduously. But no doubt it was a necessary stage. Mr. Scudamore, she felt sure, was on his way up.

So, obviously, was Mr. Peachey. His style, allowing for national differences, was not unlike Mr. Scudamore's, and with similar smooth competence he was flattering the top brass by shepherding his little flock as though it were a royal occasion. When Anthea had had her innings he brought up

John Gregorson the distinguished author, and since Mr. Scudamore did not function as a separate individual she was passed to Mr. Hart.

Mr. Hart was delighted. He was younger and very much less dedicated than his colleague and he welcomed her with a light in his eye which suggested that he was probably not destined to rise quite so high in the world. He reminded her of the dog Bracken. Sport proved an unfruitful topic. Though he had no doubt that the sport at Balgarvie rated high, it compared unfavourably, in his opinion, with hunting back home; and anyway he wasn't so keen on sport. What he liked was boats: not sailing—though if you had anything to do with boats you had to sail sometimes or appear to be nuts—but the craft themselves. This had led him to the study of history and from ships and the men concerned with them Nelson had popped up and gripped him. Mr. Hart was an expert on Nelson. He had read all the books: "And whenever I'm in London, Miss Logan, first thing I do, I go along to Trafalgar Square and say hallo."

Anthea was enchanted. "Are you often in London?" she asked, wondering if the pilgrimage was of regular occurrence.

"Oh yeah," he said carelessly. "Come over here a lot on account of the job." But though he talked freely she was left in the dark, quite neatly, as to the nature of the job. His present assignment, in orbit with Senator Cleever, appeared to be but a chapter in his professional story.

"It must be very interesting," she said, doing her best.

"Oh yeah," he said again. "We get around." The hopeful light intensified. "What do you find to do in the sticks, Miss Logan? Pardon me if I'm wrong, but you don't look the hunting type of girl to me."

She laughed and said once more that she liked the place. He was not quite floored by this, but he looked a little puzzled and she made an effort to be helpful. She liked walking, she said, and golf, and then, inspired, she added, "And I'm like you in a humble way—I like boats. Of course there are only fishing boats here, but the harbour—"

"Harbour?" said Mr. Hart, astounded. "Well, whadda you know? I've been here a week and never knew there's a harbour!"

"Didn't you notice the sea?"

"Oh yeah, sure I noticed it. But it doesn't follow, you know. There's an awful lot of empty sea and I never was down there. I don't get so much time. But now I guess I'll have to go take a look at it. Will you make a date and show me round?"

"It takes about five minutes to go round," she warned him. "It's really very small. You can spend quite a lot of time just looking, if you're that way inclined."

"I'm that way inclined all right," said Mr. Hart with enthusiasm.

Anthea's next assignment, jointly with Lady Vine, was the Frenchmen, who were showing little of the social verve for which their race is famed. Though they were polite and their English was adequate, it was up-hill work. They were tepid about Scottish sport and Scotland generally. Their visit to Balgarvie was to be brief, they were leaving in a day or two, and there was no pretence that they were sorry.

"I fear," murmured Lady Vine, when the ordeal was over, "that the young snipe have died in vain. Balgarvie has failed"—and looking very much amused she added almost in a whisper, "And I'm afraid everybody dodges the dear Senator. Poor Desmond! It worries him dreadfully that people aren't more attentive, but I really *don't* see why the men should suffer long, tedious discussions about world problems when they're on holiday. Heaven knows they have enough of them all the rest of the year. . . . Mr. Gregorson is behaving very nicely, however."

Anthea looked across at Mr. Gregorson, who was apparently giving the closest attention to Senator Cleever, and smiled as she agreed that he was behaving nicely. It was a most extraordinary experience to be with him in this company of strangers. Though Mr. Peachey's assiduous shepherding of his flock never brought them together the party was so small that they were always within sight and sound of each other, and every look, every gesture, every tone of voice was so familiar—she knew so exactly the fractional attention he was really giving to the Senator. Talking with him on the pier the years and the reserves had been barriers between them: here, among other, slightly known, people, these melted into nothing, leaving only the old intimacy.

The party was breaking up when she saw him making his way towards her. "A painstaking occasion," was his comment.

"But experience is never wasted," she reminded him. "You give a very pretty performance as a celebrity, and at least you've added to the French and American seasoning in your character stock-pot."

He looked amused. "And I now learn that Anthea Logan, writer, doesn't 'put people in her books,' which is good so far as it goes. I don't know that the stock-pot has gained much but the social credit account has risen. I can claim exemption for the rest of the season. . . . When will you come and see the Tully? Will you have a meal with me one evening?"

Anthea had thought about his invitation and reached a decision, and now, though it was with regret and some hesitation, she carried it out. She had heard from Lawrence about the Tully gramophone parties, she said. "Could I come to one of those?"

There was almost no pause and no protest. "By all means," Jock said smoothly. "You'd enjoy it, I believe —the Balgarvie music-lovers are worth meeting." He looked round. "Lawrence!" Lawrence came up, pleased and expectant. "Miss Logan would like to come to a record party. Will you—"

"Oh good," said Lawrence. "I thought she'd like it. Actually," he cocked an eye at her, "I *think* I call her Anthea."

Jock regarded his infatuated young friend with an air of patient long-suffering. "Settle it later," he advised. "You'll be able to make more of it. . . . Now, attend to the matter in hand. Will you notify your lot?"

"Will do. Everybody?"

"Certainly. We'll have the full strength." He turned to Anthea. "Which evening? Any preference . . .? Well, this is Tuesday: I'm full up to-morrow and I have some work that must go off this week—Friday do you?" Anthea said Friday would suit her, Lawrence was 'entirely at their disposal', and he smiled at the young man's pleased face. "You'll bring Anthea, then? Usual time. Now I must get off before Peachey thinks he ought to ask me to dinner. No—" as Lawrence opened his mouth hopefully, "I really have got work pressing. I'll look forward to seeing you on Friday, Anthea. 'Night, Lawrence. . . ."

They watched him take leave of his host and get clear and Lawrence turned to Anthea with most lively satisfaction. He knew she would enjoy the party at the Tully— Greg's parties were unique, nothing like them anywhere, the nicest mixty-maxty lot of people. . . . Anthea smiled and responded, concealing a heavy heart and a nagging, gritty dissatisfaction. It would have been civil and—while it lasted—such fun to go to the Tully as Jock asked her, for a meal, a talk and some records. To make her acceptance conditional was merely evasion, weak-minded, awkward—a lamentable display of dither leading to an unintentional and uncalled-for snub. And it pledged her to three more days at Balgarvie. What was she going to do in the days which expediency—pride—required her to spend at Balgarvie House?

This question was answered for her the following morning. Breakfast was an informal meal, with hot dishes arranged on a side table from which guests helped themselves, and only one girl and one of the young men on toast-and-coffee duty. Anthea was rather late that morning and when she went down most of the guests had gone out. But Mr. Hart had not gone out. He had hung about, puzzling Louisa and her colleague, and when Anthea appeared in the dining-room they were delighted to see him spring forward and attend her to the hot-plate.

"Say—what about our date?" he began at once. "Guess you want something to eat, though. What are you going to have? Fruit juice? Cereal? And there's all these cooked foods. . ."

Anthea surveyed the cooked foods gloomily. An array of food is not invariably stimulating to the appetite. "I'm not really hungry," she said. "Yes—fruit juice. . . ."

"Would you like a boiled egg, Miss Logan?" suggested Louisa. "They're here—ready to put on."

The eggs were lying in a bowl, fresh, brown and obscurely reassuring. "Yes," said Anthea, "that's exactly right," and received a quick, brilliant smile as she went to her table closely followed by Mr. Hart with the fruit juice.

"Aren't you shooting to-day?" she asked him.

"Why no," he said. "I don't get much sport right now. I'm not really on vacation. But"—his eyes were fixed on her, full of hope—"I'm only working sort of half-cock and so long's I get through the assignment the old man doesn't care when I do it. Any chance we make that trip to the harbour to-day, Miss Logan? Say—" there was a slight pause, an inevitable stage in this approach, "that sounds kinda stiff. . . ."

Anthea granted him the privilege of calling her Anthea and heard that he was Chester, Chet to his friends. She sipped fruit juice and made a few calculations. First, Jock was booked for the day to Colonel Garvie in some capacity

73

or other so he would not be messing about in *Skua*. Second, the boats were beginning to come in while she was talking to him yesterday-

"Well?" said Chet.

"I was thinking about the tide," she said. "If we go down after tea we'll see the boats come in and the fish being sold. Will that do?"

"Sure," he said. "Will you take tea with me first or—?"

"I don't know what I'll be doing," said Anthea. "Let's leave it. I'll be here about five."

"Your egg, Miss Logan," said Louisa.

"Good morning to you," said Mrs. Carruthers.

Chester Hart got politely to his feet, Mrs. Carruthers slumped rather heavily into the chair thus vacated, and Louisa sailed away. Since the lady was clearly there for keeps Chet gave a small bow and went away too.

Mrs. Carruthers had come to make friends.

"I gather from Desmond," she drawled, fitting a cigarette carefully into a holder, "that you aren't stuck on shootin' and fishin' either, so I thought we might as well get together. What *do* you do all day?"

Anthea gave an expurgated version of her well-worn piece: walking; relations; golf perhaps. Mrs. Carruthers lit the cigarette and watched her through the smoke as she ate her egg. Clearly the simple programme left her unimpressed.

"You're not an artist or anything? Writing—Desmond said something. You haven't come up here to write like this Gregorson?"

"No."

"Oh well, you may or may not have known what you were letting yourself in for. Believe me I only came to dig Bryce out."

Her voice was deep, her speech was slow, and Anthea felt surrounded. She finished her egg and as she reached for the marmalade asked politely, "Have you been here before?"

74

"No. Neither has Bryce actually, and quite frankly I'm not sure he's so glad he's here now. I mean shooting's all very well, but why be so earnest about it? He came with Desmond. They were at school together and they're the kind of old chums that baffle me. *You* know—" she waved her cigarette—"they meet. Desmond, being the out-going type, says 'Hullo, old boy,' Bryce says 'Huh,' and that's it. Nothing in common and no communication as far as one can tell."

Anthea, with a sudden, vivid picture of the two men, laughed, and a curious metamorphosis took place in the face which confronted her. Mrs. Carruthers was tall and svelte—though it was a thick svelteness like a well-groomed seal—and her large face commonly wore a bored scowl. Now, in response to Anthea's laugh, it showed a kind of minor convulsion. She did not actually smile, her eyebrows did not rise nor her forehead grow higher and wider, but all these changes appeared to happen and her eyes glimmered with reluctant amusement.

"My mother stayed here once in the old days," she said. "God, she loathed it! The men out all day and the women trudging after them through the rain or sitting about with old Mrs. G. in despair. And the evenings, says my mum, were a concert of snores and grunts and they all went to bed at ten to be ready to do it all over again to-morrow. I shouldn't think, from what I've seen, that it's changed much."

"Except that there are no obligations to Mrs. Garvie and one needn't trudge after the men," said Anthea.

"No, thank God," said Mrs. Carruthers piously. "Still, I hope Bryce doesn't want to stay long. How long are you here for?" Anthea said she wasn't sure. Not long, but she had no definite plans. "Just drifting? Here to-day, gone to-morrow—lucky you. Well look, I don't see why we shouldn't do each other a bit of good."

Mrs. Carruthers leant her elbows on the table and fixing Anthea with an earnest stare outlined her proposition. Three was a hopeless number. Anthea was on her own, which wasn't all that much fun. Balgarvie House was a morgue. However, if they got together they might contrive to amuse themselves. "Count me out for the strapping walks, and you can keep your relations and the Manse, but we can play golf and—you know—drive around . . . exploit whatever there is. . . . Ciggie?"

Anthea accepted a cigarette and, without committing herself too far, thought, as she drank her last cup of coffee, that at least Mrs. Carruthers offered a solution to one of her problems. Golf and any other amusements of a social nature would be better—and would certainly look better—than spending the next few days in the negative occupations of avoiding Jock and not going to the harbour.

"We may as well move, if you've finished," said Mrs. Carruthers. "The blonde has about had us."

They were the only people left in the dining-room and Louisa's shining head was a little bowed, but she smiled warmly when Anthea apologised, and begged her not to hurry. The two ladies had her cordial approval and good wishes. All the undergraduate staff found it maddening— more or less—that a place with so much money in it as Balgarvie House should be so dull, and Miss Logan, beautiful, glamorous and, according to Lawrence, fun, was just the person to liven it up. Mrs. Carruthers they regarded with less enthusiasm, but from scraps of conversations overheard she was judged to have the right spirit. Every revolution needs one tough organiser.

CHAPTER 6

CHET Hart fell for the harbour with instant enthusiasm. He also very nearly fell in. The work of the fleet proceeded as usual. Boats came in, unloaded and moved to their moorings, making way for others, and no notice was taken of the excited visitor with the crew-cut and the strange shoes. With a spatter of exclamations—"Gee! Willya look at the way those houses roost on that bank!"—Chet hurried about, taking photographs from every possible and impossible angle: leaning out over the water at a degree that looked far beyond balancing point, backing rapidly, camera to eye, to the edge of the breakwater.

"Chet—*come back*!" cried Anthea, feeling like an agitated nanny, and he looked behind him and grinned.

"You don't have to worry," he assured her. "I won't go in—it wouldn't be good for the film—but I can swim, you know."

"I'd hate to see you doing it."

"You would? You wouldn't just laugh?"

"Laugh," she exclaimed. "It gives me the jitters even to think of it." The face gazing at her changed and she hastened to add that her jitters were general. "I'm just terrified of edges myself and I hate seeing other people near them."

But it was no good. Chet advanced, his eyes filled with tenderness, and took her arm. "Come back then," he said, steering her away from the edge, though she was not very near it. "Gosh, you're sweet. I never saw a girl as lovely as you."

"Now Chet," she said sternly, "this isn't—"

"It's all right," said Chet. "You don't have to worry."

He led her carefully round a heap of pale lilac net. "Why'd they have it this colour? It's mighty pretty but—well, never mind. It's all right, Anthea. I'm not asking anything. I know I'm not the kind of guy for a girl like you."

"You're a very good sort of guy for any girl," she said, "but—"

"No. A girl like you rates the top. I'm just a bum that happens to be good at languages. I'll never get far. But you—you're beautiful; rich, I suppose. Different class."

She looked at him curiously and then seized on a possible diversion. "I should have thought you had got far. I don't know anything about Americans, but Senator Cleever is one of the top people, isn't he?"

"Well," said Chet, "he gets around and he knows quite a lot. I reckon he counts for something. But," he added gloomily, "you get kinda tired circling the globe and I don't really care for knowing a lot of crap other people don't. Guess I'll maybe get out after this trip. Stay home for a while and help my old man sell hardware."

"Wouldn't that be a bit dull after all the travelling and —knowing things?"

Chet didn't think it would be dull. He used to think so, but not now. Old man Hart owned a chain of hardware stores, and getting around the circuit would give him all the travelling he fancied for quite a while. "I don't know but what Pop would get a mighty slow sales clerk, though," he added with a faint grin. "I got so conditioned to not saying anything it'd be hard even to divulge the price of a skillet."

Anthea laughed aloud. "Is that why—" she began and then stopped, but he picked up her question and answered it readily.

"Nelson? Well—yeah. Matter of fact I think a lot of Nelly. He was a great little guy. I've read about him and I go take a look once in a while, but—"

"That's your gambit?"

"Yeah—my English one, that is."

"Senator Cleever just sticks to his speech, I suppose," Anthea, rather fascinated by this glimpse back-stage, and he snorted with laughter. "What about Mr. Scudamore?"

"I don't know Scud has any particular gambit," he said. "He sticks pretty close by the chief most of the time."

"Mr. Cleever has a little shadow that goes in and out with him?"

"Quote?" said Chet, interested. "Yeah, I guess that gets it. Hey—what's this?"

"This" was the appearance of two boats coming in together through the gap between the breakwaters: *Fair Weather*, green-painted and smart, with *Lea-Rig*, smaller and brown, rolling with an air of helplessness in tow. Even to a dull imagination the sight of a boat in trouble is terrible. To Anthea's lively one, *Lea-Rig's* helplessness was sickening: and no sooner had what might be called the general sickening set in—which, like her general jitters about edges, she would have felt for any boat—than the sight of Jock's black head and towering height among *Lea-Rig's* blue-oil-skinned crew gave her another, more particular jolt.

"What's adae?" roared a stentorian voice from the quay, and it was Jock, standing by with a fender, who shouted back one laconic word, "Shaft."

"Goad A'michty!" commented the stentorian voice in a descending tone of disgust and was silent.

Fair Weather manoeuvred herself and her charge into the middle of the basin to wait till room was made for them at the quay, and Anthea and Chet, hurrying round to the fish-market to watch, found themselves beside Sir Andrew Gibb and Lawrence.

The Balgarvie boats were manned by crews of five. There must, Anthea reckoned, be at least four other women— wives, mothers, sweethearts—feeling what she felt, to say nothing of family feelings and those of a close community which knew and shared the dangers of disaster at sea. There were more women to be seen than there usually were, and the two boats at the quay were being unloaded very fast, but there was no other sign of excitement and only the on-lookers talked about *Lea-Rig*.

"Say—isn't that Mr. Gregorson?" said Chet, puzzled. He had been introduced the evening before to a tidy, reputedly successful author.

Lawrence, with the complacency of one who knows about the private life of a celebrity, explained something of Mr. Gregorson's position in Balgarvie. "He worked regularly on the boats or the estate before his books began to make money," he said, "and he always helps if they're short-handed."

"I thought he was doing something for Colonel Garvie to-day," said Anthea, whose feelings had subsided into a cross sense of injustice.

"He couldn't manage it," said Sir Andrew. "One of Ecky Soutar's crew had an abscess. He had to go to the dentist."

Chet was still mystified but there was no real hope of clearing the matter up. "Lucky the other guys were handy," he observed. "Or do they always stay close—in a group?"

"They're not in a group as a rule," said Sir Andrew, "but their range is not so great—forty miles is about the limit—so they're not very widely separated. If there's trouble they're not often left alone for long."

"Unless there's a storm," said Anthea.

Sir Andrew smiled at her and agreed that it wouldn't be very nice if a broken shaft and a gale coincided. "But they're not so often in danger as they used to be," he said. "It's by no means a sheltered life now but it's very different from what it was as I remember it sixty years ago."

"*Sixty years!*" exclaimed three voices in unison, and he laughed.

"More. I'm seventy-five and I was born in the Manse up there. They had no help from radio and meteorology in those days."

"Gee!" breathed Chet. "What was it like, sir? The place, I mean."

Sir Andrew was delighted to reminisce for the three pleasant young people who shared his liking for Balgarvie harbour, and they were presently seated in a row on Anthea's favoured bench on the pier.

The two young men—Lawrence sitting back with his legs crossed, Chet leaning eagerly forward with legs apart and hands dangling between his knees—asked questions, commented and exclaimed, but Anthea sat in silence. She was listening, but only with part of her mind. *Ocean Queen* and *Crimond* moved away from the quay and *Fair Weather* worked herself and *Lea-Rig* into position. It seemed that *Lea-Rig* had fished for most of the day, for the crew set about unloading a fair shot, and at this distance Anthea could watch every movement without being noticed, and she was free, too, while her companions' attention was happily engaged, to be as miserable as she liked. If she was not saying good-bye to the harbour now she would be saying it very soon and she was angry with herself, feeling she had been a fool. About Jock, to whom she would also be saying good-bye, she had nothing with which she could reproach herself: it was bad luck but nothing more that the old pain had been revived by this meeting, as it was bad luck that he had chosen to live in the Tully, but at least she had never indulged in dreams about Jock. Of Balgarvie and its harbour she had dreamed, making for herself a kind of superstition on which she staked everything, and now that the place was to all intents and purposes closed to her she was at a loss. Her eyes went to the Tully, securely planted on its hill-side, trim, well cared-for and sure of itself, and she wondered, as she had wondered many times since yesterday, what had been in Jock's mind when he said she could have it. Sheer generosity? Perhaps. He was certainly not the man to say such a thing in a pretence of generosity, knowing well that it would not be accepted. Conscience and gratitude came in—

he felt he owed her a good deal: but could he suspect how thin was the barrier between desired freedom and desolation?

She glanced along at Chet's eager face, drinking in what Sir Andrew was saying, listening to the voice of history itself, and almost wondered what it would be like to be married to Chet and living in America. If she must laugh at his plunge into love it was affectionate laughter—indeed she was grateful. But there was no hopefulness in the gratitude. She had only to look at the black head and strong shoulders of Jock Gregorson at work unloading *Lea-Rig*'s catch and accept the truth calmly and finally. No other head and shoulders would ever mean a thing; no thought of danger for any other man would ever so tear at her vitals, and no place would ever grip her imagination and command her love like Balgarvie. But—there were other places: and plenty of women, less well equipped than she, lived and made a good thing of life alone.

". . . a great deal of superstition, of course," Sir Andrew was saying. "Much less now I dare say, but I've no doubt some of it lingers to this day. I remember my father telling me . . ." The pleasant Scots voice with its beautiful articulation went on.

"Are you cold, Anthea?" Lawrence asked suddenly.

"Cold?" she said. "No, I'm not cold."

Chet turned with quick concern and Sir Andrew looked at her kindly. "Perhaps," he said, "Miss Logan has an uncomfortably vivid imagination. Were you wallowing helplessly in *Lea-Rig*, or have I given you the superstitious creeps?"

"A bit of both, perhaps," said Anthea. She gathered herself together and got up. "But mostly—it's time to go."

When Anthea and Chet returned from the harbour, Vida Carruthers met them in the hall. There had been a little ill-feeling when, after they had spent the morning together,

Anthea left her, but she had recovered her good temper and was happy with plans for the evening.

They must hurry, she told them. She and Bryce were having a party for drinks before dinner. "And I've marked down a remote room where we can have fun—" she glanced round and dropped her voice, "without *waking* anybody. . ."

The Carruthers' party was different from Mr. Peachey's. It was as though his had been the thin end of the wedge and nonsense had now crept in. It was not rowdy but it was gay. Bryce Carruthers proved to be a raconteur and though he himself never raised his voice his stories provoked bursts of laughter. Mr. Peachey, very relaxed since this was not a diplomatic occasion, contributed a rapier-like wit, while Mr. Scudamore held his own with a salty Americanism which made Anthea giggle. She herself had not kept her end up in a newspaper office for nothing, and Vida rallied Senator Cleever.

"Now," said Vida when it was time to go in to dinner, "we meet afterwards in the—what is it, Desmond?"

"The morning-room," said Mr. Peachey.

"The morning-room—there," she pointed. "Nobody ever goes in and we'll have a lovely little gamble. You'll come, won't you, Senator Cleever?"

But the Senator regretted that he and the boys had work to do after dinner. "Don't misunderstand me, Mrs.—uh, Vida. Nothing would give me greater pleasure than to join you. A little harmless amusement is beneficial to all of us. But I have many calls on my time. In a position such as I have the honour to hold a real vacation is a very, very rare event."

"Talk about stuffed shirts," said Vida as they went in to the dining-room. She looked round the diners discontentedly. "They might as well all be dead. That leaves the four of us."

"Comecomecome," said Mr. Peachey, lightly soothing. "Don't let us despair. If Anthea plays bridge and is agreeable we may surely amuse ourselves—harmlessly. Anthea?"

83

"Not if it's the savage kind," said Anthea.

"We'll be ever so mild," said Bryce Carruthers. "Why'n't you eat your dinner with us?"

Under his stare and the persuasion of Mr. Peachey, Anthea could think of no reason except the useless one: she didn't want to. She yielded gracefully but even as she sat down she regretted it. There was, from the moment Vida sat down at her breakfast table, a feeling of being engulfed, and joining them for dinner not only meant a substantial swallow, it identified her as, so to speak, one of the gang.

They played bridge and she and Mr. Peachey lost money to Bryce and Vida, who were, she thought, very far from mild. Next morning they played golf. In the afternoon they drove in Mr. Peachey's jeep to a view-point in the hills, an occasion when everyone was very brilliant and he was also informative. "Cormorants," he would point out: or, "This is the Balgarvie march. Old Tibberley's place—gone terribly to seed. Great bore for Garvie: makes the stalking so difficult in this part of the forest. . . ." In the evening there were more drinks, more stories and a larger party for after-dinner gambling. On Friday morning there was golf again. . . . There was always Vida. And Chet and Lawrence on the side-lines, ready to rush in whenever they saw an opening.

Jock Gregorson was near but she never saw him. A prompt, polite good night on Tuesday, a general wave from *Lea-Rig's* deck on Wednesday: nothing else but the contrast between Jock and the people she did see, and the consciousness that he was there, that she might meet him round the next corner. Ness McNaughton was also there, also avoiding her. Morgan was omnipresent.

It was impossible to be unaware of Morgan. He was constantly about in the public rooms, and whereas the other students came and went with pleasant, impersonal friendliness, he gave her a creeping sensation as though a snail crawled over her. She kept finding his eyes on her, sometimes appealing but sometimes with a hint of the arrogant male which made her wonder crossly if he was enjoying an attraction—even, when his eyes widened, if he fancied a response. He was rather popular with some of the guests, who apparently liked his ready chattiness and "of-course-we-speak-the-same-language" approach, but she had more than an impression that Lawrence disliked him and that the other staff, with the exception of Ness who was demonstratively friendly, avoided contact. Remembering Lawrence's remarks about halitosis Anthea decided that Morgan was a sufferer: whether physically she hoped she would never know, but his spiritual exhalations were almost tangible and she rated Ness's charity high and her perception low.

On Thursday, when she first played golf with the Carruthers and Desmond Peachey, she asked Morgan, unwillingly but according to agreement, to fetch the clubs for her.

"Of course I will," he said gladly. "I'll get them right away. I'm afraid you'll think me a terrible fuss-pot,"—he smiled apologetically—"but—*you* know—one's doing a job." The smile became significant. "And it's a pleasure to do anything for you. . . ."

He hurried away and Vida, arriving in time for the smile, said, "Really, Anthea, you oughtn't to be allowed. I must watch Bryce."

Morgan came hurrying back, all concern. "Miss Logan, I've just looked at the balls and I'm afraid they're terrible. Not fit for you to use. See. . . ."

He displayed four dingy and imperfect spheres, much hacked, and Anthea agreed that they were unusable. "You haven't got any to sell?"

"I'm afraid not. I don't know what to suggest. I just didn't think of looking. I'm so terribly—"

"I think I've got about three," Vida said, opening the

pocket of her bag.

"What's all this?" cried Mr. Peachey, bustling up. "Good God! What disgusting pills! Morgan—what are you thinking about? Can't you do better than that?"

He spoke sharply and Morgan bridled. "I'm afraid, sir—"

"You should have seen to it—sent to Carse for new ones for Miss Logan. Never mind—just fetch my bag, will you. I always"—to Anthea—"have plenty."

"I'm rather a hacker," she said, "*and* a loser, but I will replace."

"Don't give it a thought," said he.

After the game Anthea put her clubs away herself but Morgan waylaid her before she went upstairs. "I'm so terribly sorry about that," he said in an anguished wail. "I wouldn't have had it happen for the world. Of course I was silly not to make sure there were decent balls but Mr. Peachey doesn't quite understand. I'm not a golf pro, I mean, as well as a barman. But I feel so terrible about letting *you* down. What must you think of me?"

"Don't give it a thought," Anthea said in her turn. His eyes were glued to her face and the degree of intimacy he managed to imply by the simple expedient of omitting to use her name was infuriating, but she could only ignore it.

"I can't help it," he was insisting. "I feel terrible—honestly I do—and you're being so utterly sweet about it. Shall I get some from Carse? I could go myself or—"

Anthea had a vision of a dozen expensive new balls which she did not want. "No," she said. "I'll get some if I want them. Don't bother, Morgan."

She escaped and later in the day made a satisfactory bargain with Lawrence, purchasing from him three respectable repaints. But Morgan continued to feel terrible and on Friday morning the climax came.

She went to her room after breakfast feeling tired and gloomily contemplating another day of golf and organised gaiety. And in the evening Jock and the Tully. . . . She was thinking as she climbed the stairs that this party of Jock's was like a gigantic obstacle in her path: coming up to it she could not see it clearly, she could see absolutely nothing beyond it, but when she was through—and one always contrived to brush through somehow—she would be able to turn her mind and her grip to the business of inventing a plausible reason for leaving Balgarvie almost at once. She opened the door of her room and there on the table lay a box containing a dozen expensive new golf balls. It was wrapped in brown paper and addressed in a flourishing hand to Miss Anthea Logan.

"Accept these, won't you," said an enclosed note suavely, and a masterful "M" was the signature.

"Hell and damnation!" said Miss Anthea Logan regarding it wrathfully. Should she bundle it up and take it to Mr. Saunders, thus ensuring that the silly idiot heard officially that he had dropped a major brick? Not, she decided with irritated compunction, till she had a shot at dealing with it herself. Though she trusted that power would be vouchsafed her to wither his folly once and for all, she had no wish to get him into serious trouble.

Morgan had already gone to fetch her clubs when she went downstairs, and she went after him to the games store. "Morgan," she said, "I told you not to order balls for me. As you know, I got all I need from Lawrence. What is the explanation of this?"

He had looked up when she appeared, welcoming and expectant, and as she held out the box his smile became a laugh. "Oh heavens! That's nothing. These are just—from me. I couldn't let you go on playing with Lawrence's cast-offs—he might have done better for you than that. Take them, please, and I'll know you've forgiven me and we're—friends."

The depth of the last word was almost too much for Anthea but she pressed on. "As you've bought them," she said crisply, "I'll pay for them if you can't get rid of them in some other way, but I must tell you again—I don't want them. And there is no question at all of your giving them to me."

He persisted. "*I* don't want them. I got them for you. It's just to make up for—"

"No," she stopped him. "You've made a mistake. I must say I think you should have known better, but now you must take it from me that you *have* made a mistake and we'll forget it. I'll pay for these and that will be the end of it."

She took out her purse but he put his hands behind him and backed away laughing. "Oh no," he said. "Don't worry. I may be working as a humble barman but I'm not so hard up that I can't afford to give a small present to—someone I like."

A battered kitchen table stood in the middle of the room and Anthea had a horrid vision of herself chasing a provocative Morgan round it, pound notes in one hand and a box of golf balls in the other. Nothing would delight him more. She stood where she was and put the money back in her pocket and the box on the table. Morgan misinterpreting her stillness, genuinely or not, stopped his playful retreat and advanced, chin out. Even as he came she saw the absurdity—recognised the dominant male about to disclose his passion and thought poorly of the act: but the danger— of loss of dignity, of disgusting unpleasantness—was no less because the act was corny, and she summoned all her force of will.

"You will take these back and we'll have no more nonsense," she said icily. "You're behaving like a stupid child." It sounded weak, the sort of thing one might say to sniggering schoolgirls, but Morgan paused.

"I see," he said, now openly insolent, as she picked up her clubs and turned to the door. "I'm a servant. I've—

what's the line?—I've taken a liberty. You couldn't be more mistaken, as it happens, my dear Miss Logan, but perhaps you can't see beyond the white coat. It would be all right to take a present from a *gentleman*—Desmond or—"

"If you annoy me again," said Anthea quietly, "I will report you instantly to Mr. Saunders."

She walked away, upset and with a feeling of degradation, to be rather a silent member of the gay foursome on the golf course, and an hour or so later Lawrence heard the story according to Morgan.

CHAPTER 7

IT WAS Lawrence's custom, if he was in the House in the middle of the morning, to make his way to the pantry, where coffee and companionship could be found. This year he was spending a number of mornings in on account of a little embarrassment connected with examinations, and when he put his head round the door nobody was surprised. The usual party was there, some of them engaged in cleaning silver, others present only for refreshment.

"Come in," said Biddy, Anthea's appetising little brunette, who was presiding. "Want a cup?"

Lawrence always wanted a cup. "Thanks," he said, taking a chair. "I really—well, partly—came to see who wants a lift to Greg's to-night. I don't know if I can manage everybody. . . ."

He was slightly wary. As a rule he could manage any number of passengers in his father's estate car, but Anthea could hardly be thrown on to a heap of bodies and laps and somebody might start being funny. No one did, however. There was silence as Biddy poured out his coffee, and he became aware of tension.

"I think," she said, glancing at Stewart, the wine waiter, "we're walking, aren't we?"

"Yes," said Stewart, and Louisa, who wore a large pair of gloves and was polishing spoons, beamed at them benevolently.

"I accept with pleasure, Lawrence love," she said. "And so does Alec, I'm sure. His feet are killing him and he really doesn't care for fresh air."

Alec, the dark youth, agreed cordially and Lawrence said, "O.K. Who else? Ness? Morgan?"

The tension became acute. Ness, also wearing gloves, was

sitting near Louisa polishing forks and did not look up. Morgan, present only to drink coffee, stared gloomily into his cup.

"I'm not going," Ness said shortly.

Morgan raised his eyes. "Oh look, Ness—please don't feel like that," he said. "Honestly, I'd rather you went. I mean it's sweet of you, but I can't bear to think of you missing things because of my stupid troubles."

"I'm not going," repeated Ness, polishing vigorously.

"Why not?" asked Lawrence.

Neither of the principals replied. Morgan gazed at Ness, Ness kept her eyes on the forks, and the bright, mischievous glance of Louisa went from one to the other and back to Lawrence.

"I'm afraid, Lawrence dear," she said in a low voice, "that Miss Logan has not been quite kind to Morgan."

"Oh, Louisa, don't be *provoking!*" cried Biddy. "It isn't funny. I'm quite *sure* she didn't mean to be unkind or—or rude—"

"*Rude?*" Lawrence exclaimed. "What the devil's this about? Anthea—Miss Logan—couldn't be rude—"

"It's all very confused." This was the loud public-school voice of Alec. "And we're rather upset and emotional, but we *gather* that Anthea, Miss Logan"—he said it without emphasis as if it were a title—"spoke to Morgan as if he was a waiter."

"A mere waiter," added Louisa.

Ness slammed down the current fork. "You really are *foul*, Louisa," she said furiously. "And you too, Alec. You're simply distorting the whole thing. Ever since she came she—Anthea—has treated Morgan as if he was a—a—a *serf*. Tea in her room—up all these miles of stairs . . . fetching her clubs every time she goes out . . . and never a word of thanks. And now—this morning—he'd taken all the trouble of getting new balls from Carse and she practically threw them in his face. Just said she didn't want them after all and he'd *paid* for them."

"Well, she didn't want them," said Lawrence. "And she couldn't have told Morgan to get them because she got some from me and said they'd see her through. You've made a mistake," he said curtly to Morgan. "If you've paid for them I don't mind taking them off you, but you'd better keep your mouth shut."

Stewart and Biddy, who were peace-makers and usually thought and spoke in unison, said that there must have been a muddle. Miss Logan was always pleasant, always grateful for anything done for her, and they were sure she would never be anything but kind. Morgan must have misunderstood. Ness snorted and Morgan sighed.

"I don't *think* I got it wrong," he said. "Of course this isn't quite one's normal position in life and when you're a bit worried you don't always notice things, but really, she was . . . Well," he smiled ruefully, "I was fair took aback."

Alec rose with an air of profound boredom and began collecting clean silver on a tray. "Cheer up," he said. "She may merely have felt tetchy this morning and apologise with a hunk of a tip."

"Oh heavens!" Morgan protested. "I never think about *that*."

"Don't you?" said Louisa, surprised. "I think about it all the time. So does Alec, don't you, Alec?" And she sang in a sweet high voice, "When Desmond smi-hi-hi-hiles, My heart he begui-hi-hi-hiles, With thoughts of dough . . ."

"Tips have nothing to do with it." Ness, still polishing as if her life depended on it, broke into the improvisation. "It's a matter of *fairness* and *decency*. If Morgan did make a mistake about the new balls she didn't need to get angry and make a scene: and it wouldn't have hurt her just to take them and pay for them. She spends enough on herself." She put down the clean fork and took up another. "So, as far as I'm concerned, this party's off. Actually, I think it's a mistake to get mixed up with the guests anyway."

"Thank you," said Lawrence.

"I didn't mean you, Lawrence, as you very well know. You're different, but—"

Lawrence, who was very angry, interrupted again with a flow of rapid speech. "I must say I'd have thought your cousin was just as different. I don't know why, but you've been going a mile round to avoid her all the time and if you were a man I'd say you were behaving like a damned oaf. I think this is just part of whatever bee you've got in your bonnet, because, if I may say so, I don't believe this sob-story of Morgan's." Ness opened her mouth but he merely raised his voice. "*And* what about Greg? For once he's asked us for a—an occasion instead of just letting us swarm all over his property when we feel like it, and it's discourteous, to put it mildly, to toss your head and say you're not going after all because you think it's better not to mingle with his guests."

"I look forward to it," said Louisa airily, "without fear of embarrassment."

"It's not—" Ness began and stopped. "I'll go and see Greg and explain."

"How?" demanded Lawrence.

Alec, who had a large selection of laughs, produced his uneasy one. "Uh-huh, uh-huh, uh-huh! How indeed, dear Ness? I'm glad it's your explanation and not mine. Greg's a nice easy guy but he's far from simple and far from soft."

"*Oh hell!*" cried Morgan suddenly. "I can't stand this–" and he got up and flung out of the room.

Alec clapped a tragic hand to his brow. Louisa said, "Alas, poor Morgan! So sensitive. . . . I'm afraid, Ness, you're going to have to face Greg alone, but no doubt you have courage for ten, let alone two." She turned to Lawrence. "Lawrence dear, don't think me heartless, but I'm consumed with eagerness to see Miss Logan and Greg together. You don't feel it too deeply?"

Lawrence was conscious that he had been a little too heated in Anthea's defence, and he knew Louisa well. Letting his jaw drop he gaped at her avidly and hissed, "What do you expect to see?"

There was a giggle from Biddy and the atmosphere lightened. "*Well*," said Louisa, "it *is* interesting. It could tie in. You see, our beloved Greg isn't young—he must be well over thirty. Why hasn't he married? There must, one feels, have been a woman in his life."

"Probably several, don't you think?" said Alec.

"Yes, but one special enough to keep him single for her sake. Now—could it be Miss Logan? After all, you know — why is she here?"

"I like this," said Lawrence. "Good meaty stuff. Go on, Louisa."

"Really!" burst from Ness. "You have the filthiest minds!"

Louisa's eyes were wide and earnest. "But, Ness dear, do face it. Gentlemen *are* interested in ladies. And ladies are occasionally interested in gentlemen." The eyes were modesty cast down. "Well, the point is, you can't, without risk of grave failure in tact, barge in and tell Greg you won't mingle with one who may be all the world to him, now *can* you?"

"Even Ness," said Lawrence, the light interlude over, "can hardly go round *broadcasting* tripe about her cousin."

Ness had finished the forks and drew off her gloves. "I don't accept any responsibility for my cousin," she said coldly. "Nobody asked her to come, she isn't even staying with us, and I hardly know her. Of course I won't say anything to Greg, except that Morgan and I can't go. But I stick by my friends."

94

"I think you're making too much of it, you know," Stewart said uncomfortably. "Morgan is touchy and—"

"Touchy?" cried Ness.

Biddy rallied in support of Stewart. "Yes he is, Ness. You know he is. He's always being hurt or—or slighted."

"Too, too true," muttered Alec.

"I suppose," said Ness, rising to her feet, "you just forget, or don't take in, that Morgan's life is pretty well ruined. The rest of us are just doing a holiday job—what's his future? He can't go on with university."

Lawrence felt uncomfortable but he was not convinced that it was necessary. "I thought," he said, "that if a chap got a place the State saw him through."

"So did we all think," said Alec.

"In theory," Ness corrected them. "It doesn't go so far as to support his widowed mother—"

"But—" said several voices.

"Oh," she cried impatiently, "in theory again. But he's told me what she's expected to live on. Of course for someone like her—and her health isn't good—it's pitiful. He simply has to get on and earn something."

There was an uneasy silence broken by Louisa. "Some people do have it very tough," she said soberly, "but Morgan, you know, is sometimes a victim and sometimes far otherwise—the gay young sprig being a barman for kicks. Which is it? And why should Miss Logan have it in for him specially? She couldn't be nicer to the rest of us."

Ness, who was on her way to the door, stopped. Morgan, she said, felt his position terribly, and he was terribly worried but he tried terribly hard not to be depressing about it. As for Anthea, she supposed she pushed him around because he let himself be pushed. Her hand was on the door knob and she fired her parting shot. "I'm afraid I don't care for the type of woman who spends thousands on herself and goes up in the air about paying for a few golf balls. Do you know she *actually* threatened to report him to Saunders?"

She was gone too quickly to see the heads come up. The three young men looked at each other sharply and there was a little silence.

"One of these days," remarked Louisa, "our dear Ness is going for six and I hope I may be there to see."

"She's really a good sort, you know," Biddy said unhappily. "She'd give you her last sixpence and she's honest all through."

"Very likely," said Louisa.

Stewart and Biddy, the oldest members of the undergraduate staff, had met at Balgarvie three years before and had been engaged ever since. They were both going on to do teacher training and marriage was a long way off, but they were perfectly patient and, as Mr. Saunders said, never gave any trouble. It had, however, come to be understood that on such occasions as Greg's party, friends relieved them of late duty, if they happened to be on, so that they could start early and enjoy the modest pleasure of an unhurried walk by themselves.

Ness had taken on Biddy's late duty and, as Biddy was doing her tea in exchange, she had a free afternoon and mounting her bike went in search of Greg. If it occurred to her that Morgan might have shared, or relieved her of the task she made no sign of it, but Lawrence's crack about discourtesy had got home and she considered as she went how she could excuse herself and Morgan politely and convincingly without saying too much and without lying. She went to one of the wynds and looked down. *Skua* was at her moorings and her heart sank. It would have been easier to leave a note than to face *Skua*'s owner, but she got on her bicycle again and went to do so.

Greg was at home preparing for the party. "Hallo," he said, looking pleased to see her. "Have you come to give a hand? If so, welcome. I'm getting a bit tied up one way and another."

"Good gracious!" Ness stared at the Tully's one large living-room. There were glasses and assorted bottles, cups set out ready for coffee, and beyond, in the late scullery, now a modern kitchen, signs of sandwiches. "What on earth are you doing all this for?"

His tone was slightly acid. "I thought you knew, I'm entertaining company to-night."

"Yes of course I know, but—"

Jock looked at her surprised young face. He sometimes wondered how she got on with her higher education at Edinburgh University. A pony-tail was dangling, she wore washed-out jeans and scuffed sandals, and her scorn for gracious womanhood, her dedication to loftier ideals, did not at the moment arouse his sympathy.

He said patiently, "Anthea is an old friend of mine. This will be her first visit to my house. Therefore I am taking a little trouble about it."

"Oh," said Ness. "Actually, why did you ask her with our lot? Peachey and the Carruthers are her—"

"Ness," he said, "*don't* refer to men by their surnames alone. Nothing—*from a woman*—sounds more vulgar."

"I don't see it."

"Well, take my word for it."

"It's just a foible of yours. Everybody does it."

They had strayed far from any possible point and she was still standing idle, still astonished. He sighed. "All right, it's a foible. I asked Anthea with your lot because she likes listening to music which Mister Peachey does not. Now— have you come to help or haven't you?"

Ness hesitated. "Well," she said, "I really came to tell you that Morgan and I aren't coming to-night." She swallowed,

97

remembering Lawrence on courtesy, and added, "I'm—sorry."

"Oh," said Jock. "Are you on a late shift?"

"No."

He looked at her. "I can do without Morgan," he said, "but I'll be sorry if you aren't here. Why aren't you coming?"

His dismissal of Morgan brought her head up and she coloured, but she had thought out what she was going to say. It was true, at least as far as it went, and it should cover the awkwardness, though rising doubt combined with indignation made her speak more loftily than was necessary.

"It's really quite difficult," she said, "having a relation in the House as a guest. I don't think it's a frightfully good idea to—sort of mingle." She caught sight of his face and added, "Of course it's different when she—Anthea—comes to the Manse."

"And where does Morgan come in?" he inquired tactlessly.

"Oh well—" Defensively her anger boiled up and discretion went. "You know, Greg, I can't help it if Anthea's a friend of yours. I just can't stand that sort of person."

"What sort?"

"Rich—and smart and—selfish. Snobbish. . . . I mean she runs around with those awful Carruthers people and Peach—Mr. Peachey, and that's what she's like. And she's been absolutely *foul* to Morgan."

There was a pause. Jock's eyes were on her flushed face: she stared at a tray of randomly placed glasses. Jock had formed an opinion of Morgan the first time he came to the Tully with the others and he had never seen anything to make him change it. He thought the young man was a slug and that Ness was being almost deliberately obtuse about him. It didn't matter very much what exaggerated incident had brought them to the point of withdrawing from his party, but he was concerned for Ness. She had been a nice kid before the earnest-minded phase set in, and he hoped she would be again.

"I know you haven't seen much of Anthea," he said, "but you know something about her, I suppose? She's had a tough time."

"Oh yes," said Ness. "Her father died when she was about my age and her mother this year." She was slightly ashamed when she heard herself make this bald statement and added angrily, "I'm *sorry* about it, but I must say she doesn't look as if she minds."

She didn't know much, thought Jock. But it was certainly not for him to enlighten her. "You believe, do you," he said, "that trouble, sorrow, should be carried on the sleeve for all to see?" She looked puzzled. "You don't respect the kind of courage which scorns self-pity and refuses to depress the rest of the world?"

"Oh, courage," she said. "Of course I admire it. And of course it's feeble to make a fuss about troubles. Everybody has troubles. But you can tell when people are really minding and—well, I don't believe she is."

Jock considered the charming, expensive, guarded façade which Anthea presented. Even now he was not sure whether he was making too much of his earlier knowledge of her because he wanted to be convinced of its superficiality. And yet—he had seen the facade working normally, so to speak, at Peachey's ridiculous party, and the fun was still there, the warmth when she laughed at Lawrence and the boy's response. Whatever had happened to her, whatever she had become, she was not unfeeling. Her cousin despised her—rich and smart and selfish—but in the eyes of Lawrence, who had very much more insight and intelligence than Ness, there had been none of that wary appraisal which may linger even when a very young man is considerably in love. Lawrence was having a lovely time being in love with Anthea because with it was real liking and the certainty that it held no kind of danger.

"You have a lot to learn," he said to Ness. "I think—though I may be wrong—that you should see further at your age."

"What do you mean?"

"If you can't see, there isn't much use telling you where to look," said Jock. He turned away. "All right, Ness. Scram."

"I can help you even if I'm not coming to the party," she offered. "I'm not in a hurry. Biddy's doing my tea because I'm taking her late shift."

"No thanks. I'll manage."

She looked at him. "Are you angry?"

"Fairly. At least I don't much want to see you again for a bit. And you may tell Morgan—No. Don't bother."

"Do you mean—are we not to come any more?"

"You must make up your own minds about that. If you think of it, it's a pretty extreme thing to tell me you aren't coming to my house because you won't associate with one of my friends—or Morgan won't. You have also taken it upon yourself to disapprove of Anthea, though you know very little about her, and to talk about your judgment to me, obviously to Morgan, and—you've been jiggering about with shifts—no doubt to others. Outsiders. Anthea is a member of your family."

"But Greg," she was staring at him with stricken eyes, "even though she is—*whoever* a person is—it doesn't make any difference. I've got to be honest. That's the first thing."

" 'Though I speak with the tongues of men and of angels', " said Jock, " 'and have not charity—'" He broke off. Charity. "Before you start lashing about with honesty, Ness," he said in a friendlier voice, "you have to be damned sure of your facts."

Ness had had the Bible quoted at her a good deal in her time and she always resented it. Coming from Greg, a friend of her own and not even old, it was sheer treachery. She drew herself up. "Naturally," she said icily, "I am sure of my facts."

CHAPTER 8

FROM the beginning Anthea had doubts about friendship
with Vida Carruthers, and by lunch-time on Friday she
would have given a good deal to scrub the acquaintance altogether. It was true that Vida—with Bryce and Mr.
Peachey—filled up the hours which in anticipation had
looked so empty, but the price was too high. The Carruthers
were bores—it was possible to laugh once at their amusing-
ness but no more—and, though Mr. Peachey was not exactly a bore, the cautious love-light behind his spectacles
threatened to become a nuisance. And they were exigent.
Keeping Vida happy was never a light task, and at Balgarvie,
where it was exceptionally heavy, Anthea was so valuable
that the natural thing was to annex her. Bryce was willing
to buy her any number of drinks and cigarettes, to make
himself as agreeable as in him lay, but she could not be allowed to detach herself: her time and attention, her com-
pliance with every plan, were necessary for his comfort.

The Balgarvie golf course, as Morgan said, was not much
of a course, but it was exceedingly beautiful. With the sea
on one side and the moors and hills on the other, with
heather colouring the rough and fairways carpeted with
delicately blowing harebells and drifts of tiny, jewel-like
flowers, it was not necessary to take the game very seriously
and it was quite difficult not to be happy. But on Friday the
foursome sank into failure and ill-temper. Anthea, fresh
from her scene with Morgan, tried her best but could not
reach the required pitch; she was dull. Vida was off her
game and the course had nothing to offer, so to speak, but
itself—no other players to criticise, no acquaintance, no
club interest. She had played golf at Balgarvie twice and she
had *had* it. Bryce grew correspondingly irritable and Anthea

reached the end of her tether. Deliberately she drove her ball to the left, Vida's being lost in the heather to the right, and walked after it away from the snarling voices. Deliberately Mr. Peachey drove his ball after hers and the four-ball match became an exercise in evasive action.

Mr. Peachey was not unhappy himself but he saw that it was time to think of something new. He thought of the island. The island, which formed part of the local sea-scape, offered a lighthouse and a bird-sanctuary for inspection, and a two-hour voyage which was delightful in fine weather and impossible in bad. He proposed to collect a party and make a day of it. Striding lithely along by Anthea's side— head up, chest out—he contrived to make it sound quite a daring sort of enterprise and Vida responded with some enthusiasm. It was discussed all the way back to the House and, as Anthea could not fail to overhear, all through lunch.

"Gregorson's our man," Mr. Peachey said, knowledgeable as always, whenever the discussion came round to the appropriate point. "The fishermen couldn't be less interested in pleasure trips—they make too much money, these chaps—but Gregorson has this boat. He'll rally if it's put to him nicely . . . I *think*. He's not invariably obliging."

Anthea had contrived, by being very smart about getting rid of her clubs and tidying up, to begin her lunch at her own table before the others came into the dining-room, but she had missed none of the discussion, the voices being loud, and now Vida raised hers further.

"Anthea," she shouted across the gap, "let's go and leer at Gregorson this afternoon, darling. After all, you know him. If you bring out the old wiles he could hardly resist, could he?"

"Sorry," Anthea replied with a mixture of more subdued voice and head-shaking. "Can't. Going out. . ."

She had finished her meal—hurriedly—and was on her feet as Vida's protests began. "But where are you *going*? You never said—I thought it was fixed we were going to do something—you *know* the men are shooting. . . ."

Very few people were lunching indoors, but the Americans were there and one or two ladies, and Mr. Peachey's sense of decorum came to Anthea's assistance with jocular cries about the penalties of popularity which quite skilfully wafted her away.

"What am *I* to do?" she heard Vida say angrily as she went out of the room. "Where the hell's she *going*?" She couldn't have told her. All she knew was that she had to escape and in order to do it she must go somewhere.

In the end she went to Carse, the local metropolis, which was seven or eight miles down the coast. It was a dull little town and had nothing to attract a visitor, but as she was pledged to go to the Manse for tea it would fill in the time as well as anything and she could do some shopping. She paid a courtesy call on the harbour, a larger, less attractive harbour than Balgarvie, with a clutter of warehouses, stacks of timber and what were known locally as bings of coal, and boats which were simply boats: visiting trawlers and small freighters, battered-looking and rusty. Anthea soon moved on to the shopping centre—which was not much more attractive. Her shopping was not extensive. She bought soap and cigarettes, peppermint creams for Cousin Maud and a pair of stockings, and was idling along with her parcels in her hand, looking for a shop with a stock of paperbacks, when she heard a loud blast on a horn and saw the Carruthers signalling urgently from Mr. Peachey's jeep.

Anthea acted promptly. With a bright, busy smile she waved back and lengthening her stride whisked round a corner and bolted for her car—taking to the hills before Vida could be decanted from the jeep and Bryce break for freedom. Getting out through the narrow congested streets was maddeningly slow and she kept a nervous eye on the mirror, but there was no sign of pursuit and when she was clear of the town she put her foot down, laughing at the absurd lengths to which one could be driven by persistent friends. She hoped Vida would find a lot to interest her in the Carse shops.

The episode had raised her spirits—the ridiculous usually did cheer her up—and it struck her that in the last few days she had allowed herself to be driven to absurd lengths in another direction. She was going to leave Balgarvie in a day or two. What would take its place, where she would go next, she did not know, but meanwhile, why be so dramatic about it? What had she accomplished by her heroics—being distant with Jock and avoiding the harbour? Nothing. She had merely become entangled with the Carruthers. And she had wasted time. By now she should at least have begun to think about where she was to go, what was to replace the Balgarvie plan, and she resolved to begin at once. She would go to the harbour now and, accepting the loss once and for all, resign herself to it and look ahead.

A sturdy fair-haired youth was walking along the road in front of her. Hearing the car he looked round hopefully, and then, seeing a girl alone, hesitated and walked on; either afraid of her or expecting her to be afraid of him. Anthea pulled up. "I'm only going as far as the village," she said. "Any good to you?"

"Oh aye, that'll dae fine," was the reply. "Ta."

He got in and sat staring determinedly in front of him, so suffused with blushes that it would have been cruel to take any notice of him. They drove on in silence. Anthea thought her own thoughts, he presumably thought his, and at the top of the Water Wynd they parted.

"Well, cheerio. Thanks," said the boy with a bashful side-long smile and walked away. Anthea said, "Cheerio," the universal Balgarvie farewell which she always enjoyed using, and went down the steps and path of the wynd. As she reached the quay she heard Vida's shout. "Hi! Anthea —*wait!*"

It was too much. It was persecution. And this time there was no question of pretending not to hear and making a bolt for it. Anthea stopped and turned round.

They were both following her down: Vida negotiating the steps with an awkward crab-like gait, making exclamations and clutches at Bryce's arm; he striding boldly and taking no notice of her fuss; both talking as they came with the loud voices and the air of owning everything in sight, including the natives, which had made Anthea blush for them before and which she found particularly offensive here. They stared briefly at the harbour and thought nothing of it. "Ugh—fish!" said Vida and turned to attack.

"If you were only going shopping in Carse, Anthea, I must say I think you might have said so. I could have gone with you without putting you out much, I'd have thought, and let Bryce get his shooting. Or were you meeting up with a boy-friend? We saw you ahead of us with a man in the car."

Anthea said laconically that she had given a lad a lift.

"Then you did a damn' silly thing, if I may say so," said Bryce. "I don't give lifts myself—don't see why I should provide free transport—and I absolutely forbid Vida to stop when she's driving alone. Asking for trouble. Who was this fellow? A local?"

"I've no idea," said Anthea. "Probably. He was harmless anyhow and everybody gives lifts here."

Vida moved on. "What are you down here for? If you've got no more pressing private business you might tell us where to find Gregorson and his boat. We're supposed to be fixing up this trip. But of course," she added, heavily sarcastic, "we wouldn't want to *intrude.*"

The harbour was very quiet: the tide was low and the only boats in sight were *Skua* with her companions and *Lea-Rig* lifeless at her mooring, the only people a few women and babies and the old men who spent their days sitting on the benches by the fish-market. But for once the strangers were being noticed. Heads turned at the sound of the loud voices and the sight of such obtrusive foreignness, and Anthea's sole desire was to keep the Carruthers quiet. She didn't know where Greg was, she said, but she could show them his boat if they liked.

They walked along the quay to where the *Skua* lay deserted. Bryce and Vida looked at her without enthusiasm, telling each other that she was much smaller than they expected and more utilitarian. "I suppose he'd clean it up," Vida said doubtfully. "Would we be hiring it or what?"

Bryce was not sure. Desmond hadn't really said. He fancied they wouldn't exactly *hire* it but slip over a wodge of notes— no doubt far more than the job was worth, but that was how it went when you got involved with chaps who were neither one thing nor the other, vaguely friends. . . . Vida stated unequivocally that friend or no friend, host or hireling, Gregorson would have to clean the nasty little tub *thoroughly* before she set foot in it. Bryce asked jeeringly if she had expected a yacht, and Anthea stood wondering how the negotiations would proceed if they ever got as far as Jock himself.

It surprised her that Desmond should have let the Carruthers go so far astray. Though they were not "readers" they might have been better informed about "Gregorson." But then it surprised her that he put up with them at all. If asked, Mr. Peachey would have told her that his was a complex character. He could appreciate John Gregorson's work, he could admire the man and even, now and again, envy the kind of life he led; but he had another side. Without being particularly avaricious himself he loved the rich and enjoyed expensive amusements. As they stood on the pier Anthea symbolised one half of Mr. Peachey very fairly, while the Carruthers, staring discontentedly at *Skua*, very fairly represented the other.

Bryce was supposing that the boat would do. "Damned uncomfortable but apparently there's no choice. How the hell do we locate Gregorson? He wasn't at the hotel and he's not here. . . . I told Des I'd get hold of him. Damn! Where is this place he holes up in?"

Anthea pointed out the Tully and the path to it and he scowled. "You can go round by the road if you want to," she said.

"This island idea of Desmond's is a brainstorm, if you ask me," said Vida. "Can he have *seen* this wonderful boat? Leave it, why don't you?"

Looking again at *Skua* with disparaging eyes Bryce hesitated, and then found a solution. "You'll be seeing him, won't you?" he said to Anthea. "Gregorson, I mean. Isn't there some sort of party? Easier if you ask him. Put it to him as an old pal, but just drop a hint that nobody expects him to lose money on the deal."

Anthea shook her head. "Not me," she said. "Desmond had better ask his own favours."

The Carruthers both stared at her, hostility mounting. "Favours?" said Vida angrily. "Where do you get that? Nobody expects him to do it for nothing. Anybody'd think we were trying to *exploit* the man."

"It's not often," said Bryce in more measured tones, "that I'm accused of looking for *favours*. As far as *favours* go it seems to me I give quite enough but I don't often get in on the receiving end."

He looked meaningly at Anthea, a look which held all the drinks and cigarettes he had pressed on her, and she cursed herself for the careless word. She said, "Desmond would agree that it's a favour. There wouldn't be any trouble about money but I don't think Greg could spare the time very easily. He's busy."

She spoke peaceably but it was no good. The Carruthers were affronted, and when they were affronted they hit back, whether they were in the middle of Piccadilly or on Balgarvie pier. Vida cried scornfully that she saw no difference between taking them to the island and going out with the guns or fishing parties from the hotel.

"I suppose you think it's humiliating to *you* talking about paying *your friend* for the hire of his horrible little boat, but it doesn't look as if he's all that big a friend seeing he's never done a thing about you. And you needn't tell me he does those hotel jobs as a *favour*. For all you and Desmond rave about his books they can't be worth a lot. If he was making any money he wouldn't be here, would he?"

Bryce agreed. "You wouldn't think so. But Balgarvie has its little mysteries." He paused, smiling significantly at Anthea. "Some time, Anthea my dear, you really must do us a *favour*. Tell us why you're here—and don't give us the Minister. . . ."

Nothing on earth would induce Anthea to quarrel with Bryce Carruthers. For one thing, in the words of the old saying, he could spit farther than she could: for another, bullying and deliberate insolence are only extensions of more harmless teasing and the best defence is no defence—refusal to rise. Happily the build-up had been on the slow side, and the smile, the snide tone of facetiousness, made it possible to clown her way out. It was not very good clowning but it was enough, with its assumption of good-humoured farce, to make it difficult to continue the attack. The Carruthers, still angry but momentarily foiled, went away, and as their resentful backs disappeared up the wynd she went along to her bench to compose her mind before tea at the Manse. So far, she reflected, the day of Jock's party had been a peach.

To Ness, Greg's reaction to what she still felt was a perfectly fair and rational attitude towards Anthea was a severe shock. As Alec had remarked, Greg was neither simple nor soft, but up to now, though he laughed at her a good deal, she had only met the easy tolerance which was so comfort-able, and the contrast was both wounding and puzzling. It was a terrible thing to be at odds with Greg, but it amazed her that he failed to see her point, and she could only sup-pose that Anthea, in the manner of light-minded, probably over-sexed women, had contrived to upset his judgment. When she left the Tully she went for a vigorous bicycle ride which did less than she hoped to relieve her feelings: then, grateful for once that the sanctuary of home was at hand, she went in, and found Anthea herself sitting down to tea.

Being well brought up she forced a stiff smile and said "Hallo," and her mother, delighted to see her, said, "We did-n't expect you, dearie. Get yourself a cup, will you?"

"I won't bother with tea, thank you," said Ness. "I just looked in—I'm going up to do a bit of reading."

Her father eyed her sternly. "We have a guest," he said. She met his eyes and went to fetch a cup.

"She's at the stage," Mrs. McNaughton said apologeti-cally, "when everything that happens at home seems an in-terruption. Of course she has got a lot of—"

"So long as she is at home," said the Minister, "she will conform to the ways of the house. There is always time for civility."

Anthea had tried to work at home in her time and she did not agree, but she did not say so. "I expect," she said peaceably, "that she finds it quite difficult to get through her reading while she's doing this job."

"She always finds time for what she wants to do," replied Mr. McNaughton.

Ness came back from the kitchen, where she had spent a minute or two grinding her teeth, and sat down looking remote. The fireplace in the Manse dining-room was all black. On the black marble mantelpiece stood a black mar-ble clock with a staring white face, and flanking it on each side were identical knights in black armour, eighteen inches high. Against this background she was an incongruous little figure with her pony-tail and jeans, and Anthea was sorry for her. It was not pleasant to hear the girl chidden, as Lawrence would have said, for discourtesy to her, and it outweighed the discourtesy itself and brought the scales down on Ness's side.

She did her best for her. She talked to Cousin Walter about the economics of the Balgarvie fishing fleet and to Cousin Maud about the scones. When Ness might be presumed to have recovered her poise she introduced the House and the undergraduate staff and met a glance of pure hatred.

"They thoroughly enjoy it, I think," said Mrs. Mc-Naughton, picking up the conversational ball. "Most of them are here for at least the second time, aren't they, Ness?"

"Louisa's new," said Ness. She helped herself to cake. "And Morgan." Anthea asked how they were recruited and she replied, without looking up, that they mostly brought each other. "Louisa came because of Alec—they know each other at Oxford. Alec actually came through Lawrence."

"Morgan," her mother told Anthea, "is an Edinburgh friend of Ness's. She recommended him to Mr. Saunders. But it is so unfortunate for the poor boy: he has had to give up his university career."

"What a pity," said Anthea. "Why is that?"

"It is difficult to see how it can be necessary," said the Minister. "I have offered to look into it but—"

"He doesn't want people looking into it," Ness interrupted him. "He's made up his mind it's the right thing to do and there's no use going *on* about it."

"If his heart was really in it," he persisted, "he would hardly give up so easily."

Ness opened her mouth again but her mother cut in. "Walter, is there a cigarette for Anthea?" she asked and went straight on. "I hear there's a party at the Tully to-night. Isn't it strange, Anthea, that we have known Mr. Gregorson for so long without knowing that he's a friend of yours?"

"I suppose it is," Anthea agreed. "But we had lost touch altogether. I haven't seen him since I left London."

Mrs. McNaughton talked gently on, keeping the ball in her own hands. Anthea must have missed her friends when she left London: it is always difficult to keep up from a distance: no doubt, however, she had quickly found new ones: however, again, it is always pleasant to meet old friends. She glanced at her daughter's jeans. "Don't forget to take a frock with you, dear. You can't go to a party like that."

"I could," said Ness, "but actually I'm not going."

"Not going? But why? I thought—"

Ness stood up. "Will you excuse me? I have to get back. There always has to be somebody on the late shift, you know. Morgan and I are doing it."

"But you often go on after the late duty! And surely, as Anthea is to be there, Mr. Saunders—"

Anthea also stood up, and as Cousin Maud's protests faded for lack of response she said, "If you're going back now, Ness, I can give you a lift. You look quite tired. We can put the bike on the back of the car."

Mrs. McNaughton, successfully deflected, thought her daughter did look tired and embarked on a little worry. Ness glanced at her father and civilly accepted the lift, adding with only slight venom that there was no need to risk Anthea's lovely car. "I'll borrow a grid to come home, or hitch a ride."

"As you like," said Anthea.

They got into the lovely car and she started it and drove away with a farewell wave to the Minister, who looked censorious, and his wife, whose face as usual reflected conflict within. Cousin Walter's chilly disapproval, Cousin Maud's eager desire to make allowances—which assumed the need for allowances—were so irrelevant as to be ludicrous, and yet she could not protect herself by any process of rational thought from the soreness. That gentle talk about keeping up with London friends and quickly making new ones—had they no imagination? They could accept the unseen in their religion all right, but in the world, in the lives of people even as close to them as she was, it appeared that nothing existed, or held the possibility of existence, except what they could see with their own eyes and hear with their own ears. As for Ness . . . Ness had not spoken to her since the meeting with Jock at the harbour, and she, Anthea, was not going to start a conversation now. Something—Morgan presumably—had fanned the first antagonism to a flame, but it must die down or go on blazing. She was tired of the McNaughtons.

She drove along the village street with no sound except the friendly purr of the engine, and then, turning into the road, stopped suddenly. A flock of black-faced sheep was pouring along it, a river of bobbing grey backs herded by men, boys and dogs, with a sad pandemonium of bleating punctuated by yells and whistles. The road was narrow and absolutely full. The man in charge signalled that his goal was a gate three or four hundred yards ahead and Anthea put her car into low gear and followed at sheep's pace. A woolly bundle near the back leapt suddenly into the air and flounced towards the car. She blew her horn to turn it but it leapt again and bolted past and a black and white collie streaked after it. Ness spoke.

"You'd be far better to stop. They won't be very long and you're only flustering them."

"They're so flustered already that I don't think we're adding much," said Anthea, crawling on.

Ness looked long-suffering and in a moment spoke again. "Do you know Greg well?"

This was a tediously familiar question and Anthea gave her usual answer. Quite well at one time. They had lost touch years ago.

"So you really didn't know he was here?" said Ness.

Anthea looked round at her. "Ness," she said, "I don't know if you mean it, or are aware of it, but that was offensive. I have already told you—and you heard me tell your mother—that I haven't seen or heard of him for years—seven years, if you want to be accurate."

"Sorry." Ness was scarlet but obstinate. "But you must have heard of him—seen his books."

"His books don't publish his whereabouts so far as I know."

"Well, of course not." Logic was not Miss McNaughton's strong point. "He doesn't want a lot of fuss and publicity. Do stop! These poor sheep!"

A panic party, whether spontaneously or by arrangement, broke and tore past them towards the village. Whistles sent two dogs in pursuit and a very hot boy pounded by with an embarrassed grin. Anthea grinned back—her sympathies were not with the sheep—but Ness had turned right round and cried again:

"Oh poor things! It's *wicked* driving them like that."

"They're silly creatures," said Anthea.

"They can't help it. It's their nature."

"So it is, and so they have to be driven. Or do you think each one should be consulted about moving to a new field and led—with a blue ribbon?"

"Of course not." Ness turned to face front again and glanced at her cousin. "Don't be silly."

Anthea said without emphasis that she didn't think she was being silly, and as the situation seemed to be worsening with the spread of the idiotic panic, she stopped the car and in preparation for another spell of silence lit a cigarette.

But Ness, with an air of determination, went on, or rather,

like the sheep, back. "I really didn't mean to be offensive—"

"All right," said Anthea, bored. "Say no more."

"But—I have to. I mean, people are talking, and now Greg's furious and I've got to know where I am." Anthea had turned to look at her and she added defensively, "Why *did* you come to stay at the hotel?"

Anthea was no longer bored. "What are people talking about?" she snapped.

"Well, of *course* they wonder why you're here. Women don't come by themselves. The hotel's for people who want to shoot—or fish—and it's terribly expensive. You must have *some* special reason."

"And why is Greg furious?"

Ness was not sure how it came about that she was undergoing a hail of questions: she resented it and she was reluctant to answer this one, but she did so—rather confusedly. Because of his party, she mumbled. At least because she was not going—at least—

"That doesn't sound much to be furious about," said Anthea. "It's not like Jock—Greg—to be huffy because someone refuses an invitation."

"It isn't that exactly. I mean, I *was* going, but I'm not now, because of Morgan."

"Morgan?"

Anthea's tone brought Ness's chin up again. "You must know perfectly well," she said, "that after this morning Morgan couldn't possibly meet you in a friendly way—socially." Anthea agreed that it would be awkward, and wondered what Morgan's version of the morning's encounter was, but the accusing voice was going on. "I believe in being absolutely honest. I think this morning was well, unspeakable. And not only this morning. Ever since you've been here you've treated Morgan like a—a lower type of being, and I'm afraid I feel it too much to be able to meet you as a friend myself."

114

The sheep were again more or less under control and Anthea put the car in gear and moved slowly forward. "You believe in honesty, Ness," she said, "so I may as well say that I think Morgan *is* a fairly low type of being. You needn't begin on class," as Ness's mouth opened. "You're all students and I know nothing about anybody's social position except yours. Morgan is simply an unpleasant individual. You've heard his version of this morning's scene: I don't want to hear it and I don't propose to give you mine, but I will tell you that he behaved very badly. Quite seriously."

"What nonsense!" Ness cried loudly. "You simply pour out money on things like cigarettes and drink and clothes and went up in the air because you didn't want to pay for a few golf balls. It was a mistake. You completely misunderstood."

"There was no misunderstanding," Anthea said dryly. The van of the sheep procession had reached the gate and as they jostled and jibbed at the bottle-neck she stopped the car again and glanced at the hostile face beside her. "It's no good. You may as well accept it: if I succeeded in snubbing Morgan finally I'm delighted. He's quite lucky not to be out of the hotel on his ear."

"That's just not true," declared Ness. "You simply have no idea what Morgan is like. He's *too* conscientious and sensitive and his life is simply tragic. He has so much real trouble to bear," she added with some triumph, "that it isn't surprising if he makes mistakes about golf balls. There *are* more important things in the world."

"Very true," said Anthea. "We'll leave it at that." The road was clear at last and she shot forward, raising a hand to the shepherds as she passed. The gates of the House were already in sight and she finished with Ness briefly. "I gather from Lawrence that Jock Gregorson is a pretty good friend to you all. It isn't surprising if he's angry with you—cutting his party for such a phoney reason with the maximum display. What object do you suppose I could have for snubbing Morgan if he hadn't asked for it? As for the other thing that's troubling you—I came to see Balgarvie and my relations again." She turned in at the gates and drove fast round to the yard. "There you are," she said, pulling up.

Ness got out of the car. She was still flushed—bloody, Anthea thought, but unbowed. "Thanks for the lift," she said stiffly. "I'm sure you mean to be honest and I don't suppose you meant to hurt Morgan as you did. You just don't understand. You're too different."

"Well, Ness," said Anthea, "as you said of the sheep, it's my nature. I can't help it."

CHAPTER 9

NESS stalked away to the staff entrance. Anthea put her car into a shed and went straight to the manager's office. She could bear no more of Balgarvie. Which straw of the many had finally broken her back she did not know, but she was through. What, after all, was there to stay for? And if her sudden departure caused speculation, she would never see the speculators again.

"I'm sure," said Mr. Saunders politely, "we shall all be very sorry to see you go."

Anthea thought that Lawrence and Chet would probably be a little sorry, and as she left the office she met Chet himself looking solemn. "Say," he began, "I was looking for you. Could you come out and walk around a little?"

It was past six o'clock and she longed for solitude, but Chet clearly had some load on his mind and she went with him. At a little distance from the house was a walled garden, a pleasant place unknown, like the harbour, to most of the Balgarvie guests, and he led her to it briskly and said nothing till they were inside. Then he took her arm and slowed to a saunter. They had strolled in the garden before and she was used to having her arm or her hand taken and to the endearments which were partly protective habit, partly the expression of his undisguised but unexpectant fondness for her. She was going to miss Chet—and Lawrence—she thought sadly, lavishing affection and admiration on her, being glad to see her. But this stroll had a definite purpose.

"Look, honey," said Chet, "I wanted you to know I'm going away and I'm not just sure when I'll be back."

"Are you?" She looked up, rather surprised. "Are you all going?"

"No. No, it's just me." He gave her the apologetic grin which always accompanied any reference to his job. "I told you I'm an errand boy. I have to go and meet a guy. Probably be back Monday. Well—you'll be here when I do get back, won't you?"

"No," said Anthea. "I'm afraid I won't, Chet. I'm going myself to-morrow."

He was aghast. "To-morrow? But—how come? I thought—you never actually said, but I thought you were here for some while yet."

Anthea said no again. Chet looked at her sharply and conducted her to a semicircular seat which fitted into a niche in the wall.

"Here," he said, and taking his handkerchief from his pocket dusted the slats. "We'll park. Smoke?" She accepted a Lucky Strike, which was the brand of smoke he favoured, and he lit up and proceeded. "Why are you going to-morrow? You weren't planning to, were you?"

"Well—I thought I'd go on Monday, actually, and then —to-morrow just seemed better."

"You haven't—" he hesitated, "you haven't had any trouble, have you? There's nothing driving you away from here?"

"Oh—no, Chet."

He looked at her hopelessly. "Talk about clams . . . you don't open up much, Anthea, do you. You worry me. I don't think you're happy. I can feel you're having it pretty bad some way and I don't know how. You know, don't you, that I'd—well, I'd give everything I have to make you happy?"

Chet was tall and untidy: he carried himself carelessly and the only thing that was notable about his face was that it was pleasant and unmistakably American, but his eyes were a clear blue, honest and kind, and Anthea turned away.

Looking down at the cigarette in her hand she said, "I've had a bit of trouble one way and another, but it's—nobody can do anything about it. It's no good talking about it."

He half turned and put his arm along the back of the seat behind her. "Anthea," he said, "will you marry me?"

Anthea looked at him. "Dear Chet," she said, almost in tears, "I can't. I like you so much—I wish I could. But I couldn't marry you without loving you and I don't love you."

"I know you don't," he said sadly. "I guess there's somebody you do love, but it doesn't seem like it does much for you. I—well, I could take care of you." She shook her head and he nodded, accepting final rejection. "Well, I'm not going to forget this, you know. I mean, could be you'll get all fixed up and married pretty soon, but supposing you don't, we could meet sometimes when I'm over here, couldn't we? You'll give me your address, won't you?"

There was a pause and then she said again. "I can't."

He was taken aback. "Why not? Anthea—you're not scared of me? You couldn't be—you know I wouldn't do anything to hurt you—"

"Of course I know it," she cried. "I haven't *got* an address—I don't know where I'll be. . . ."

She stopped, dismayed by the way it had come out, and before she found the words to tone it down, Chet's arm moved down from the back of the bench and he drew her close to him, gently and without looking at her.

"So that's it," he said. "No home. No folks closer than what's-it the Minister. I wondered how come you were travelling around by yourself this way." He glanced at her with a sort of comic sweetness. "How about the dough? Is that real?"

Anthea laughed weakly. It was extraordinarily comforting to be held in a firm masculine grip, and the comic glum made her plight seem less formidable. "There isn't much dough," she admitted, "but I have a fair earning capacity."

"Well then, you'll have a bank." His tone was relieved and practical. "You give me the address of your bank—O.K.? And I'll give you all my addresses. . . ."

Releasing her he felt in the side pockets of his coat and Anthea watched. Chet's system, or lack of system, in the matter of pockets was already known to her and always a pleasure. From the left-hand pocket came a handkerchief, his packet of cigarettes, a lighter and two boxes of matches, and what looked like a few old bills. From the right came a handkerchief, a box of matches and a bundle of papers which burst from his hand.

"Hell," said Chet mildly and gathered them up, turning to make a face at her giggle. He produced a card from the confusion and gave it to her. It had on it official-looking addresses in Washington and London, and a street number in an unknown town in Connecticut to which he pointed. "That's home," he said. "If you ever feel like a trip to America you just go there and they'll be looking for you. But any of these'll get after me pretty quick."

"Thank you," she said and gave him the address of her bank. As he wrote it in a plump note-book which he brought out rather triumphantly from another, inner, pocket, the clock over the old stables in the yard struck seven.

"Hell," he said again. "I've got to go in—there should be a phone call." He put the book away and turning back to her put his arm round her again. "I'll leave you here," he said. "This is good-bye for now, Anthea, but don't forget there's one clean-living guy that loves you. . . ." He kissed her gently three times, patted her shoulder and got up. "Guess I better hurry," he said hoarsely. "'Bye, honey. . . ."

He bolted. Outside the garden, on the path which was hidden from both garden and house, he stopped and angrily yanked a handkerchief from his pocket. He used it and after a pause stuffed it back and hurried on.

When Ness left the Tully, Jock returned to his preparations with strong distaste. Since he had asked Anthea to his house and she had politely indicated that she would prefer to come in a party, he had arranged it, but he had known all along that it was artificial, and now, after Ness's little scene, it seemed so unreal that it was simply silly. He observed the arrangement of glasses and cups, wondering what the hell was wrong with them: moved them into straight or straightish rows, tried artistic grouping, scowled at a handsome bunch of sweet-peas donated by the landlady of the Sun Tavern, and gave it up. When Anthea began talking about parties he should have scrubbed the invitation. People who had known each other as well as they had, who had loved each other, must either begin again on a basis of intimacy or not at all. She, it seemed, had decided that there was a third alternative—strictly social. She was friendly enough; she gave no sign that she felt herself injured by him, but she gave no sign either of recognising—or perhaps admitting was a better word—his concern about her. He would rather know what had happened to her in those years, how she was placed in the world now, and never see her again, than go through the farce of meeting like casual acquaintances in crowds.

But however repulsive the prospect, the party was on, and he remembered the sandwiches. He strode into the kitchen, where the materials—and already some crumbs—were spread out. He had just got going when Ness arrived and the impetus was lost. Why had he thought of sandwiches? The hotel served an ample dinner. Then he picked up the bread-knife resolutely. The kids were always hungry and he would carry out his plans however misconceived.

"Oh Gre-heg!" sang a high voice outside. "Anybody home?"

"Louisa!" he shouted. "Come in—quick!"

Louisa had borrowed a bike from Ian McNaughton, though Ian was not yet aware of it, and like Ness she was wearing jeans. But hers were not high-minded jeans, they were pale blue and they fitted: so did her white jersey, and above were lively blue eyes and shining hair which owed almost everything to art.

"I just dropped round," she said, giving the place an amiable glance from the door, "to see if there was anything a little girl could do to help Daddy. I see that there might be a trifle or two."

"You're darn' right," said Jock. He flung an arm round her shoulders and hurried her in. "Louisa, you restore my faith in humanity."

"Oh?" said Louisa. "Ness has been, has she?"

He gave an involuntary laugh and she twinkled at him and with a deft movement or two arranged the cups and glasses.

"What is it all about?" he asked.

"Well really, we hardly know," was the reply. "Dearest Greg, may I suggest two vases—at least—for the sweetpeas? You won't be hurt?"

"Ten if you like—if you can find them."

"Oh, I'll find something," she said and carried the flowers to the kitchen. Jock followed, feeling greatly relaxed, and watched while she rummaged about his cupboards and came up with an earthenware jug and a pewter tankard. "Morgan, you know," she said, easing the tightly packed sweet-peas out of their vase—"these are really heaven, Greg, aren't they—Morgan is very, very sensitive and there was a mix-up about some golf balls. Apparently he *first* failed to provide some and got his ears bent by Mr. Peachey: and then, after everything was settled and Miss Logan had bought some repaints off Lawrence, he upped with a dozen new. Whereupon, says Ness, Miss Logan very unkindly flung them back in his face." She stood back and looked critically at the flowers arranged in the tankard. "We feel that the story lacks authenticity. One doesn't quite see Miss Logan pelting Morgan with golf balls."

122

"Not quite," Jock agreed. "Is that all?"

Louisa said it was and it wasn't and carried the tankard through to the living-room. "You know how earnest Ness is," she continued when she came back and began on the earthenware jug. "And Biddy says she's much more so this year because of becoming a leading bomb-banner and because nobody likes Morgan very much and her crusading spirit is up. This will do, I think." She shook the remaining sweet-peas into place and took them away while Jock lit a cigarette and leant on the kitchen table waiting for enlightenment. He enjoyed Louisa and took time off to reflect on the interesting fact that girls who are most obviously ones for the boys are so often good—and comfortable—about the house.

"Sandwiches now, Greg?" said Louisa coming back. She looked at the loaf. "Shall I butter and cut and you fill? What have you got? Cheese and shrimp—clever you."

"No need to be tactful," said Jock. "I know I can't cut thin."

"You've done fine," she said and picked up the knife. "Where were we?"

"Ness crusading."

"Oh yes. Well, you can imagine it goes against the grain a bit. Here's Miss Logan, everything she disapproves of most—glamorous and beautiful and *gorgeously* expensive looking"—a wistful note came into the clear voice—"and not in the least earnest. And she's her cousin. *And* even worse, of course, all the men falling over their feet in pursuit." She looked up innocently.

"All?" Jock's voice was hollow and he met her wide-eyed gaze with one so scandalised that she giggled.

"Well—not *all*. Lawrence and the young American—Mr. Hart, he's sweet—are flat on their faces. Mr. Peachey and Mr. Scudamore are—I think *smitten* is the word, and dear sweet

123

Sir Andrew and Mr. Cleever cluster purely round and—Now, that's a funny thing." She paused, bread-knife poised. "I've only just thought of it. The French *didn't*. Why?"

"You tell me," said Jock, spreading the cheese-andshrimp mixture. "I'm out of my depth."

"Are you? I thought writers knew all about human nature."

"A fallacy."

She sighed. "Another illusion gone. . . . But it's common knowledge that the French go big for *l'amour* and one would have expected them to be rushing the queue. But no: they were quite disinterested."

"*Un*-interested, Louisa."

"Oh? You do know about grammar? Very well—uninterested. They've been very antisocial all round, as a matter of fact. We can't think why they came—the boys say they can't shoot. However, they've gone. . . . I've rather lost the thread."

So had Jock. "I think we'd got Miss Logan surrounded by admirers. But why should Ness mind that? She doesn't want them, does she?"

"No, indeed she doesn't." Louisa held up the knife again to emphasise her point. "That's just it, you see. The top priority of all that Ness deplores is sex. She bristles like a porcupine whenever she sees a manifestation."

"She seems to tolerate Stewart and Biddy all right."

"Oh she does, but that's different. Stewart and Biddy are so sweet, they love each other so much that it's sort of sublime. The carnal aspect isn't apparent," said Louisa. Jock turned away to fetch more sandwich filling and she glanced at him sharply. "You know quite well what I mean, Greg. Of course Miss Logan isn't the carnal type. The nicest people fall for her and they *like* her and she's fun—she's lovely to Lawrence. But Ness doesn't see that. She just thinks it's dalliance vile: sexy and horrid."

124

They worked in silence for a little and then she said, "That's enough cut, don't you think? What about a nice cup of tea? I'll finish spreading if you put the kettle on."

He yielded up the spreading gladly and filled the kettle, thinking about Anthea surrounded by admirers. She was worth admiring. The Anthea of seven years ago was not the kind of girl who attracted all the boys—there were prettier girls and far more competent girls—but even then those who were attracted found her fun: she was lovely to them and they liked her, and even those whose feeling for her was slight never forgot her. Now she must be almost irresistible, though for him the young Anthea was still so vivid that he felt he could not see clearly what she had become. He got out the tea things and made the tea while Louisa swiftly finished the sandwiches.

"Did you know her—Miss Logan, I mean—well?" she asked. "It's odd that you should meet here, isn't it?"

"You will find as life goes on," said Jock, "that you meet people everywhere." He added, with what he felt just then was profound truth, "No, I can't say I know her well," and then qualified it, "I saw a lot of her at one time."

Louisa put the sandwiches carefully into polythene bags. "That's the lot, Greg. What do we do with the bits?"

"Dan," he said and whistled to the dog, who came in hopefully and waited with waving tail as the scraps were put into his dish.

"You're a precious love," said Louisa, embracing him fondly. "How nice and *straightforward* dogs are. Not sensitive—no moods. . ."

"They don't demand much," Jock agreed. "Sit, Louisa." He poured out tea and passed it to her. "Biscuit? I feel better about this party—I think. I don't know that it was a very clever idea."

Louisa sat down and looked at him kindly. She was glad she had thought of coming. A few weeks ago, when she arrived at Balgarvie and met Greg for the first time, it had

125

seemed inevitable that she should fall hopelessly in love with him—that it would, indeed, be sheer waste not to. There was his appearance: black, brown, tough and yet so far from a hunk. There were his books, already known to her; the thrill of knowing the writer and the romantic way he chose to live at the Tully. And, of course, his advanced age and presumably vast experience. Looking at him now as he sat on the kitchen table smoking and drinking tea, she was quite surprised and more than a little pleased with herself that she had resisted the inevitable. But she was realistic: Alec, who was also realistic, had pointed out that it's never much good aiming too high, and she had switched, without great difficulty, to motherly affection.

Finishing her biscuit she reached for the tin and said she thought the party was a splendid idea. "We're all looking forward to it madly and our best frocks are pressed and ready." She glanced at his doubtful face and away again. "It's funny how a drip like Morgan spreads a blight—in ever-widening circles, as you might say. But it wears off."

"Or is dispelled," said Jock, "by those who are not drips. Don't stint yourself. At least half my biscuits are yours."

"I'm gratified," responded Louisa, "but I must now go and don the garments of servitude. One more . . ." She chose a biscuit with care and got up. Jock slid off the table and went with her to the door.

"I really am grateful," he said. "You're a dear good girl and a treat to look at. If this party doesn't flop, the credit is yours. Is Miss Logan enjoying herself up there?"

Louisa's curiosity about the relationship between Mr. Gregorson and Miss Logan had been lulled. Greg was in a slight state about his party, which was significant, but on the other hand he had not been visibly moved to hear of the admirers and he had said he did not know her well. Now, however, her interest revived.

"Well, yes, I think she's enjoying herself," she said, wheeling Ian's bicycle on to the path. "She has quite a lot of fun—though I can't think why she came." She paused, wondering about Anthea's enjoyment, and added, "She looks rather saddish sometimes when she's not talking to anybody: but then, as I said, Morgan does create an atmosphere and Ness is so aloof it isn't true." She grinned suddenly. "Actually, Alec thinks Ness is getting a bit tired of boosting the underdog and that's why she's specially fierce."

Jock thought that neither Ness nor Morgan was likely to affect Miss Logan so powerfully as she supposed, but he only remarked that Alec seemed to be the expert on human nature.

"Oh yes," said Louisa. "Alec knows a lot. Public-school education can't be so sheltered as they make out."

Jock agreed. "They do exaggerate. Is this Ian's bike? You'll never make it."

"Yes I will." She put her foot on the pedal and swung her leg spaciously over the saddle. "Whoops!" There was a nasty wobble and she recovered neatly. "Safe! See you, Greg. . . ."

She pedalled away along the narrow unfenced track—decently surfaced since Jock began to make money—which led across a field to the main road. She was pleased with her good work and almost sure there was something between Greg and Miss Logan. She would tell Alec to look out this evening and see what he thought. Did she, she wondered doubtfully, *want* to see signs of romantic attachment? It would be a loss if Greg got married. No house with a wife in it would ever be so wide open as the Tully was now. But at least he wouldn't be thrown away on Miss Logan, and it was comfortless for him to be alone all the time. Turning into the main road Louisa decided that she and Alec would throw in their weight in support of romance. Ness's annoyance alone, she reflected, would be worth it.

CHAPTER 10

ANTHEA sat still for a while after Chet left her in the garden. She could still feel his arm holding her, his heart thudding steadily against her shoulder, and she wished she could have stayed in the sheltering warmth. She would never again be alone, she would never need to worry about what to do next: Chet and the hardware would take care of everything. But it was no good. It was just as well, she supposed, that Jock Gregorson had made it impossible for her to love anyone else. It saved a lot of trouble and when it was accepted one knew that life could be full and, given the right work to do, satisfying, without love. Only there were moments when it came near, and the lack, the coldness it left behind were fully felt.

It was half past seven when she got up, and as she went into the hall Lawrence, tidily dressed, came running downstairs.

"Hallo," he said. "You're late." She said flatly that she had been in the garden and his welcoming grin vanished. "Anthea darling—is anything the matter? You look—are you sad?"

She pulled herself together. "No, darling Lawrence. That wasn't my sad face, that was my thoughtful face. I suppose I haven't time for some sherry? No—I must go and doll myself up for this party. I see you've got on your good suit."

"Decorations will be worn," said Lawrence. "Tell you what—you go on up and I'll bring you a sherry."

A few minutes later he entered her room carrying an outsize glass. "Brought you a double," he said complacently. "Clever? You haven't got far." He looked at her innocently. "I thought you might have got farther."

"You'd have liked to see my dressing-gown perhaps," said Anthea. "Well, you'll see a very nice frock instead if you'll go away and let me concentrate." She took the glass, smiling at him. "Thank you, Lawrence. You're a blessing."

He smiled back, but a little doubtfully. "All the same, darling Anthea, I'm not sure that you're not a bit sad. Is—" He hesitated, rather embarrassed. "Look—Morgan isn't being a nuisance, is he?"

"No, no," she assured him quickly. "He's been a slight pest—which isn't the same thing—but it's nothing, and all over anyway. I'm all right. I'll come reeling down in about ten minutes."

Without saying anything more he kissed her cheek gently and went away. Anthea watched him go, and as the door closed she put the untouched glass of sherry carefully on the table and sat down. The sweetness of Chet, the sweetness of Lawrence, in contrast to everybody and everything else that had happened to her during this horrible day was too much for her. She cried for five minutes. Then she got up, drank the sherry, and set to work to repair the damage and dress for Jock's party.

Though she was quick it was past eight when she put the things she carried with her into the appropriate handbag and picking up a light coat left the room. But the repairs were entirely successful. She was wearing a frock which was definitely pretty, full-skirted and of a rather dark blue which took more make-up than she usually wore. Her hair shone, her face showed no trace of tears or what Lawrence called sadness, and her head was well up as she went downstairs and through the hall to the dining-room.

One small hazard for which she had to look out was the unpredictable mood of the Carruthers. Would they ostentatiously cut her dead, or would they have forgotten all about the near-scene at the harbour? They hadn't forgotten, but neither did they cut her.

"Oh, *there* you are," said Vida loudly. "You're so late we were on the point of sending out a search-party. Have you been at the Manse all this time?"

Anthea said she had been in the garden for a bit, and Mr. Peachey, frankly feasting his eyes and, she thought, not unconscious of the uncertain climate, came in with an impassioned complaint.

"How gladly would I tear Gregorson limb from limb!" he declaimed. "*Why* am I not asked to his party? I asked him to mine."

Anthea laughed. "It's the truest kindness," she said. "He's sparing you the symphonies," and she went to her table, smiling at Chet and with a tiny sketch of a lurch for Lawrence.

After dinner and an interval in which the dining-room staff cleared its feet and rushed into civilian clothes, she was driven by Lawrence along with half a dozen assorted undergraduates and schoolboys to the Tully, where almost everybody in the neighbourhood who liked listening to music was assembled. She was the only guest who was not perfectly at home, and Jock and the dog met her at the door with the ceremony proper for a first visit.

In the living-room, which was surprisingly large, she met the doctor and his wife, Colonel Garvie's head keeper, who was eighty, and a scarlet young under-keeper, the possessor of a bass voice famous throughout the north of Scotland. And beside the tough, bright-eyed octogenarian was Sir Andrew Gibb.

Jock had contrived his large room by taking in the byre which adjoined it, and it contained everything he wanted and nothing superfluous. It had book-lined walls, rugs on a stone floor and an upright dowager of a piano. The typewriter stood beside orderly piles of paper on a solid table near a window, and though the furniture was shabbily comfortable, having been picked up at local auctions, the electric fire and the record-player were magnificent. It was a pleasant room, so characteristic that Anthea thought she would have known it to be Jock's if, without Lawrence's warning, she had had the temerity to look in when she passed on her first day. The atmosphere, too, of a place where hard work was done, and the austerity of the working arrangements—no gadgets or fancy touches—were characteristic, and, most of all, the party: the mixture of old and young, all trades, not separated by their variety but contributing it.

Anthea said, "No wonder you're content with the Tully. You've made yourself uncommon snug."

"Huch, he's ower snug, jist," said the old keeper. "I'm aye telling him. It's no fair on the lassies—a fine wee hoose and a no-bad man jist wasted."

Jock replied without heat as if he was used to it. "I'm aye telling you, Fergus, nobody wants a writing man and it's a fine house for one."

"Havers!" cried the doctor. "You've the cart-shed to take in yet, and plenty room to build. Ample for a wife and half a dozen bairns."

"What about the peace and quiet so essential to the creative artist?"

The doctor snorted, having no patience with the pernickety, and Sir Andrew said, "I don't think an artist should marry early—he needs to be free to find his feet—but a single life is a lonely one."

"And forbye," the old keeper added with a lewd chuckle, "ye'll be sorry in the hinner end if ye've begotten naething mair lively than a wheen books."

"This is an unseemly attack—in mixed company," said Jock.

"Not just the thing," agreed the doctor's wife, who was knitting busily while her eyes went with keen amiable interest from one face to another. "I think myself that peace and quiet can be *overdone*, but it's a personal choice after all. Where's Ness to-night, Ian?"

Ian started, and replying automatically to the real question said he didn't know. "At least," he corrected himself, "she's at home. I mean' I don't know why she isn't here."

"Verra likely awa' oot for a bit walk wi' that lad Morgan," said Fergus who was not easily repressed. "Art's fine in its way but it's no the first thing for everybody."

Resigned glances passed among the student contingent. Ian began uncomfortably, "I don't think—" but the clear voice of Louisa broke in.

"Do you want to have coffee now, Greg?"

"No," said Jock, "we'll have some Bach."

"Aye," said the old man giving over. "We'll hear what he has to say."

The room settled into silence. All the chairs were occupied, boys and girls sat on the floor and Anthea was on a low stool by the fireplace with Ian and Lawrence beside her. Sir Andrew, the old keeper and the doctor were filling their pipes with slow, deliberate movements, the doctor's wife was relaxed and contented with her knitting, and peaceful happiness enclosed Stewart and Biddy who had preferred to walk. Though it was not yet dark outside, little of the evening light came through the small windows, and the lamp which Jock switched on by the record-player made the room shadowy.

Anthea was glad of it. She was wondering what had possessed her when she thought it would be an easy way out to come to Jock's house with a lot of other people and listen to music. Across the room his black head and intent face were lit by the lamp as he bent to put the needle on the record. He straightened, forgetting, it seemed, to tell them what he was playing, and the concerto for two violins began.

She must have moved involuntarily, for Ian, who was close to her, looked round to see if he was in the way. Ian was shy; he had none of his father's conviction or his sister's zeal, but he had his mother's kindness and it had led him to his cousin Anthea's side in case she needed support in the crowd of strangers. Anthea had not failed to appreciate it, and as he turned his fair head and made a move to give her more room she put a hand out and pulled him back. He smiled, offering his shoulder for a "lean," and she turned away from the room and listened to the Double screened by his solid person. Jock sat down near the player, and taking a pipe from his pocket he began to fill it, his movements as deliberate as those of old Fergus, his eyes on his hands. Anthea, breathing carefully in time with Ian's steady in-and-out, wondered if Jock knew what he was doing. If he had chosen this record on purpose it was a strangely heartless thing to do. If he had merely forgotten that they had listened to the Double together once before and together been moved as by a revelation, it was, if not even more strange, a painful and humiliating coincidence.

The first movement went its way, gay and serene, and the faces in the shadows reflected its mood with a clear, innocent sort of pleasure. There was a pause in which nobody stirred, and then the second movement began, the two violins in question and answer, pain and reassurance. The faces now held a reflection of sorrow, in memory or foreknowledge, and Anthea, in spite of herself, looked across the room and found Jock's eyes on her. He was looking at her intently, pain in his face and also, it seemed, a question. She knew one thing—he had not forgotten: but why he had done this and what the question was she did not know.

The jocularity of the last movement brought smiles and a sense of release, but Anthea was beyond release. The Double was in the nature of a last straw and she fell into a daze of fatigue and heard no more music. After the last record— whatever it was—the student body got up and served the refreshments which Louisa had helped to prepare, and Anthea roused herself to take part in the general talk.

Jock was talking to the doctor's wife, who emphasised

133

her own remarks with stabbing movements of her knitting needle and nibbled its end as she listened to his. Presently, commanding him to lean forward, she seized the free needle in her teeth by its middle and spread a large sheet of heavy knitting—heather mixture—over his back, patting and tweaking it into shape as she measured. Sir Andrew, delighted that Miss Logan shared his liking for music as well as his liking for the harbour, drew her away from the doctor into a three-sided conversation with old Fergus on the subject of Scottish music. She had to confess that she had never heard any, beyond the occasional pipe band, and he turned to the young keeper as if she had given him an excuse he wanted.

"You hear that, Tom?" he said. "Here is Miss Logan who has never heard a Scots song. Will you sing for her?"

"Oh aye, if ye like," was the laconic response. "If Greg'll play for me."

"He'll do that," said Sir Andrew and turned back to Anthea with a pleased face. "I must say very few things give me such pleasure as the old Scots songs—if they're well sung, Tom. I don't know how much is sentiment. I know I can't judge these tunes dispassionately."

"Weel," said Fergus, "they're no a bad basis. I never heard ony ither till I was fifty years of age or therebye. Then it was you, Andra, tell't me tae get a wireless. Back in the thirties that was."

"And what did you say?" demanded Sir Andrew. "We won't repeat it, but the one thing you would *never* do was to get a wireless."

"Aye, that's so," he admitted, "though I dinna mind jist what I said. But I got it in the end and ye see what I mean aboot the basis," he told Anthea with some triumph. "I can tak' pleasure in onything—Bach, Beethoven, the Romantics as they ca' them. But I canna jist dae wi' they modrens."

"Plenty of time," said Jock, arriving beside them. "You'll

come round to them yet." He turned to Anthea. "Do you approve of what I've done to the Tully?"

She said, "Completely. What you've done and what you've not done. Do you ever leave it?"

"Oh yes. I'm very glad to leave it sometimes—and very glad to get back. Come and look. . . ."

Accompanied by the young habituées, who took a proprietorial pride in the arrangements, the newcomer was conducted round the house, but back in the living-room the crowd was shaken off and Jock took her over to his work table, like a fellow-craftsman, to tell her about the book in progress. But he hardly mentioned the book.

"Anthea," he said, "we must talk. I don't want to harry you, or intrude, but I can't—"

"Greg, my dearie," called the doctor's wife across the room, "do you know what time it is? If we're to hear Tom sing it must be now. We should really be in our beds."

"Please don't hurry away," said Jock and went to the piano.

For half an hour he accompanied Tom's velvet voice in songs very familiar to some of the audience and surprising to Anthea. Her daze and preoccupation had kept out the accustomed sounds of recorded music, but the presence of the singer, the unexpectedness of so lovely a voice coming from the sturdy, red-faced figure, and the beauty of the songs themselves, drove everything else from her mind and she listened with curious intensity, as if she must catch and store the whole and every note of what she heard. Afterwards she responded to Sir Andrew's pleasure and, when she thanked the singer, found that he was very little affected by compliments, regarding his gift with detachment as something that had been issued along with his curly hair and strong muscles.

"If I had a voice like that," Lawrence said discontentedly, "I'd wreck everything by rushing off and being trained for a pro."

"But why should that be wreckage?" she asked, surprised.

Lawrence had heard Tom often and had thought about it. "Because," he said, "if he went and got trained it'd be just one more good voice. To hear him sing like that—his own kind of songs—*here*—is quite something; but he'd lose that—bound to—and what would he gain?"

"Anyway, Tom would hate it." Ian, who was sitting near them with the dog between his knees, joined in unexpectedly. "He just likes singing for fun."

So that was it, thought Anthea, feeling in her fatigue that she was seeing an immense distance into the mystery of beauty. The harbour was beautiful by accident, young Tom had, by chance, a good voice and liked singing. If the harbour gave up its job, if Tom ceased to be a keeper, the valuable quality in both, the beauty itself, would be lost. . . . She thought. But it was difficult to know whether she was being profound or merely light-headed, and Louisa was approaching.

"Miss Logan," she said, "we usually clear up a bit before we go. Would you mind if we kept you waiting for a few minutes? We won't be long."

"Come and look at the view," said Lawrence and received a withering glance.

"Not you, Lawrence dear," said Louisa and herded him to the sink.

The last of the daylight had gone but there was a majestic moon making a radiant path on the sea. Anthea went out and crossing the short turf which Jock had levelled and bounded with a dry-stone wall, she stood looking at a night view of the harbour, below and to her left, which she had never seen before. Behind her was the old white cottage, the lights from its windows and open door yellow and warm. Inside was a talkative bustle of clearing up: outside, sounds of departure, cars starting and voices calling good night. Before her was the sea, black where the moonlight did not touch it, and perfectly still.

"The boats will be going out on Sunday night when it's chappit twelve," said Jock's voice. "Will you come with me and see them go?"

"I won't be here," she said. The cool air and the tiredness were making her shiver and she was full of sorrow.

Jock put a hand on her shoulder saying, "Sit—it's quite clean," and they sat down on the wall. "Cigarette?" He lit cigarettes and then asked, "Why won't you be here?"

A large figure wheeling a bicycle called, "Good night, Anthea," and with a warm tone of affection which made Jock smile she called back, "Good night, Ian." Then she turned to the task of putting less than the truth across to an uncomfortably acute listener.

"Well, I never meant this to be a long holiday," she said, truthfully so far, and as easily as she could. "I've seen Balgarvie again and the McNaughtons—and you, for a surprise bonus— and the hotel is damned expensive. So I move on to-morrow."

There was a pause and then Jock said, "Did you get my message?"

"Message?" She looked at him blankly.

"The Double. You didn't think it was accidental, did you?"

"Oh . . . I thought it might be one of those unconscious associations—"

"No you didn't, Anthea," he said. "We looked at each other. I put it on because I wanted you to know that *for me* it hasn't lost its significance. This may sound like a writer talking, but if it does I can't help it. Since that time I've never heard it, probably never will hear it, without weeping: not, thank God, where it shows. Inside where it hurts. And I thought it was time that—whatever happens—we heard it again and wept together."

She said, "You showed a good deal of faith in my self-control."

"I have faith in it—with reason. But I noticed that Ian

137

came in useful. Anthea, I don't know anything about your life—what sort of job you have, what ties . . . what love. But why need you make a mystery of it? If you don't want me you can't think I'd—Damn!"

At least some of the clearing-up party had been conscious that they were keeping Miss Logan waiting and took credit to themselves for being quicker than usual. "Coming, Anthea?" shouted Lawrence's voice.

"Coming," she answered, and simultaneously Jock roared, "*Wait!*" and put a restraining hand on her arm.

"*You must say something*," he said urgently—and angrily. "I have not changed. Have you? For my sake and your own, darling, be honest with me."

There were interested eyes on the two figures now standing by the wall, and Louisa, with ready tact, created a diversion with some mild assistance from Alec. She lost her handkerchief and set everybody else to a thorough search of the car while she herself rushed noisily back into the house. Jock, unaware of the help being extended to him, nevertheless took advantage of it and held Anthea still.

"Well?" he said.

"Jock," she said, "I can only say that in a way I haven't changed. I think I'll always love you, we'll always love each other—a bit. But in every other way I have changed, and if you're asking me to—to begin again, the answer is no."

As she spoke she began walking slowly forward across the grass and they had taken half a dozen steps before he asked, "Does that mean that it's your intention to disappear again?"

"Well—I suppose that's what it amounts to."

"Why?"

"It's better, that's all," she said. "Don't be *angry* with me, Jock. At least—I suppose you may as well be angry as anything else. But I wish you weren't. . . ."

Her voice faded and he took her arm and pressed it

against his side. "All right," he said and as Louisa came running out of the house displaying her handkerchief they walked on and reached the car.

"Good-bye. Jock," said Anthea. "Thank you for a lovely party. You have very nice friends."

"He's a very nice man," said Louisa, hanging out of the car window. "Can we come again soon, Greg?"

"Any time you like," he said and looking directly at Anthea he added, "the door of the Tully is always open."

Lawrence, light-heartedly honking his horn, drove away. There was a loud chorus of good nights and thanks, and then only the diminishing sound of the car as went across the field. It turned on to the road and was gone. Jock stood still on the grass and Dan stood beside him, his nose wrinkling delicately as he savoured the smells wafted from the shore below them, from the harbour and the village. . . . There was nothing particular, just the usual smells, and the day had been a long one.

He enjoyed having friends in and always played his part as co-host, but it would be nice to get to bed. He gave Jock's leg a nudge and turned suggestively to the house. At the door he paused and looked round to make sure he was coming, which he was—slowly. There was a disturbed, troubled feeling. . . .

"Good night, old dog," Jock said to the face gazing up with loving concern. "Thanks for your co-operation. Dan, I have made one hell of a hash. What do we do now?"

Dan's reply, though silent, was eloquent. A brief, moderately sympathetic wag of the tail dismissed knotty problems, let alone histrionics, as unsuitable for the time of night, and picking up his paws he trotted briskly into the house and made for the living-room hearth-rug. Jock stood hesitating for a moment, wondering if he might get some work done since he didn't feel much like sleep. Dan stood on the rug willing him to go to bed. He met the stern eye, made a face at it and went. Dan gave a short sigh of relief and lay down.

CHAPTER 11

JOCK was accustomed to getting through a lot of work in the early hours, and on the morning after his party he was, as usual, dressed and shaved by six o'clock. But he knew that no work would be done. He was puzzled by Anthea, he was angry with her: and, having found her again, he could not bear to let her go. Whether, if she had not turned up on the pier that day, he would have lived the rest of his life contentedly without her, he did not know. In a way he had always believed that she would come back to Balgarvie and appear suddenly before him just as she had done, and he knew that if she went away now his life would be a failure. He would stay on the tram-lines, a writer gradually running out of juice, with—as old Fergus gracefully put it—nothing more lively to his credit than a row of books.

He opened the door to let the dog out and stood for a while smoking, looking at his view and noticing automatically that the weather had gone to bits. It was cold and a wet haar was being jostled by a vicious little wind. Shivering he went back to his bedroom and pulled on a heavy sweater and then went to the kitchen. He filled the kettle and proceeded, without thinking about it, to brew up his first pot of tea.

He felt ill. Leaving Anthea alone for these three days had been the action of a fool; resentful and—he was not sparing himself—conceited. Why the hell should he, who had left her flat seven years ago, expect that she would instantly re-admit him to the status of intimate friend—confide in him and trust him? *Why* had she come all the way to Balgarvie for a few days' visit? *Why* was she going to-day? He would swear that none of the young staff—or Lawrence or Ness—had any idea of it. At least he now knew that she was related to the McNaughtons, but if she meant what she said about vanishing again there was no guarantee that they any more than himself would hear what became of her.

The lid of the kettle set up an agitated, maddening rattle and water streamed down its sides. He swore and switching it off began to pour the boiling water into the teapot before he realised that he hadn't put the tea in. He was beginning again, wondering if he shouldn't go up to the House and sit on Anthea's luggage till he got some sense out of her, when he heard a car coming along the field track and saw her white convertible.

He and Dan were out of the house and beside the car as it drew up. Anthea got out. She stooped to pat the dog briefly, as a naturally kind person under stress automatically will, and looked at Jock.

"All my money's been stolen," she said baldly.

He dealt with first things first. "All right, I can lend you whatever you need," he said. "Come in."

She went with him into the living-room and he switched on the fire. The kettle was noisily boiling over once more and he swore and dashed to the kitchen. When he came back, carrying a tray and another sweater, she was still standing as he had left her and Dan gave him an alarmed glance.

He handed her the pullover. "Put this on."

"Oh—thanks," said Anthea. "It is rather cold. . . ." She hauled it on over her own thin jersey and absent-mindedly rolled the sleeves up over her hands. "I'm sorry to bother you with this," she said formally. "I wouldn't have come, but I really don't know what to do. I should have gone to the Manse, I suppose, but—"

Jock was pouring out tea. He had hardly looked at her; it was better not to and there was no need. She was not going to cry or faint. She was, indeed, well controlled, her eyes and voice steady, but she had changed: the golden colouring was dimmed and she was very nearly ungainly. He said:

141

"Let's skip this bit, Anthea. You and I are two of a kind and we both know it. And," he added, "we're not, either of us, given to blackmail—of any kind. Sit down and drink your tea."

His matter-of-fact tone worked. She sat down obediently and took the cup and a cigarette from him.

"Now," he said, "how much money?"

She put a hand to her head. "About four hundred pounds," she said.

There was a slight pause, and then Jock sat down in the chair facing hers across the fireplace saying, "Well—if you're travelling, staying in expensive pubs, I suppose it's not so much to carry—"

"Don't be silly," she interrupted him irritably. "It's all I've got—available, that is. You know perfectly well I'm not the kind that *ever* has that kind of money."

"Well—I thought your standards had risen pretty steeply," he admitted. "Where was the money? Have you any idea when it went?"

"It was in a small locked case—in the wardrobe. Nothing else was taken. There are one or two things—my mother's engagement ring and so on—but only the money has gone. My papers had been read, I think. It was all right at lunch time yesterday, because I took some out. I was going to Carse."

"So it was between about two o'clock and the time you got back from here—soon after midnight. I think there's a chance you may get it back, you know. It isn't a nice thought, but I'm afraid it must have been an inside job. Burglars are pretty rare in these parts."

"I know," Anthea said miserably. "I've been thinking about that. It's really wicked to leave money lying about in people's way."

"It was hardly in people's way—a locked case in a wardrobe. You didn't think of giving it to Saunders to keep in the safe?"

"*Afterwards*," she said. "It never occurred to me *before*. Of course it was damn' stupid—the whole thing was stupid." She looked at him anxiously. "If you could lend me a bit— enough to pay the hotel and—just float me—I can pay it back all right. Only it'll take a little time, I'm afraid. Some days."

"No rush," said Jock. "It'll be easiest if I cash a cheque for you." He glanced at his watch. "We'll go along in a minute and set old Saunders to work." A look of extreme distaste crossed her face and he said, "You weren't thinking of driving off as planned without saying anything about it, were you?"

She shook her head. "Not quite. Very nearly, though. It's so—foul."

"Never mind," he said. "We'll clear it up. Drink your tea." She drank it and he got up to pour out second cups. "How did you get like this?" he asked. "Wandering around with every, appearance of affluence and nothing in the bank . . .?"

His tone was so casual, taking for granted a reasonable explanation of behaviour which might seem mildly eccentric at first glance, that Anthea gave a sudden involuntary laugh. But she only said, "Oh well, it's a long story. Quite dull—and pretty silly."

Jock sat down again and took a pipe from his pocket. It was early. Mr. Saunders would hardly be awake yet and the matter of the theft could wait for a little. He blew a clearing blast through the pipe and said, "I should have told you on the pier that day, I know about your brother. Randal."

She looked up. "Do you? I thought you probably would and then I thought perhaps you didn't. I don't know when you got back to England that time."

"Not for about a year, but of course I heard about it. William told me. He didn't know what had happened to you, though." William Humbolt was the editor of the *Trumpeter*, at one time "the boss" to both of them, but his name brought no response from Anthea. "He was very concerned about you," Jock went on. "And he couldn't fathom why a girl like you, with all the guts in the world, had to cut and run just because her brother was jugged for selling information to the Communists."

"I know he couldn't," said Anthea.

"But of course," said Jock, "he hadn't all the facts. And William sees what's in front of him. He saw you and knew that with his help you could have weathered it: he didn't see the wider destruction."

Anthea put her hand to her throat as if speech was physically impossible—which was nearly true. The room was very silent and after a moment Jock began talking again, and telling her story.

"I met Randal once—remember? We ran into him somewhere—at some party. Clever as hell—and conceited. The rules didn't apply to him. Unfortunately his simple-minded parents couldn't keep up with his broad, enlightened views. Your father died at once. Your mother took longer and you, I suppose, kept her and yourself afloat. There couldn't have been much left after the trial." He paused. "He got seven years, didn't he? He must be out now—where is he?"

"I don't know," Anthea said hoarsely.

"Didn't you see him when he came out?"

"Once. Just after my mother died."

"Looking for money, was he? Did you give it to him?"

She nodded. "Mother had a little of her own. I didn't know. I suppose she was holding on to it—perhaps for Randal. I gave him half of it." Jock didn't speak but she looked across at him as if he had—almost angrily. "It wasn't so soft as it sounds. For one thing, if you'd known Randal you'd know it just wasn't worth while trying to refuse: he could wear anybody down. But the main thing was he needed it to get away—out of the country—and he promised that would be the end. He'd never come into my life again. 'You have no

144

brother' was what he said. I can't tell you what a relief it was," Anthea said vehemently. "It was finished. I was free."

"Yes," said Jock. "Worth any money—if true."

"It is true," she said. "I know him. He's gone—I don't know where and I don't want to—and he'll make a new life for himself."

Jock said, "Well—he's capable enough—and tough enough," and there was another silence.

They were two of a kind. It was not necessary that he should know the details of her life in the last seven years: the drudgery of a teaching job which, with a brother in prison and a sick mother to look after, was not a good one; the drab, half-dead seaside town where neighbours did not know each other, and the stuffy little flat with the curious, persistent smell. He could imagine it all—the awkwardnesses, the strain of meeting people and the swiftly-developed skill in talking without saying anything—evasion. Above all, he knew of the creeping, insidious tide of dullness, deterioration.

Suddenly, as if the talk had been continuous, Anthea said, "It wasn't *hardship*, you know. One got used to it. There was even a kind of contentment. Bed and a library book were wonderful."

"I know," said Jock. "Like going to sleep when you're lost in the snow. The wonder is that you ever got out. It must have taken a hell of an effort."

She made a little sound, a not very amused laugh. "Randal did it," she said. "I *think* I'd have made it without his bit of dynamite but it would have been more gradual. More sensible, perhaps."

There was some amusement in the laugh and she was more relaxed, sprawling in the big chair with her legs stretched out, a tired, characteristically Anthea sprawl, graceful in spite of her. Jock threw over cigarettes and matches and ventured to ask in what way Randal had assisted. She caught the packet and groped among the folds of the enormous pullover for the matches.

"He told me I looked like a half-drowned cat," she replied, "and advised me to give up martyrdom and seek rehabilitation." She lit a cigarette and threw back the materials, looking at Jock with eyes in which the amusement had grown. "It wasn't *news* to me that I looked like a half-drowned cat," she added. "I even took a kind of pride—the martyr's pride, I suppose—in my dreary bun and hopeless clothes, but hearing it *said* had a galvanising effect. I took a look at myself and—gosh!—it was an eye-opener."

Jock thought that Randal—the bastard!—might be allowed a couple of million years off hell for that, seeing the results were good, and said so. Anthea agreed, in the same dry tone, that it had been salutary. "So," he said, "you broke out?"

"Yes— I *burst* out. I threw in the job—gave notice next day in fact—sold the furniture and took off with everything I'd got. Except about a thousand pounds which is still invested."

"What was your plan—or didn't you have one?"

"Oh yes, I had one. But first—" She broke off and shot him a half guilty, half comic look. "*First*, I just wanted to *spend*—car, hair-do, clothes—and wallow in luxury for a bit. So it seemed to be a good idea to combine that with coming to Balgarvie. Having a holiday."

"I can imagine that—wanting to splash—very well," said Jock. "And then? Your book's been accepted . . .?"

There was only a slight hesitation and then she said levelly, "Well, I haven't got down to details, but I had roughly the same idea as yours. I'm going for a non-brainwork—and I don't mind if it's non-U—job which will keep body and soul together while I see what the writing amounts to." She paused, but before there was time for any reply added, "I

146

can't make much of a guess about that, but I do know it's what I want. To be free—and write."

Jock smiled. He was giving thanks for the spirit, the guts, which had reacted in a good healthy burst of extravagance, of pleasure in her good looks and such riotous living as Balgarvie House afforded: and at the moment there was nothing he could do about the rest. He could not announce that he was going abroad and offer her the Tully rent free.

"Good for you," he said warmly. "How sensible you've been."

Anthea's head came up. "*Sensible*? You call it sensible?" She waved a hand in the direction of Balgarvie House, taking in the white car on the way. "Even . . .?"

"Certainly. You needed your extravagance—it was an essential part of the rehabilitation. I don't know if you can make a living from books or not, Anthea, but I'm sure you're right to have a shot at it. You can live on very little if you set your mind to it—stick to what's necessary for you and for the job and the hell with what other people think. Your four hundred would go quite a long way—let you get your next book written."

"Yes, perhaps," she said, but the shadow had come and she stirred and frowned. "This damned business . . . isn't it time—"

The telephone exploded, a shrill relentless clamour. She started violently and Jock leapt to stop it. "Damn you, shut *up*!" he shouted and seized it. "Gregorson," he snapped.

Anthea heard a man's voice, a quacking sound of question and Jock said, "Yes. Why?" very curtly. The voice quacked on, agitated and urgent, and presently he said, "Hang on, I'll ask her," and turned round putting a hand over the mouthpiece.

"Peachey," he announced laconically. "Cleever's lost a letter—or Hart's lost it for him. They want to know if he dropped it in the garden and you picked it up."

147

"No," said Anthea. She had got up from her chair. "At least, he did drop a whole lot of papers but he picked them all up again. There was nothing left so far as I saw. Desmond Peachey, you say? Why is—should I speak to him?"

"Don't bother," said Jock. "We'll have to go along anyway and report your little loss." He turned back to the telephone. "Peachey? No, she didn't see it." Mr. Peachey quacked again at some length. Jock's responses were mainly grunts. "We'll be along in a few minutes," was his conclusion.

He put the receiver down and came back across the room with a face that Anthea could not read. "Is it an important letter?" she asked. "What was all that about?"

Jock said sourly that it was important in the eyes of Senator Cleever and Mr. Scudamore. Disgusted was the word, thought Anthea, eyeing him. "Silly idiots," he went on. "I'll swear it's lying under Hart's bed—or a sheep may have eaten it—and that it's about as hot as a wet Sunday anyway. However, they're off the ground. Scudamore's one of these security maniacs and Cleever's bleating for the Special Branch. Peachey's had to call in the police to hold them."

"Mercy!" said Anthea, rather entertained. She had never found it possible to take Senator Cleever very seriously, though she was quite fond of him, and she could believe anything of Mr. Scudamore when his blood was up. "We'd better go and help look," she said. "I'll bet they haven't gone through Chet's pockets properly. He keeps them in such a muddle it isn't true. What's the matter?"

Jock's face was still cross—disgusted. The mirth died in Anthea's eyes. Neither of them spoke—there was no need. She had recovered, at least to a great extent, her normal grace and colour, and he looked at her, dreading to see her change again, to see fear. His thought was, " Oh God, my poor girl! Of all the damnable outside chances. . ."

But to Anthea, being linked with Randal Logan, a convicted

traitor, was something she had lived with for a long time. She had always known that as well as being an irrecoverable misfortune it was potentially a danger if unscrupulous or, in certain circumstances, scrupulous hands got hold of it. She had dreaded it, anticipated it, and therefore it was unlike the unforeseen, fortuitous blows which had culminated in the theft of her money. If this was it she was already braced to meet it.

She picked up her handbag and straightened her shoulders, an upright, quite unconsciously gallant-looking girl who had forgotten that she was wearing a huge masculine sweater, and looked at Jock with a small smile.

"Poor old Chet," she said. "It's really silly, isn't it?" She made a face. "Not that I wouldn't prefer to be elsewhere—say Land's End."

"Never mind," said Jock. "It may not happen—the bloody thing may turn up any minute. And if it doesn't, it'll be no worse than a damned bore. We may as well get along and see."

"There's no call for you to get mixed up in it, you know," said Anthea.

He put a hand on her shoulder and turned her towards the door. "Try and stop me," he said. "I revel in excitement. Besides, if it comes to a fight I'm a sharper second than the Minister. Dan—do you want to stay in or go out?"

Senator Cleever had lost a letter—or rather, Chet Hart had lost it for him. The central facts were that Chet had put the letter in his pocket before he went down to intercept Anthea in the hall the evening before and in the morning it wasn't there. On the perimeter the facts were more numerous and less simple. The letter was in reply to a request for information connected with a recent phase in the Senator's travels, and it was the errand which was to take Chet away from Balgarvie that day. He was to take it to London and hand it to a messenger, obtaining a receipt.

149

The whole business bored him very much. In a way he enjoyed his job with Senator Cleever for it gave scope to his talents—his flair for languages, the ability to grapple with codes and ciphers and to write good, well-worded reports. The Cleever set-up, as he saw it in his more cynical moments, was that Mr. Scudamore told the Senator what to say, and he, Chet, said it. But the more he saw of politics the less he believed in them, and he resented this particular letter hotly. It was, in his informed opinion, wholly superfluous. The personage who asked for it was merely ministering to his own self-importance; sending it by messenger—in code—was a come-back asserting Senator Cleever's importance; the information wasn't worth a dime, and he didn't want to leave Balgarvie so long as it held Anthea Logan.

All these, Chet was unhappily aware, were contributory causes. He had been careless about the letter—so careless he wasn't even sure which pocket he had put it in. The only thing he was sure about was that when he saw Anthea's car drive into the yard the letter was in his hand—he had just stuck it up—and he shoved it in a pocket. After that he didn't give it a thought till morning.

He reported the loss as soon as his first hasty search failed, and at once the balloon began to fill. High among his grudges against politicians in general and Senator Cleever and Mr. Scudamore in particular was their unvarying habit in security matters of by-passing the probable and going bald-headed for the sensational barely possible. It was as useless to point out that Balgarvie was an unlikely pitch for an agent as that no agent would be much interested in the lost letter. Senator Cleever's natural tendency to see what he called the enemies of the free peoples under every chair, fanned by Mr. Scudamore's zeal, sounded the alarm and the hunt was up.

"The content of the letter is not crucial," said the Senator. "You say you've looked all where you went last night and it's *addressed*. The theory of accident may hold —it is my earnest prayer that it will—but we dare not wait."

They did not wait. Mr. Saunders was summoned, a signal was flashed round the staff and a posse of the tall young ghillies sent to search the grounds. A messenger—Louisa— was despatched to ask Miss Logan, with apologies, if she had picked up the letter in the garden. She very unwillingly reported that Miss Logan's room was empty: Morgan, wide-eyed, reported that her car was not in the yard. Mr. Peachey of the Foreign Office was summoned and Chet discovered what his carelessness had done.

"Anthea Logan," said Mr. Scudamore, hunting. "Out, was she? This time in the morning? They don't have early-morning services in Scotch churches, do they? She was in the garden with Chet last night . . . she knew Chet was leaving this—"

"She didn't know why," shouted Chet unavailingly.

She had decided—just last night seemingly—to leave to-day herself. . . . What was she doing at Balgarvie anyway . . .? He turned to Mr. Peachey. "Wasn't there a Logan convicted seven-eight years back?"

Chet was struck dumb. Senator Cleever's eyes bulged and Mr. Peachey, who shared Mr. Scudamore's enthusiasm for security, looked at him with the respect of one expert for another. But he was filled with consternation. "Yes. Yes, there was," he said. "Randal Logan. He was a chemist. But it would be an extreme coincidence—it isn't an uncommon name and it never occurred to me . . . There is absolutely no reason to connect . . . She isn't, after all, a stranger to Balgarvie. The Minister . . . And I do feel very strongly, you know, that anything other than accident is so improbable."

Mr. Scudamore smiled. "The attitood every agent prays for," he said sardonically. "Not that I'm saying there is an agent here, but we've got to act on the assumption there could be."

"Naturally it can't be ruled out," Mr. Peachey agreed, nettled. But though he had suffered a snub he was not demolished, and came back with some authority. Action must not include contravention of the law. If there was any question of suspicion, let alone accusations, it was a matter for the police.

Before eight o'clock the meeting had transferred to Mr. Saunders's office to await the police, and it had multiplied. Mr. Saunders himself was there, Colonel Garvie and, rather mysteriously, Sir Andrew Gibb. An agreeable smell of breakfast pervaded the House and the early risers were already well on with their meal, but the party in the office was unfed and explosive.

Colonel Garvie on the one side and the Senator and Mr. Scudamore on the other faced each other across a gulf of total non-comprehension. The Americans had expected grave concern, willingness to act promptly under their own experienced instruction. What they got was open disbelief. The Colonel didn't hold with sensationalism. Spies, if that was that they were hinting at, didn't occur at Balgarvie and he was not prepared to subscribe to bizarre phantasies. This letter would either turn up or not and in his view it didn't much matter which. If it didn't they could write another. The Senator on responsibility and the enemies of the free peoples left him embarrassed but unmoved. His temper, however, at all times tried by the unfamiliar and by behaviour which left the rails of his own standards of common sense, could almost be heard to sizzle, and the busy Scudamore went too far. If, said the Colonel at the pitch of his voice, he had known that Senator Cleever carried a lot of damned secret documents everywhere he went he was damned if he would have let the Senator put a foot inside his House. And he would remind Mr. Scudamore that American senators were not the only—or the most—important men in the world. They were merely guests at Bal-

152

garvie and they would behave themselves or leave. He would not have his other guests annoyed and that was final.

Mr. Peachey strove to induce calm, but his weight was insufficient. It was left to Sir Andrew Gibb, whose own calm remained unruffled, to bridge the gap. In a quiet, undramatic voice he explained each side to the other. No accusations were made and he had gone some way in persuading them that they were all reasonable men with the same reasonable object when the police arrived: Superintendent Wilkie from county headquarters, attended by a pink young constable and a beefy older man, Sergeant McNab, who had reached the pinnacle of a useful but not too exacting career as guardian of the law in Balgarvie and district.

Wilkie was a big man with sandy hair and a plain, sandy face sprinkled with freckles, and as he removed his cap small grey eyes, looking out from whitish lashes, took the assembled company like a camera. He greeted those he knew —the laird, the manager and Sir Andrew Gibb—was introduced to the strangers, and took charge.

Like the Colonel, he had no faith at all in anything more sensational than what Senator Cleever called the accident theory. It was too improbable. Like Mr. Peachey, however, he knew that the improbable can happen and that the Senator, if he wanted a fuss, must have it. He listened impassively while the letter and the circumstances of its loss were described—a description of extreme discretion as far as the letter itself was concerned—and the Senator and Mr. Scudamore gazed incredulously at the uniforms, the checked hat-bands, the brawn: the whole display of provincial force.

Senator Cleever, feeling perhaps that the story had hardly made the impact it deserved, raised his grey head and repeated his homily. "The contents and the urgency of the letter," he said rather defensively, "are not crucial. But at the present time, Superintendent, the enemies of the free peoples are everywhere. A man in the position it is my privilege to hold knows that only too well. Responsibility is a heavy burden to carry in these difficult times. Every hour of every day I am conscious—and I assure you those who work with me are conscious—that ordinary care will not suffice. From some unexpected quarter, from some hand none could suspect, the blow may fall." He looked sombrely at his hearers. "Gentlemen, neither you, the British, nor we representing America, dare take this lightly."

CHAPTER 12

SENATOR Cleever had dressed hurriedly that morning. A white stubble covered his chin, his hair was imperfectly brushed, and at all times his oratory hovered near the brink of the ludicrous. But he had dignity. He was an honest man who believed implicitly in the views for which he stood and the work he did. There was a little silence when he finished speaking, and then Wilkie proceeded.

He asked, "Was there anything, sir—even some small trifling thing—that made you suspect the letter might have been taken—deliberate, like?"

Mr. Peachey coughed and the Senator looked uneasily at Mr. Scudamore. "Well—yes," he said. "It's slight, but there is. . . . There's a young lady, a Miss Logan, whose circumstances seem to us to—uh—warrant research."

"Kin tae the Meenister," hissed Sergeant McNab to his superior in a scandalised whisper. Mr. Saunders's mouth fell open and Colonel Garvie's face grew black.

"Why would that be?" Wilkie asked the Senator.

Mr. Scudamore took over. He was hotly resentful of this example of the British way of doing things—amateurism. In a case which rated top-level action—swift, ruthless, specially trained men—they got the local cops and a rigid concern for the rights of everybody except the victims. Mr. Peachey's cold eyes reminded him, however, that whatever he felt about the system, this was British soil, and he gave, dispassionately, the reasons for suspecting Miss Logan which were, so to speak, public property already. They were enough to go on with. Randal Logan could wait.

"You say she went out early this morning?" said Wilkie. "Has she ever done this before? Gone to the Manse for her breakfast or the like of that?"

There was a knock at the door. It opened and Anthea came in with Jock close behind her. Her short hair was ruffled by the wind, she was wearing an enormous royal blue pullover, clearly not her own, and she was rather pale.

Mr. Saunders leapt to his feet. "Miss Logan," he protested, "I must ask you . . . this is not a convenient—"

"I have come to tell you," said Anthea, "that a large sum of money has been stolen from my room."

A blank silence followed. Colonel Garvie broke it. "Money?" he said. "Stolen? But how could—" Mr. Saunders cried distractedly that the hotel could accept no responsibility for money or valuables left in guests' rooms. Why, he demanded, had she not had it put in the safe?

Anthea had disliked Mr. Saunders at sight. His affable teeth combined with what she felt to be excessive managerial watchfulness repelled her, but she knew that in this matter his wrath was justified. "Of course I should have had it put in the safe," she admitted, "but it just didn't occur to me that it was necessary."

"And it shouldn't have been necessary," moaned Colonel Garvie, who was not a hotel manager. "Our people—our nice young students—I can't believe any of them—"

"Good God!" burst from his manager. "A lot of money lying about in a bedroom! How can I—how can *anybody*—be responsible for young staff when that sort of carelessness—"

"It wasn't just lying about, you know," said Jock. "It was in a locked case in a wardrobe. Whoever found it was looking for it."

A thought struck Colonel Garvie. "But," he said, "why would anybody just go to the one room? We haven't had any word of other losses." An expression of deep disgust came over his face. "Except this letter."

"I doubt," said Wilkie, "we'll have to wait for him—or her—to tell us. Have you any idea when it was taken, Miss

Logan? You've heard, haven't you, that Mr. Cleever here has lost a letter?"

Mr. Scudamore gave a sharp cough which acted like a goad on the Senator. He stirred restlessly. "I deeply regret," he broke in, "that Miss Logan has sustained this loss, but perhaps she—and you, gentlemen—will pardon me if I remind you that a crime even more serious may have been perpetrated. A crime which—in its implications —must urgently affect, it is hardly too much to say, the whole human—"

"Just so, sir," said Wilkie. "But there's just the possibility the two might be connected. We'll ask Miss Logan and Mr. Gregorson just to remain here while we run through the main facts you and—" he consulted his papers, "Mr. Scudamore and Mr. Hart have given us about this letter that's missing, and then we'll ask Miss Logan for a brief wee statement and see where it leads us."

There was another protest from Senator Cleever. He was extremely reluctant that any information should be revealed to any person whatsoever except those already necessarily informed. A cold glance rested on the intruders, Logan and Gregorson; a baleful glare singed Mr. Peachey of the Foreign Office, and the police officers were eyed with more than doubt.

Behind Mr. Gregorson's polite, unhelpful face, Mr. Peachey caught a gleam of unholy joy and turned angrily away from it. He could only wait and pray that Superintendent Wilkie knew his job. But, though he did know his job, Wilkie looked for a moment uncertain of his lines and it was again Sir Andrew Gibb who moved in. He entirely agreed with Senator Cleever that the investigation called for the greatest discretion and therefore—as the Laird had said earlier—the least possible disturbance: but in the interests of speed—which, as the Senator pointed out, was vital—it was desirable that the basic facts of both cases should be known to all who were present. "The *basic* fact, that you have lost an important letter, sir, is already known. Anyone may be able to help us and the theft of Miss Logan's money is a curious coincidence—if it is coincidence."

It was touch and go, but the calm face and quiet voice won. "Very well," said the Senator and transferred his gaze from Sir Andrew to the superintendent without calling in on Mr. Scudamore on the way. "Seems like we're in your hands," he said. "You better handle it."

Wilkie handled it with considerable tact. He made no reference at all to the character of the letter. He was concerned only with what had happened to it, who could have got at it, between the time it was written and half past six this morning when its loss was discovered. When Senator Cleever and Mr. Scudamore returned from the moors about half past five, Mr. Hart discussed the letter with them. He left them soon after six with the letter in his hand. "What did you do then?" he asked Chet.

Chet cleared his throat before he spoke. Without looking at Anthea he said reluctantly that he had met her in the hall, he guessed it would be between a quarter and half past six, and they had been talking in the garden till just after seven. He reaffirmed that he had put the letter in the pocket of his jacket before he went downstairs, and it was still his opinion that he had dropped it, probably outside. He could have pulled it out with his handkerchief or ether papers.

"You took out your handkerchief to dust the bench in the garden," Anthea reminded him. "And you pulled out a lot of papers and dropped some of them when you were fishing for your addresses. You picked them up and I didn't notice anything left on the bench or the ground, but—have you *looked*?"

Her conviction that men simply don't know how to look for lost objects was so obvious, her tone so like that which Chet frequently heard from his mother, that his eyes were faintly amused. "Oh sure, I looked," he told her. "Went straight back to that seat first thing when I couldn't find the letter this morning." He had also searched the path by which they had gone to the garden and he had returned alone, though he was not going to dwell on the return journey.

"So you have no idea when the envelope left your pocket," said Wilkie. "Would it have been possible for anyone to enter your room during the night without you hearing?"

"No," said Chet. "The door was locked."

"Did you leave it at any time? Did you have a bath before dinner, for example? Or before going to bed?"

Chet shook his head. "Nope. Took a bath and changed before they came in from shooting. No, s'far as I knew it was never out of my sight. I don't see anybody could have got at it. I *must* have dropped it."

It was Anthea's turn again and "to fill in the picture like," as Wilkie put it, she told them how she had spent the day. She had played golf in the morning with Mr. and Mrs. Car-ruthers and Mr. Peachey: after lunch she got some money from her case and went to do a little shopping in Carse. She had tea at the Manse and afterwards saw Mr. Saunders to tell him that she intended to leave the hotel next day—that was to-day. She met Mr. Hart and walked to the garden with him: he told her he was going away for a few days and as she expected to be gone when he returned they exchanged addresses. She lingered in the garden after he went in and was rather late for dinner. The evening was spent at the Tully.

"There was nothing out of the way at all, then?" asked the superintendent.

She hesitated. There was Morgan. She disliked doing it but it was factual enough to be mentioned. She said that he had been troublesome and described the final scene—with restraint, reminding Mr. Peachey that she had to borrow a ball from him the first day they played golf and not making much of it. "It was very silly of him," she concluded, while a disapproving cluck from the Colonel boded ill for Morgan. "He made far too much fuss and it was ridiculous to imagine that I would let him give me a dozen new balls—but he was very persistent and I'm afraid I had to snub him quite hard. I don't suggest that it has any bearing on the theft, but I mention it as being out of the way."

"I've no doubt he resented the snub," Jock said dryly. "In fact I know he did."

The superintendent glanced at him. "You know the lad, Mr. Gregorson?"

"I know most of them," was the reply. Mr. Saunders said rather stiffly that any of them would have felt it: Morgan was inexperienced but he had no doubt meant well. But the Colonel would have none of it. "Piece of impudence," he snorted and begged Anthea's pardon.

"Was it a sudden decision to leave to-day?" Mr. Peachey asked her. "You hadn't mentioned it—at least in my hearing."

"'I've been very vague," she said. "I had meant to go on Monday and then—well, to-day seemed better." She stopped. If she went on it was going to lead into the long story which she did not want to tell them. It seemed that it would have to be told; but not, she hoped, to so large an audience.

It was an abrupt conclusion, and a pause followed. Mr. Scudamore was the first to speak. He turned to the Senator and, so to speak, addressed the company through him. He didn't altogether understand how things were handled over here, he said with a stiffness which made it plain that he thought nothing of what he had seen of British police methods so far, but it seemed to him that there were some questions which needed answering at once. "I don't want to speak out of turn, but this could be a very, very serious business and I have to say that I think Miss Logan should be asked to give more evidence of her movements. And I don't mean just yesterday."

The tension in the room tightened. Chet, who was leaning against the wall, stood upright, Senator Cleever turned a startled face to Anthea, and other eyes were on Mr. Scudamore. Anthea herself looked at him and said, "Why?"

The direct question seemed to affect him like a breach of decorum. He hesitated and Wilkie, his small eyes unexcited, asked, "Have you anything particular in mind, sir?"

"Well yes, I have," he said. "Miss Logan will just have to excuse me, but I'm deeply troubled. There's one or two things, little things that kind of add up. Miss Logan was the only person outside ourselves that knew Mr. Hart was going to London to-day—"

"You've nothing there," Chet broke in. "She didn't know anything about why."

"No, you wouldn't say—I know that—"

"She didn't ask, either."

"No—sure, but there's this money and her decision to leave. . . . It seems that was sudden and—well, I've wondered all along why she was here in the hotel." Mr. Scudamore paused. The eyes of Mr. Peachey were on him but he had made no accusations, he had mentioned nothing that wasn't already obvious, he had merely ensured that Anthea Logan would not be overlooked. "I'll be a whole lot happier," he concluded modestly, "when these points are cleared up."

Anthea's quick anger died. Of course the points added up and they must be in other minds besides his. And there were other points. . . . Colonel Garvie blew his nose, a long trumpeting sound of angry defeat.

"Well, gentlemen," said Wilkie with a bleak gleam of amusement, "you can see we have some way to go, but I won't keep you any longer just now. We'll all be the better for a bite to eat and we've to get a thorough search organised."

He got to his feet and the first stage was over. Mr. Saunders hurried away to see that breakfast was ready for the unfed party. Colonel Garvie paused to remind the superintendent that the police must not enter the guests' rooms without permission, and then went sadly to the yard from which everybody had already gone. It was a relief in a way; but he had never before missed seeing them off.

As the room emptied, Senator Cleever raised a sombre head and addressed Mr. Peachey. "Is it still your opinion that there is no need to call in this—Special Branch did you call it?"

"Yes, Special Branch," said Mr. Peachey and looked at the superintendent. "What is your feeling?"

"Well, sir," Wilkie said, "we can get them here in a matter of hours if we want them. I would say we could go on a wee bittie farther first. There's still the hope that the letter will just turn up. Things get lost in queer ways sometimes." He, in his turn, looked for support. Old Sir Andrew Gibb was the man for him: he hoped to keep Sir Andrew close at hand as long as he had Senator Cleever to deal with. "What do you say, sir?" he asked, rather jovially, since he was not seeking advice.

Sir Andrew responded nicely. It was always easy for the man without the responsibility, he said. "But I don't suppose any of us want to call the fire brigade before we've made sure there's a fire."

Mr. Scudamore's lips tightened. The Senator sighed and allowed himself to be led away to such comfort as eggs, bacon and coffee could afford.

In case anybody had seen it, or picked it up, put it somewhere and forgotten about it, a brief, unemotional announcement had been made that Senator Cleever had lost a letter, but the guests listened without much interest. Gaps in the dining-room were unnoticed, or at least aroused no comment, and the superintendent's car and Sergeant McNab's motor-cycle had significance only for those who recognised them. But the staff, if not much better informed, could not fail to be aware that something more was up, and the observant Lawrence, as soon as he finished breakfast, made his way to the pantry by his usual devious route.

The weather was unpromising. The chilly little wind was bringing drifts of sea haar inland, and Lady Vine and Mrs. Carruthers smoked their cigarettes in the hall with an air of discouragement.

"I can't think," said Bryce Carruthers coming towards them dressed for a cold day on the moors, "where the hell Desmond's got to. He's not in his room."

His dark scornful face was bad-tempered and Lady Vine glanced at it with dislike. She could not do with peevish men, and she was already bored by his wife, who had attached herself to her immediately they left the dining-room.

"Is his jeep out?" Vida was asking in a voice less languid than usual.

"No, I looked. It's in the shed. Anthea's car's standing in the yard. The place seems even more cluttered with vehicles than it normally is."

Vida exclaimed. "God! What's going on? I wonder—" she turned to Lady Vine, "should I go up and see if Anthea's all right?"

"I don't see why you need," said Lady Vine, who did not like busybodies any better than peevish men and considered that the hotel could look after its guests without assistance. She had not been excited by the gaps in the dining-room and she was not going to subscribe to excitement now.

"What the devil am I supposed to do?" grumbled Bryce. "How long do I hang about waiting for Desmond?"

As he spoke Sir Francis Vine came up. He was no more excited than his wife but there was a glint of private amusement in his eyes. "Oh, I wouldn't hang about waiting for Peachey if I were you," he said. "He'll be crawling all over the house on his stomach looking for poor Cleever's lost missive. I don't know how the Foreign Office manages to instil this boy-scout spirit of helpfulness into its chaps. Aren't you ready?"

The question was addressed to Lawrence, who appeared from the direction of the pantry looking solemn, and simultaneously Lady Vine, with an unwilling stir of uneasiness asked, "Is anything the matter?"

"Er—no, I don't think so," said Lawrence.

"If you've been hobnobbing backstairs," said Vida, "haven't you picked up any clues? Where's Anthea, and what on earth are Desmond and the Yanks doing?"

"I really don't know anything," said Lawrence and wished ardently that Bryce and Vida would go away. Backstairs everybody was behaving well, but under the surface, curiosity bubbled, and an old friend like himself heard what little was known. He wanted to tell his parents about the police cars in the yard, about Greg's car standing beside Anthea's, and the party in the manager's office. "If you don't mind, Dad," he said, "I'm not coming out to-day. It's foul and I may as well get in some reading."

Bryce Carruthers turned to Sir Francis. "In that case, can we join up? I don't feel like wasting my time, whatever Peachey does with his."

"By all means," said Sir Francis civilly.

"What *can* be going on?" Vida demanded again as the two men went out together. "Don't you know *anything*, Lawrence?"

Lawrence said, "I'm afraid I don't." His mother got up and went towards the stairs and he followed her, but Vida was still in the hall when the party in Mr. Saunders's office broke up.

Anthea found herself strangely exhausted and with a wavering tendency in her legs when she got up from her chair. She trailed out into the familiar hall, surprised that it was still there looking just the same. Jock seemed to have disappeared. . . . She wondered what would happen next. What was she in for . . .? How long would she have to stay at Balgarvie . . .? She caught sight of Vida alone in a corner and turned away before their eyes could meet. What was she supposed to do now and where was Jock . . .?

"Come along," said Mr. Peachey at her side. "You must be quite faint." He took her arm, firmly disposing of a vague idea of escaping to her room, and led her to the diningroom. "Coffee first," he told Biddy who came forward. "A lot of strong, very hot coffee, and then food. If you'll sit here, Anthea, I'll join you in a minute."

He went to speak to the Americans, who were sitting down at their table, and Anthea lit a cigarette and leaned her weary head on her hand.

"I'll pour you a cup, Miss Logan," said Biddy's voice, subdued and concerned. "Do drink it while it's hot—it'll do you good."

It occurred to Anthea that as she was under suspicion until Senator Cleever's letter turned up, so Biddy, Stewart and all of them were going to know themselves under suspicion unless the mystery of her money was solved. She wanted to say something—to apologise—but there was nothing that could be said, and Mr. Peachey was coming back. As he sat down, Jock appeared at the door and a peremptory wave invited him to breakfast. Biddy, giving no sign of curiosity, took their orders and went away.

The two men looked at each other. "This is an imbroglio," Jock observed moderately.

Mr. Peachey agreed and drank some coffee. He was without any trace of his social self and Anthea regarded him with uneasy respect: a tough and rather formidable man was Desmond Peachey under the glossy veneer which had become so familiar to her in the last few days. "It was bad enough," he said, "before you came in with your burglar, Anthea. Now, I confess, I'm bemused."

Jock asked, "How did Gibb get roped in? Garvie?"

"Garvie. He feels that a man who has governed parts of the late Empire can deal with most crises. In which," added Mr. Peachey raising his coffee cup to his lips, "he is not far wrong." He drank a little coffee. "And not alone, incidentally," he added. "Cleever also appears to have some faith in Gibb."

"For which you have reason to be thankful," said Jock.

Biddy reappeared with toast and fresh supplies of coffee, Stewart behind her with a tray of hot food. They carried out their duties in sober silence and departed.

Anthea slowly ate her lightly boiled egg. It was an effort and she was not enjoying it much but it was no doubt doing her good. Jock and Desmond ate like hungry men and she felt a faint resentment at their unimpaired appetites, but their minds were not solely on their food.

"Do you really think there's anything in it but flap?" Jock asked. His tone was extremely sceptical and he added, "It's too bloody silly."

Mr. Peachey, whose mouth was full, raised his eyebrows and shook his head. "It looks like it and I hope it is," he said when he could speak. "But you must see, Gregorson, that the other possibility must be taken seriously. I'm concerned to *contain* the flap, but the letter hasn't turned up."

"Pity he didn't just pop it in the post."

"I couldn't agree more. I wish to God he had. But no doubt prestige required him to send Hart post-haste in some direction or other."

"Jock thinks a sheep has eaten it," said Anthea.

"Yes, well there you are. It may be reduced by the gastric

juices of a sheep or blown out to sea—Hart seems to have been pretty off-hand about it, I must say—in which case we'll have the whole works." Mr. Peachey became intent on the rather liquid yolk of an egg and when he spoke again it was on a different tack. "Anthea, have you any idea at all about the theft of your money, or are you quite blank?"

"The only thing that occurs to me," she said carefully, "is that I know Morgan is a liar. There's quite a juicy story going round about our scene yesterday." He looked surprised and she explained that it had come back to her through Ness.

"Of course," he said. "I'd forgotten that Ness must also be related to you. But isn't she rather extra friendly with Morgan?"

"She has a mission about Morgan," said Jock. "She thinks he's a victim. The others don't—at least they certainly don't believe he's been victimised by Anthea."

Mr. Peachey composed his next forkful thoughtfully. "I can't say I've ever noticed Morgan particularly, but you have them at your house—can you see him as a thief?"

"I can see the little swab looking round for a way of getting back on Anthea for a well-deserved snub. I think he might pick up cash if he got the chance."

"But you can't *possibly* see him as an agent placed in the hotel to pick up Cleever's letter?"

Jock laughed aloud. "Not possibly. He's not in that class. Anyway I'm afraid I don't believe Cleever's in that class either."

"*I* can't believe," said Anthea, "that the two things have anything whatever to do with each other." She said it without much hope but Mr. Peachey expressed qualified agreement.

"On the evidence we have," he said emphasising it, "it seems unlikely that they're connected. It's difficult to see why an agent, if an agent exists, should go straight to your room and swipe a few hundred pounds. However, it's an odd coincidence and they'll be investigated together. And as like as not," he added, glancing at Jock, "investigated by some tiger from Special Branch."

"The more vigorous the investigation the better," was Jock's response. "But properly conducted investigation. You can't have everyone sitting around putting in their unofficial oars all the time."

"And how would you propose to discriminate?" Mr. Peachey asked coldly. "I agree that crowds are undesirable, but my own status is questionable: I can only try to be helpful."

"Police authority must deal with it," said Jock. "If we stick to the constabulary and the rules we won't go far wrong."

" 'We' ?" Mr. Peachey looked up from his plate. "What is your status? We don't want the Press."

"You won't get it—not through me. I have no official status, but I intend to establish myself. Allegations have been made—or at least suggested. Either I watch the proceedings on Anthea's behalf or you wait till the lawyer of her choice is here to do it."

"If a watcher is necessary, shouldn't it be McNaughton's business?"

"Yes and no," Jock said. "I don't doubt his goodwill, but I know more than he does."

There was a silence. Anthea sat by feeling like a package, as if they merely argued whether to send her by post or rail. Mr. Peachey, who was keeping an eye on the Americans and who was hungrier than they were, went on eating swiftly, but he was thoughtful in a new way which isolated him from the two who shared his table. He finished his toast and marmalade and drank his coffee.

"More?" said Anthea, who had taken charge of the coffee pot.

"Please." He passed his cup and watched her fill it, and then as he took it he looked at her directly and said, "Anthea, does the name Randal Logan mean anything to you?"

She replied without hesitation. "He's my brother."

He gave her a little bow, acknowledging the information without comment, and turned away to light a cigarette. Anthea was mildly surprised that it passed with so little fuss. She only observed—dispassionately, as though it had nothing to do with her—that he hated the guts of people like Randal Logan and that his hatred would, inevitably, extend in some degree to everybody connected with them. With the end of her cigarette she pushed a neat little heap of ash together in the ashtray in front of her, wondering what it was that made the difference. Jock hated treachery, he probably felt a pretty hearty dislike for Randal, but he could separate her, the rest of the family, from the guilt and feel only compassion for the ruin Randal had brought upon them. Mr. Peachey could not, though he would know he ought to and would pretend that he did. It would be assumed—unconvincing and uncomfortable for all concerned. Why? Was it a difference of imagination? Or did wisdom, as opposed to cleverness, come in? Insight . . .

"You will appreciate," Jock was saying, "that it is important that the investigation be conducted properly. We want no hysteria."

"No indeed," said Mr. Peachey. The Americans got up and he drank his coffee hurriedly. "I must go."

Jock said, "I'll come along in a few minutes and talk to you and Wilkie if you can arrange it," and he nodded.

"That'll be best. I'll head them off if I can. Cleever will want to shave, poor devil." He rose, excusing himself to Anthea without quite looking at her, and bustled away.

CHAPTER 13

JOCK and Anthea, left alone in the dining-room, looked at each other. "Can we find a corner?" he asked. She nodded and remembered Vida sitting in the hall. They would have to pass through very quickly and find their corner—the morning-room where the lovely little gambles had taken place would do. But before they had got up from their chairs Vida was coming across the dining-room towards them.

"Anthea," she said, "whatever is going on?"

Anthea, determined not to be pinned at the table, went to meet her and said, "You know Mr. Gregorson, don't you?"

"Oh—yes, of course. . . Hallo," said Vida. "But look—what—"

It was Jock who replied: Anthea was thrown out for the moment by the difficulty of saying anything brief enough and the memory of the near-quarrel the day before. He said, "Two things are going on. Senator Cleever has lost a letter, as you've probably heard, and there's been a burglary. Miss Logan has lost a considerable sum of money."

"What?" Vida's mouth was open and her eyes round. "But how extraordinary! My poor Anthea! Do they think, then, that the letter's been stolen too? I thought it was just—"

"Look, Vida," said Anthea, "there's nothing we can tell you. It's all complete mystery still. Will you excuse us?"

She walked away with Jock, followed by a powerful beam of resentment which she felt but could do nothing about, and they found their corner in the deserted room and sat down. The haar outside pressed against the windows and the light that came in was cold and cheerless. Anthea, sinking into a chair, sighed and Jock looked at her and smiled.

"Quote—'My poor Anthea!'—unquote," he said. "How many hours since you got up? It was a long time ago that I saw your car coming over the field."

"Weeks," she said and neither of them spoke again for a few minutes. He lit his pipe and sat back, his long legs stretched out, and Anthea, weary and a little light-headed, pushed reality away and indulged in a short daydream. The last seven years hadn't happened: they were back before the Festival Hall and she refused to *have* the next sequence. . . .

"I disliked young Morgan at sight," Jock remarked presently, "and I can't swallow the sob-story about the widowed mum and his self-sacrifice. I may be wrong, of course, but I don't think so. I wonder if he was ever a member of the University of Edinburgh—or any other."

"I thought Ness knew him there."

"On the fringe perhaps. She's being wonderfully silly about him."

"He's spiritually halitoxic," Anthea murmured, and explained to his raised eyebrow, "Lawrence said Ness would be sweet to me if I had halitosis."

He agreed. "I've no doubt she would—and a doggone pest you'd find it. But according to Louisa quoting Alec, who is respected by all for his powers of observation and knowledge of the world, signs are visible to the discerning eye that devotion to Morgan is becoming a bit of a strain."

Anthea said that in that case hers could not be a discerning eye, and he asked, "Has she quarrelled with you?"

"I suppose it could be called a quarrel. She was not sweet. None of this is evidence of criminal tendencies in Morgan, however."

"It's suggestive, though," said Jock. "He has a grudge and he's not honest. But I can't see him whipping Cleever's bumph—unless by accident, which is unlikely."

"Who can you see whipping it?"

"Nobody, really. I can't believe anybody would take the trouble. If we must have a crime the only thing to do is pin it on the man you dislike most. Scudamore gets my vote."

"You dislike him, do you?" Anthea considered it. "Well, I can't say I dislike him, but I'd rather have the crime pinned on him than on me. Or Chet, who's *incapable* of crime. But it won't stick. You might as well go for Simp himself."

"What will stick? You say not Hart. . . . Lord Justice Burnley? Sir Francis Vine? The Bishop or Sir Andrew?"

She laughed. "It's really absurd when you look at it, isn't it? On your principle I think I'll vote for Mr. Saunders. I don't like his teeth."

"No," said Jock, "I can't support you. A man isn't responsible for his teeth and I've known Saunders too long. There's Peachey himself, of course—not that I dislike him."

Anthea returned to reality. "And me. I'd vote for myself without hesitation if I didn't happen to know I didn't do it."

"Yes," he agreed. He took out a packet of cigarettes and gave her one and when he had lit it he went on, "He isn't a bad chap, Peachey. Moulded by his job, of course, but fortunately his tendency to suspicion is more than balanced by terror of any sort of stink. He'll be very canny indeed, will Desmond. And Wilkie's reliable. He'll have been to the Manse by now and—"

"To the Manse?" she exclaimed, startled, and he went on in a firmer admonitory tone.

"Anthea, you *know* the investigation is going to be thorough. You heard Scudamore. You know there's enough, even without Randal, to make the police want to find out all they can about you. Obviously they'd go to McNaughton. For your own sake more than anything they had to go to your cousin. He can tell them—what's the matter?"

Anthea was looking rather sick. "He won't do much to set their minds at rest," she said.

Jock opened his mouth to say "Nonsense!" but he did not say it. He had known the Minister for years, in the pulpit and out of it, and he could not altogether scout the idea that he might give an impression which was not favourable. "He's an honest man, though," he said, "and known to be utterly scrupulous—over-scrupulous. He'll be an asset all right, if not a very comfortable one." He looked at his watch. "Now, the next thing. I'm going along to get hold of Peachey and Wilkie together and give them the whole works—if you will authorise me to do it. It's the quickest way, I think, and the easiest." He looked at her. "May I do it?"

"Oh, Jock—*yes*!" she said. "Please. . . . I'm so—so grateful. I really don't know how I'd have coped—*survived*—if you hadn't been here."

"You'd have coped. . . . Well, as soon as that's done, Wilkie will want to talk to you, I expect. Will you stay around?"

"Yes," she said again. She had a vision of Mr. Saunders's office full of men, and a song swam into her mind. "Old Uncle Tom Cobley and all . . . Old Uncle Tom Cob—" She switched it off. "Who will be there?" she asked.

"No gapers," Jock replied briskly. "Police, Peachey, self. And I'm in favour of using Sir Andrew, if you don't object. He's a very wise, experienced old bird."

"He'd be a comfort, I think," said Anthea and he nodded and got to his feet.

She got up too and he looked at her as she stood beside him. It was no good saying anything sympathetic or even kind. Strength was what she needed, to keep calm with her wits about her, and a matter-of-fact, unemotional tone was the best help he could give her. But in her face was a look, not so much of fear but dread of fear: the look of someone who has been hurt before and waits, knowing all about it, to be hurt again, and he wondered if Randal Logan had any idea at all of what he had done.

"You'll be all right, Anthea," he said. "Don't worry. It will pass, I promise you. Wilkie's a good chap. Just tell them everything and don't resent their questions—they have to do their job."

She nodded. "It's nothing like so bad," she said, "if I don't have to *break* it to them—watch them taking it in. I'll go up to my room till they're ready for me."

The door opened as she finished speaking, and Mr. Peachey came in. "Wilkie's back," he told Jock, and turned to Anthea, unsmiling and formal. "I'm so sorry, but I'm afraid the police want your permission to search your room. You will understand that it must be done and it will be better if you give permission. For the moment they've sealed it. If you want anything it can be fetched, of course."

It was no good wasting time protesting that all she wanted was that the police should get on with it. "They'll want my keys," she said opening her bag. Deliberately she opened it wide and held it so that he could see inside it as she took out the keys and gave them to him, and saw a small, appreciative gleam as he received them.

"Will you be here?" he asked.

She glanced round. It was chilly and dark and smelled of damp: the hall would be full of Vida, of people coming and going. . . .

"Hang on a minute," said Jock.

She watched them go, Jock's black head towering above Mr. Peachey's dapper briskness, and then turned forlornly to a window and the drifting white haar.

"Hi," said Lawrence's voice a moment later and he came across the room carrying cups of coffee. "You left your car out, did you know? Hood down, keys in—I put it in the shed."

"Oh thank you," she said. "What a blessing you are. I forgot about it. *More* coffee?"

"We drink coffee all day long when the weather's like this," he explained, putting the cups down carefully. "The pantry just keeps on brewing and drinking. Here are your keys." He handed them over and went to the fireplace. "There should be an electric fire behind this elegant screen . . . yes."

"It's a great thing to know your way about," observed Anthea as he removed the screen and switched on the welcome warmth.

"Just a kind of gift," he said modestly, and as he sat down he looked at her directly for the first time. "Greg said I was to keep you company, drive off intruders and ask no questions. What shall we talk about—or would you rather be silent? I'm capable of it."

Anthea leant back in her chair and deliberately relaxed, grateful for the warmth and the coffee and the boy. There was no point in trying to think, nothing to be gained by imagining the ordeal that was coming; nothing easier than talking to Lawrence.

"We'll resume the hearing of your views on current satire," she said.

"Where were we?" said Lawrence.

Mr. McNaughton had been a Justice of the Peace for many years; he often had business with the police and he was not greatly surprised when Wilkie arrived. But in the study, which contained the round table of yellow walnut, the roll-top desk and the sombre books which had furnished his father's studies in other manses, the superintendent stated his present business and did surprise him.

He found it very difficult, not merely to believe but to take in. Wilkie's voice when he talked to an old and trusted acquaintance was low and confidential, and as the homely accents flowed on there was a period of confusion in which the Minister saw hundreds of pound notes belonging to Anthea Logan winging their way across the Atlantic, while foreign powers and Communist agents occupied Balgarvie House. But the superintendent went on talking.

"So you'll see, sir," he concluded, "if the letter doesnae turn up we'll need tae check on every one o' thae folk jist."

"Yes," agreed the Minister in his bewilderment. "Yes, I suppose you will."

The interview went on and he found himself being delicately questioned, as part of the check, about his wife's — he could never remember whether the child of a first cousin was a second cousin or a first cousin once removed—Anthea Logan. Unhappy but conscientious he unfolded the story of his wife's other relative, Randal Logan, Anthea's brother.

"You'll understand, Wilkie, it's a painful subject. The father, poor fellow, died almost at once. A cold man"—a flash of mirth was stifled by the superintendent—"though not unpleasant. I never saw the boy. How it came about that he fell into this temptation we'll never know, but it was a terrible thing. Terrible. The poor mother—and this girl."

Superintendent Wilkie thought it was a terrible thing. He clicked his tongue sadly. "T's, t's. And what did they do, the poor things?"

Mr. McNaughton said that Anthea—the girl—had been working as a journalist with a London paper and was believed to be doing well, but she had very sensibly given it up and taken a teaching post. She and her mother had lived together till the mother died early this year. "Never got over it of course, poor woman. My wife understands that she was quite an invalid, never went out."

"This is a very nice-like young lady," observed Wilkie. "There would likely be a wee bit money?"

The Minister's long upper lip seemed to lengthen. "Well, I don't just see. . . . We heard they were left very poorly off. The mother—my wife thinks there may have been a little. A thousand or two, perhaps—no more. I suppose Anthea—the girl—may have saved something."

"Aye, she might," agreed the superintendent civilly. He

was used to the common tendency to overestimate the salaries and underestimate the expenses of other people, and he did not expect the clergy to display much sense in worldly matters. The Minister and Mrs. McNaughton, he went on to suggest, would have been keeping in fairly close touch, like, with the poor ladies. They would know pretty well what sort of life this real bonny girl had been leading?

"Well, no. That's just it," was the reply. "We don't know. I blame myself. I blame myself very much. I feel now that we should have gone to them when the—the tragedy happened. But it was difficult to see what good we could do. . . ."He talked uneasily about the long expensive journey. "They didn't suggest it themselves, and the relationship is not close." He paused and then went on to say that they, he and his wife, had really almost lost touch with the Logans. Anthea had, of course, informed them of her mother's death, but they knew nothing of her own life. "It was quite a surprise to us when she wrote saying she was coming here. She had only been once before—eight years ago or thereabouts. Mrs. McNaughton wrote at once asking her to stay with us, but she had booked accommodation at the hotel. I was uneasy," said Mr. McNaughton, frowning. "Very uneasy."

Wilkie, who knew him well, looked at him closely. Was this merely general uneasiness because Balgarvie House was an expensive place to stay and had a bar where intoxicating liquor was sold? Or uneasiness over any young woman staying in any hotel alone? Or something more specific? He thought it was specific and he was right. Mr. McNaughton raised his head and directed the frown straight at him.

"Far be it from me," he said, "to impute evil where no evil is, but I was astounded, Wilkie. Astounded. That expensive car. The—a—her appearance, clothes and so on. The cost of the hotel alone . . ."

"Of course, sir," said the superintendent, feeling a good deal of sympathy for the culprit, "like you said, these young ladies earn good enough money at school-teaching and with a wee bit, like enough, from her mother it's no such a *wild* expense for a holiday."

"Possibly not," said the Minister coldly. "I am not in the way of knowing what professional women normally spend on holidays. However. What really troubles me is that she has given up her post."

"Oh," said Wilkie. "Is that a fact? Why would that be?"

Mr. McNaughton said he was at a loss to understand it. It was quite a good post. "What she intends to do, I do not know. She says she wants to write, but I cannot see what she will live on, or why she could not write in her spare time. The holidays are long."

There was a pause, full of thought, and then Wilkie said, "As far as you know, the brother just disappeared when he came out? He never got in touch with her at all?"

"So I understand," Mr. McNaughton agreed and added punctiliously, "but I cannot say I have precise information. The subject is distasteful, and since it only concerns us remotely we feel hesitant about pressing her to talk of it."

Anthea and Lawrence were not left to their discussion for long, but when Mr. Saunders appeared to conduct her to the police Anthea found that the relaxation paid off. Her mind was clearer and she felt a stronger self-command. She smiled at Lawrence as she got up, grateful for his well-mannered tact and easy companionship, and dealt firmly with Mr. Saunders, who was uncertain in his attitude.

The police would be obliged if she would spare them a few minutes, he said. "If you'll just come along—"

"Certainly," she said. "Are they still keeping you out of your office?"

"A—no." He was surprised and could hardly approve of what was almost levity. "No, we have put another room at their disposal. This way if you please. . . ."

Anthea found herself crossing the hall in the direction of the gun-room area. She was wondering why Jock had not come back to have a word with her—but she had not finished with Mr. Saunders.

"By the way," she said, "I obviously won't be able to leave Balgarvie to-day—"

"No," he agreed. "I'm afraid the police—that is, I hardly expect—"

She interrupted him. "The point is, will my room be available or not? I could go to the Manse if necessary, but I would prefer to stay in the hotel until this matter is cleared up."

The managerial manner wavered. The situation was so confusing. Miss Logan's position was peculiar and it was not impossible that she would sleep that night in a police cell. On the other hand there was the Manse connection and Colonel Garvie's chivalry. He assured her civilly that the room was, of course, available, and was about to open a door when it was opened from inside and Jock came out.

He closed the door behind him and a nod dismissed Mr. Saunders. "Anthea," he said, "it will be better if I'm not in on this. I've done the paving and Sir Andrew's there." He dropped his already low voice further and added with a gleam of amusement, "It'll make it easier to reduce the audience. Don't try to get rid of Peachey." She nodded and he took her hand in a brief, firm grip. "Don't worry, Wilkie's very intelligent. On you go—" and letting her hand go he opened the door for her.

The room which Anthea now saw for the first time had been the housekeeper's room and bore a strong period resemblance to the Minister's study: it was a shabby, old-fashioned apartment which nobody had looked at or thought about for many years. At the moment it was nearly as full as Mr. Saunders's office had been earlier in the morning and Anthea stopped short just inside the door. Sergeant McNab was absent, so was Colonel Garvie, and Jock, having ushered her in, withdrew: but the three Americans were present as well as Wilkie and his constable, Mr. Peachey and Sir Andrew Gibb.

She looked at the seven men. Her private affairs were about to be uncovered, stripped to the bone, and here indeed were Uncle Tom Cobley and all. Chet looked up with a smile which was meant to be reassuring, and Sir Andrew was calm and kind, but Senator Cleever bulged with suspicion while Mr. Scudamore and Mr. Peachey, carefully expressionless, conveyed a sense of purpose, determined and, if necessary, ruthless. She hesitated, wondering what her rights were: if Jock had meant that it was her job to protest, and if it would be worse to make a fuss or put up with the audience. But Superintendent Wilkie began speaking.

"Miss Logan," he said, "we have asked you here to make a statement in connection with your own loss and the loss of Senator Cleever's letter and we hope you'll be willing to answer some questions. Now, you could refuse, but I don't think you want to do that. And you *could* say"—the emphasis was slight but unmistakable—"that you would prefer to talk just to me, say, or mebbe to Mr. Peachey or Sir Andrew here and me."

Senator Cleever stirred. "I am bound to repeat my strong opinion," he said, "that in the absence of our own security men and your specially qualified officers we should be present throughout all interrogations."

"I believe, sir," said Mr. Peachey, deferential but firm, "that at this early stage it is a matter for Superintendent Wilkie. The preliminary investigation is bound to reveal a great deal which has no bearing on the case and it is for the police to—so to speak—screen it."

So that was how it was done, thought Anthea. She said politely that though there was nothing she would wish to conceal if it were relevant, she would find it easier to talk to a smaller number, and her audience was reduced to four; Mr. Peachey, Sir Andrew and the two police officers.

It was six years since Jock Gregorson came to Balgarvie to look for Anthea and failing to find her fell in love with the place—a curiously complex love of which association and a kind of fatalism formed part. In that time he had become what was called "weel kent and weel respectit." It was not unnatural that a young man who chose to live in Balgarvie should be judged uncommonly sensible; and then he was without affection or conceit, the same to everybody and a good friend who accepted help and gave it with a lack of fuss which assumed that this was how men live. Superintendent Wilkie knew him well: they met on curling rinks, at white hare shoots, and there was a Burns Night when Jock, as another literary Scot, had proposed the toast, "The Immortal Memory," in a speech which would be recalled with tears of joy as long as any of those who heard it survived. But beyond all this, Wilkie was one of those who had an inkling of the difference between the kind of writing which puts commercial success first and the kind that doesn't. He respected the spirit which, recognising that you can't often have it both ways, chose a way of life which depended little on financial success and even more he respected the realism with which it had been carried out. Mr. Gregorson was no ascetic for asceticism's sake, no mere visionary: and in practical affairs and judgment he was no fool at all. He had paved the way for Anthea better than she knew.

The grilling, as he had called it, was conducted in a manner which was by no means oppressively official, but Anthea was grateful for his foresight which had prepared her to face detailed probing without resentment or fluster.

The beginning was easy enough—her personal timetable of the evening before—and the talk with Chet was not difficult. He had been friendly enough, she said, not to want to go without saying good-bye. He had told her nothing beyond the one fact that he was going, and hearing that she would be gone before he came back he had given her his address and written down the only one she could give him, which was that of her bank. Then there were the time checks: Lawrence bringing her sherry, her arrival in the dining-room. But with the question, "It seems it was a sudden decision to leave to-day, is that so?" she was on the stony ground.

Wilkie had told her that he had seen the Minister, and it was, she recognised, better that he had. But she recognised, too, that Cousin Walter's evidence had not been favourable. It could not be. Her plans and her burst of extravagance would only seem reasonable to someone who happened to have the same sort of outlook as her own: and at this point she took the initiative herself. She explained briefly the plan, which Jock had called sensible, to allow herself a time of freedom in which to try to develop her writing.

"He would understand that very well," Sir Andrew put in, "since he's done it himself with such success."

"Oh yes, he understood it," she said, "but the success wasn't bound to be repeated, of course. It was a sudden decision to leave to-day," she went on, looking directly at Wilkie. "I had meant to leave soon—I thought Monday. For one thing,"—there was a flicker of her comic gleam— "the hotel is expensive, but really I had come to see that Balgarvie isn't the place for me. I'd had an idea that I might find somewhere very cheap and stay here, but—" She broke off and shook her head. "You can't make a new life where there are people who remember—who are associated with what you want to leave behind."

"And what made you decide on to-day?"

She shook her head again. "Nothing particular. Just an accumulation of small things and a feeling I'd made a mistake. Staying here, in the hotel, I was in a false position. I didn't really mean to pose as what I'm not—rich and well-placed—but I found I was deceiving people. It's sort of assumed, and you can't wear a label. I just—I wanted to get away."

"Quite so," said Wilkie. "Now, the head at this school you worked in, she would confirm you've been there these seven years, wouldn't she?"

"Yes," said Anthea. She gave the address of the school and said she thought the headmistress would be there. "She doesn't usually go away for long."

The address was written down and Wilkie turned to her brother Randal. He took her through the whole case and she, conscious of the young constable writing in the background, answered with meticulous accuracy.

"The Reverend McNaughton," said Wilkie, "he has the idea you never saw your brother or heard from him after he was committed for trial, but from what Mr. Gregorson says —and yourself—I take it you have seen him. Not so long ago."

"That's right," she said, and described her brother's visit.

"Do you believe you'll never see or hear of him again? You really don't know where he is?"

"I don't know," she said, "and I do believe it. He was never a liar. If he'd thought that I'd be any use to him, he'd have said—oh, something like 'You'll be hearing from me.' As it was, he just said it was the final break and I know it was."

She had been in the room for a long time and she was very tired when Wilkie at last said he had no more questions to ask her at present. He gave her a sort of bow, formal but not unfriendly, and added, "I have to thank you. You've been very helpful."

"Indeed you have," Mr. Peachey endorsed it and Sir Andrew went to open the door for her.

"A nasty disagreeable business," he said and patted her shoulder kindly.

"The only thing that matters is to get it cleared up," said Anthea.

"I'm sure it will be cleared up," said Sir Andrew.

CHAPTER 14

ANTHEA made her way back along the dark, dingy passages to the hall. It was tenanted only by the antlered heads and dead Garvies, and they all gazed over her head, sad and remote, as she wandered across to a window and stood looking out. The wind had dropped and the haar had turned into a busy persistent drizzle which made no sound. She thought with vague worry about her car and remembered that Lawrence had put it in. Then her mind reverted inconsequently. She wondered how they were feeling at the Manse and how far Cousin Walter's disapproval actually went. Had anybody believed what she told them about why she had given up her job? They all knew about Jock, but the very fact that he had done so exactly what she had planned to do made her story, if anything, less credible. To anyone who didn't know the background it must be almost inconceivable that two writers should pick Balgarvie as a refuge from the wage-earning world—even if they could swallow the idea that a writer needed a refuge.

Her mind swung to and fro. It was so unreal: and yet . . . if that damned letter stayed lost, how could she prove that she couldn't be less interested in international politics? That she loathed her brother's views and what he had done? She noticed the rain again and thought of people coming in for lunch . . . Vida. . . . Wondering if she was free to go out—if she could think of somewhere to go—she turned from the window and saw Jock coming towards her.

"If you agree," he said at once, "we'll go to the Tully and contrive some lunch there. Tins, eggs, bottles. Lawrence is coming to keep you company because I can't stay long. He's gone to fetch a coat for you."

"How about the police?" she asked doubtfully.

"They're quite happy. I've told Lawrence all he needs to know—which isn't much. I thought you'd rather have him around than anybody and you can be peaceful at the Tully."

"I was wondering where I could go," said Anthea.

"Never mind," he said. "It won't be long—I hope," and then Lawrence appeared carrying a duffel coat.

The next hour remained in Anthea's memory as an oasis. To be driven away from the hotel, the people and pressures, and taken to Jock's house: to be cosseted by him and by Lawrence, who found it impossible not to be rather cheerful, was a relief so intense that it was a kind of bliss in its own right. One thing about having a bad time, she reflected, was that you really knew when you were having a good one, and, knowing how brief and isolated the interlude must be, she let herself savour it.

Over the first glass of sherry, when Lawrence went to the kitchen to rummage for tins and break eggs, she told Jock about the interview with the police and heard what he had been doing while she was under fire in the housekeeper's room.

"I got on the blower to William," he said and smiled at her astonished face. "The solidarity of the Press embraces even those of its children who stray from the fold—except under certain circumstances which don't apply."

Anthea's expression was more than sceptical. "I thought I had been shot out of the fold," she said. "That was certainly the impression I got last time I saw William."

"He was annoyed with you—"

"*Annoyed*! He all but took me back by the scruff of the neck and the seat of the pants and threw me downstairs. The whole building shook."

Jock said, "His understatement, not mine. However, he's not going to tolerate any kick-back now."

"How does he propose to prevent it? It's happened," Anthea said. She was not unmoved by William's readiness to take action on her behalf, knowing well that his violence seven years ago had come from concern for her as well as annoyance that his advice was rejected, but at this distance of time and space she did not see that he could do more for her now than he could then.

"Well," said Jock, "he will Telephone People Up." He grinned and she involuntarily grinned with him as the quotation brought the man before their eyes. "And the police digging up the gen on your blameless life in Flatford-on-Sea, and Randal's movements from the moment he left the prison gates, will be assisted—unwittingly—by a couple of William's smartest boys. So . . ."—he paused to raise his glass—"good hunting. We now wait—calmly as always. . . ." And then Lawrence announced that he would not be responsible for the omelet and they took the bottle and went to join him in the kitchen.

They heated soup and made the omelets and ate their meal talking about Jock's books, gossiping about agents, publishers and habits of work. It was almost like the companionable days in London before the Bach Double Concerto fired the train of disaster: the days when coffee was brewed in a jug and there were no clouds. But the illusion, though it was good, was illusion. After lunch Lawrence offered to wash up, an offer promptly accepted by his host, and the time had come to leave the oasis.

"I mustn't be much longer," Jock said, coming to join Anthea as she stood by the fire.

"What are you going to do?" she asked.

The short answer was that he was going to watch the proceedings on her behalf. In the presence of Mr. Peachey and Sir Andrew Gibb he had repeated to Wilkie what he had already said to Mr. Peachey: either he sat in as her representative or they called in the Minister or they waited till she had legal advice. They could take their choice. Wilkie and Sir Andrew had no hesitation. Mr. Peachey, that rising man, felt that it was extremely unorthodox, but Mr. Gregorson, though no longer of the Press, probably retained some influence with it, and he had joined Sir Andrew in reassuring the Senator and Mr. Scudamore.

She said, "I think, perhaps, I should go to the Manse. They must be in a bit of a spin." Then, frowning, she added, "But I really don't know if they'd rather I went or stayed away."

It was surprising, Jock thought, that the Manse had made no move to come to her. He did not believe that in any circumstances the Minister would deliberately dissociate himself and his wife from her, but the restraint they were displaying was extreme and it could not be allowed to go on indefinitely. She must have, and be seen to have, the McNaughtons' support. But for the moment, peace was what she needed most.

"Stay here with Lawrence for a bit," he said. "I'll see what they're up to at the House and if there's nothing stirring I'll come back and take you to the Manse later."

"All right," said Anthea. "If Lawrence won't be bored."

The restfulness was such that Anthea, Lawrence and the dog were all nearly asleep when, an hour or two later, an elderly Austin came over the field and Mr. and Mrs. McNaughton alighted. They had been to the hotel, explained Cousin Maud, who was rather flustered. It had been a little time before they were able to discover where Anthea was. She looked at the Tully nervously.

It was baffling for them. The theft of a large sum of money, a lost letter and police questions about their young cousin were bad enough: now, in addition, was Mr. Gregorson's position both with regard to the cousin and the crime, and her presence, thoroughly at home in his house, alone with Lawrence Vine. Anthea felt for their bewilderment but she could do very little about it. Lawrence greeted the parents of his old playmates, Ness and Ian, with cautious politeness, and retired with the dog to the kitchen. In the living-room there was a difficult little silence.

After a moment Mrs. McNaughton laid her ears back and plunged. "My dear," she said, floundering a little, "how dreadful all this is. . . . Losing your money—to *think* of anybody going into your room to steal . . . It's so terrible I can't . . . And this American's letter—so *extraordinary*! Surely it will turn up—has it been properly *looked* for?"

Anthea said she believed so. "The police have been at it and I don't suppose they scamp the job."

The Minister cleared his throat. "I am afraid you have lost a large sum," he said. "No doubt you are realising now that it was hardly prudent to keep it with you."

"Of course I am, Cousin Walter."

"Are you—what are you going to do?" asked Mrs. McNaughton worriedly.

In both faces Anthea saw fear that she was going to borrow money. The hotel bill, even for the few days she had been there, would throw the Manse budget out quite badly but it was not that consideration which worried them. It was an inborn hatred for borrowing or lending money.

She hastened to reassure them. She would have enough for her needs, she said, and turned to the Minister. "I'm in a more awkward position about the other theft—if it was a theft. And I want to say to you both how sorry I am to —to have involved you in this. I really don't know if Randal's name will—get out. A good many people will have to know about him, I'm afraid, and even though your connection is remote it's—unfortunate. I'm so sorry. I shouldn't have come, of course."

Mrs. McNaughton cried, "Oh, my dear child! It isn't *possible* that anyone could seriously suspect you of a thing like that. And we're *glad* you came, darling. If only—"

In more measured tones the Minister said, "I sincerely hope you will soon be cleared of suspicion, but it would not be true to say that you are not in an awkward position now." He paused, looking very bleak. "Everyone connected with your brother must to some extent suffer the consequence of his sin. For us, public knowledge of the connection would hardly entail more than unpleasantness, and you would be wrong to suppose that we were not glad to welcome you back among us. That, however, was much in my mind in the matter of your staying in the House. In your position it is necessary to be more than ordinarily careful—discreet. A quiet, regular life, avoiding, on the whole, strangers and all cause for question, is your best protection. But I feel sure the police will not allow your brother's case to influence them. Wilkie is a good man."

"It would be very wrong if they did," said Mrs. McNaughton in a stout but trembling voice.

"I don't see how they can help it," said Anthea.

"Naturally they must take it into account but they will not be *influenced*," the Minister corrected them. "They are trained men. That troubles me less," he went on to Anthea, "than your present unsettledness. The fact that you have resigned a safe appointment without having secured another; the scale of your expenditure in relation to what I believe your financial position to be—these could not be made to look well."

Anthea thought drearily that it depended on the point of view, but it was not worth while to say so. After a little pause Mrs. McNaughton said that they must have faith. Everything, she felt sure, would be made plain—the letter found.

"But don't you think, dear, it would be more comfortable for you to be with us?" She looked doubtfully at Mr. Gregorson's living-room. "Cousin Walter thinks—we both feel it would be advisable—"

"It would be suitable," said Cousin Walter. "Your relatives' home is the natural place for you while you are in difficulties. It will enable me—your Cousin Maud and myself—to give you the support you need and which it is right that you should receive from us."

"Mr. Gregorson, you see, dear," Cousin Maud chimed in, "however kind, is not an *intimate* friend, and he—well, he is quite *young*."

"He is an intimate friend," said Anthea, "and there's nobody from whom I'd rather accept help. But it's not a case of putting myself under anybody's protection—his or yours. I'm only here for lunch and a—a rest."

"Oh, my poor darling child!" Mrs. McNaughton cried again, forgetting discretion and duty. "Anthea, are you all *right*?"

Her eager, anxious face was now all kindness and Anthea smiled at her. "I'm all right, Cousin Maud," she said. "But it's a muddle and I'm going to stay at the hotel till it's cleared up. I'm not going to run away even as far as the Manse."

Very shortly after Anthea's interview with the police, the pink young constable, greatly to his chagrin, was sent to assist in the search which was still going on in the grounds for, as he put it, a wee bit paper, and the three who were left in the housekeeper's room took stock.

Before the superintendent were two lists: the guests and employees of the hotel. Sergeant McNab had checked the staff with Mr. Saunders, and Wilkie did not expect to find anything of interest—as far as the case was concerned—in the list of guests. There was nobody that hadn't been coming about the place for years, bar the foreign gents, Miss Logan and Mr. and Mrs. Bryce Carruthers.

"They're friends of yours, sir," he said to Mr. Peachey. "You'll be able to vouch for them, I dare say."

"No," replied Mr. Peachey promptly. "I'm not prepared to vouch for anybody."

A gleam of amusement appeared in the eyes of Sir Andrew Gibb, but the superintendent, who was less familiar with Mr. Peachey and his kind, was inclined to be huffy. It was as good as saying that he, Wilkie, was relying more than he should on what Mr. Gregorson said about Miss Logan. "But you know a good deal about them?" he said stiffly.

Mr. Peachey did know a good deal about the Carruthers and he gave the information readily. He and Carruthers had been at school together and though their ways had parted from time to time they had never quite lost touch. "We're in the same set," he concluded, "and we share the same regrettable characteristics." He smiled at Wilkie's face. "We're entirely selfish, we have expensive tastes and we're easily bored. Still," he added blandly, "I don't go in for selling information and I should be very surprised if Carruthers does. For one thing, he's a stockbroker and wouldn't have any to sell. For another, he's very comfortable and wouldn't bother."

Superintendent Wilkie didn't much like the sound of either Mr. Carruthers or Mr. Peachey, but he responded as he normally did to showing off. He remained impassive and went on with his work. There was no doubt that if Senator Cleever's letter had been stolen—and it became less improbable with every hour that passed—Miss Logan stuck out like a sore thumb. But he didn't like it. Though quite a lot could be piled up against her there was not a single hard fact. To every question she had an answer, and if some of them were out of the ordinary, a bit fantastic, they would be even more fantastic if she had made them up.

He leant back in his chair and lit a cigarette. Mr. Peachey also lit one. Sir Andrew sat still, upright but relaxed, his hands folded on the table.

Without Senator Cleever's loquacious fuss and also without Mr. Gregorson, who was openly partisan, it was a good moment for discussion. The minds of all three men were on Anthea, and the superintendent began to speak of her without introduction.

"She was very frank," he said. "It wasn't a nice thing having all that brought out: the disgrace . . . even the bit silliness of wanting just to spend—to have things nice for a while." He blinked his colourless eyelashes. "She behaved well, I thought. Like a lady should. Dignified."

Sir Andrew said, "Yes," and Mr. Peachey also agreed.

"She was. Perfectly dignified and very convincing. All the same . . ." He paused, making a grimace which expressed reluctance. He was, in fact, disliking Anthea a good deal: he felt he had had a narrow escape from her dignity, her beauty and her appeal, and he was convinced that in some way or other she was at the bottom of this deplorable imbroglio. He also felt that the two older men with him at the table were just a bit innocent. "All the same," he resumed, smiling with friendly ruefulness, "one has to remember that it's a terribly wicked world. When all's said and done, Miss Logan's presence here *was* deception, whether calculated or not."

"Do you think so?" said Sir Andrew, mild and interested. "You mean it gave the impression that she was richer—or grander—than she is? It hadn't really occurred to me."

"How did you place her, Sir Andrew?" asked Wilkie.

"I don't know that I thought about it." Sir Andrew's hand went up to give his head a little scratch and then smoothed the neat grey hair. He peered into space, searching his memory, and smiled faintly. "She gave me great pleasure, I must confess. An old man maybe takes the more delight in young beauty and charm because it's so far off. I think I put her down as a professional girl doing well. Certainly not a girl born in the purple. She hasn't the manner, and something

193

about her, I think, shows that she has made herself what she is—that she relies on herself. Don't you agree?" He looked at Mr. Peachey and smiled again. "And, after all, though it's true that there are very rich men among the Balgarvie guests they're not all rich. I fancy the Bishop saves up for his one holiday and I'm a poor man myself. Indeed I wouldn't be here if the Laird didn't insist on favourable terms for old times' sake. Are you rich?"

"Indeed, no!" Mr. Peachey's reply was prompt if not entirely convincing. "But here, in the hotel, a certain *position* is rather taken for granted and I'm afraid I must—very unwillingly—remind you that from her own account Miss Logan is *not* a professional girl doing well. I still feel that in her circumstances as she described them, this hotel and her car, her clothes and so on, are *too* disproportionate, and not, I should have thought, worth it." Unless, he added silently, she hoped to land a well-placed husband.

The ball was again in Sir Andrew's court. "But do you see the alternative as worth it?" he asked. "I mean to say, if Miss Logan has taken Cleever's letter she must have come here especially to take it. She could not herself know that he would be here, so organisation at quite a high level must be presumed. Would it have been worth it? According to Cleever himself the letter is not of much consequence."

Wilkie cleared his throat. "Young Hart—"

"Yes," said Mr. Peachey. "Though they are very careful about the men selected for jobs like this."

Sir Andrew laughed. "Poor laddie! Do you not think his efficiency was just temporarily impaired by a broken heart? He looked to me to be in the kind of *dwam* where he'd as likely as not tear up the letter and put the blotting-paper in his pocket."

"It looks as if his career is seriously impaired," Mr. Peachey said severely. "I really *can't* believe he would be so irresponsible. And I do wonder why Miss Logan rushed to Gregorson at six o'clock in the morning. Why didn't she immediately raise hell here, rousing Saunders to do his job?"

Wilkie thought it was understandable. "She knew him well at one time and he's what you call approachable."

"And you don't immediately think of raising hell," Sir Andrew put in, "if you can't pay your debts. Saunders would be the last man she would want to rouse before she saw her way round that corner."

Mr. Peachey began, "All the same," for the third time. ". . . the letter," he said, "doesn't come to light, does it? And nobody has searched Gregorson's house which Miss Logan visited this morning and is, we understand, visiting again."

Huffy was now too mild a word to describe Superintendent Wilkie's emotions. He was annoyed. "I can assure you, sir, that I and my men are not overlooking any possibility," he said. "But if you are dissatisfied with the conduct of the case, or you feel it's time to ask for help I'm quite willing to put your recommendation to the chief constable."

"Oh I'm sure it's too soon for that," Sir Andrew said quickly. "It's only a few hours. And I don't think that's what was in Mr. Peachey's mind." He looked at him. "Was it?"

The significance of the word "recommendation" had not escaped Mr. Peachey and he did not hesitate. "Oh God, no!" he cried very frankly. "Let's put that horror off as long as possible. I'm sorry, Superintendent. I keep thinking all the time of Cleever and Scudamore—their reactions. Think of all this as my untrained mind failing to express itself clearly."

"That's all right, sir," said Wilkie.

Chester Hart was spending the most miserable day of his life, and the fact that he had only himself to blame made it no easier to bear. Lectures on Responsibility from Senator Cleever and freezing from Mr. Scudamore might have been the rumble of traffic and a drop in physical temperature for all the effect they had, but his own ineptitude—his blank spot—worried him badly and he was in a panic about Anthea.

Chet was highly trained and his conditioning to secrecy and suspicion had not been in vain. There was a time, a very bad time, when he had to ask himself if it was possible that Anthea was an agent: if she had picked his pocket while she was sitting on the bench with him, so sad and so lovely. The shrewd, realistic side of him rejected it for the same reasons as Sir Andrew and Jock Gregorson, rejected it with more knowledge: an agent in connection with that letter was just too bloody silly. He had too high an opinion of the intelligence of those who employ agents to credit it. And for Anthea herself he used his native common sense, the instinct for truth which had not been trained out of him so thoroughly as might, perhaps, have been wished. If Anthea had ten fellow-traveller brothers he wouldn't believe that she was other than she appeared—lovely, lovable and true.

That was a comfort but it left him just where he was about the letter.

The moment which kept bothering him was when he stopped on his way back from the garden. Every time he thought of it he gritted his teeth, but he did look at it. Whether he was unusually emotional for a man he didn't know, but he had to stop, to jerk out his handkerchief and blow his nose. . . . He hadn't noticed anything fall, but he had to admit, at least to himself, that if the Woolworth Building had dropped at his feet just then he probably wouldn't have seen it.

He went back to the spot—he remembered it exactly, vividly—over and over again, but neither it nor the garden itself had anything for him. Not long before lunch he went once more and this time a young plain-clothes cop in a wet mackintosh met him on the path.

"I was just coming to look for you, Mr. Hart," he said pleasantly. "You did say you stopped about here on your way back to the house and took out your handkerchief, didn't you?"

"Yeah. Blew my nose," said Chet.

"Could you show me the exact spot, do you think, sir?"

Chet said he could and they moved on. "Right here." He stopped. "I remember that tree with berries. Why? Have you got something?"

"Well, not the letter," said the detective. He glanced at the rowan tree in the little thicket which screened the spot so well. "You didn't see anybody?"

"No!" The word snapped out.

"And you didn't leave the path? No. . . . Well, there's been some chap. . . . If you'll come I'll let you see."

He led the way among the trees and the dismayed Chet followed. In a spot even better screened than the path, where the ground was always slightly damp yet protected from direct rain, were footprints, male and female. It looked, the detective pointed out, as if two people had stood there—the man had sunk in quite deeply at one point and he had smoked a cigarette. Not an American brand.

Gloomily Chet displayed his packet of Luckies and compared a large American shoe with the prints, which were much smaller. The policeman, with a friendly grin, said it looked like one of the girls had popped out for a minute with her boy. "But at least it's something to report."

"That's right," Chet said heavily and went back to the house.

It was part of the Balgarvie House routine that as soon as a day declared itself wet, as distinct from uncertain, fires were lit in the hall and at least one other of the public rooms, and when Chet came in Lady Vine and Vida Carruthers were sitting near the fire in the hall.

"Chet," Vida called peremptorily, "we're *consumed*. Do tell us what's going on. Have they found the letter yet?"

Chet went forward reluctantly and gave his small polite bow to Lady Vine, whom he found remote but likeable, and Vida, whose amused stare always made him feel half his size and very irritable. He said they hadn't brought home the goods yet. It was a wet day, wasn't it? Had the ladies been out?

"Oh Chet!" Vida protested, half playfully. "Don't be so utterly clam-like. Everybody knows a crime has occurred —two crimes, poor Anthea. At least tell us who they've got in there. A top cop came, didn't he—it?"

"I'm afraid," said Chet, "I can't tell you anything." He began his leave-taking bow and paused. "I wonder—do you happen to know where Anthea is?"

Vida mimed mystification and a touch of worry, but before she could speak Lady Vine, who was embroidering a chair seat and looked as if she would have no part of the scene, glanced up and addressed Chet briefly.

"Anthea and Lawrence have gone to lunch at Mr. Gregorson's house."

"I see," said Chet. "Thanks," and he completed his bow and went away.

"God!" exclaimed Vida, staring after him. "He looks *distracted*, doesn't he. It must be something pretty hot. I wonder what. . . ."

Lady Vine felt that fate was using her unkindly. She never grumbled about wet days at Balgarvie, indeed she rather enjoyed them, provided there were not too many in a row, but a wet day and Vida Carruthers hungering for companionship was too much. Vida was at no time her favourite young woman, but to-day she was an offence: obviously one of those, thought Lady Vine with a shudder, who would be in the front of the crowd after an accident and drive miles to see the house where the murder happened. She smothered a yawn, deciding that she would go upstairs and rest after lunch and wondering when Lawrence would be back.

"I expect," said Vida suddenly, "that you think I'm being ghoulish, but actually I'm frightfully worried."

There was nothing Lady Vine desired less than to become even remotely involved in Mrs. Carruthers's problems. She said that her own custom, when in doubt, was to consult her husband.

But Vida was not put off. "Oh I know," she said earnestly, "but Bryce—well, I haven't much social conscience, but he hasn't *any*. He'd just say keep out of it. But"—she was very serious—"I'm not sure. It'd be so ghastly, and yet—I mean this may be frightfully serious—"

"If you have anything to tell which might *help,*" said Lady Vine, not mincing her emphasis, "Desmond would be the one to advise you."

"Yes, I suppose Desmond," said Vida doubtfully, "but that would be so sort of final. Do let me just unbosom, Lady V. I really feel quite zany. You see, it's Anthea. I mean they're bound to wonder about Anthea. . . ." The well-trodden ground was traversed once more. What was Anthea doing at Balgarvie? She was so cagey about herself it wasn't true, and by all accounts it was a surprising amount of money. . . . "Well," the narrative continued, "I don't know if you remember, she was very late for dinner last night. Bryce and I had seen her down at the harbour earlier and . . ."

Lady Vine felt a little sick. Her first reaction to the news that Anthea's money had been stolen had been irritation with Anthea. To leave a lot of money about was simply inviting someone—a youngster, perhaps, hard up and not too strong in character—to steal it. And there was this vague mysteriousness. But she kept seeing Anthea's gold-flecked eyes and the charming, humorous mouth which looked as if she had been badly hurt at some time or other. She said coldly, "I simply can't imagine Anthea having anything to do with—"

She stopped. Desmond himself was coming across the hall, looking tired and keeping his smile in place with an effort. "Lordy, lordy!" he sighed, humorously resigned. "How much nuisance can a piece of paper be? You look a little bored, Lady V. Are you oppressed by all this crime and mystery?"

"Well," she said, "it would be a wet day, wouldn't it?"

Vida gave an exaggerated shiver. "*And* cold! One's blood runs thin. I suppose—or *is* it the atmosphere? Des, darling, let's go and have a drink. I have a problem."

CHAPTER 15

IN THE pantry, people were inclined to be funny about Senator Cleever's letter and rather edgily reserved about the theft of Miss Logan's money, but on the whole they avoided both in general conversation. Morgan was the exception. He and Miss Logan, he told everybody earnestly, hadn't got on. He admitted he'd felt sore; quite honestly he felt that she had been a bit—well—unfair; but he would never believe she had taken a confidential letter. Gracious! he said. When you *thought* what that would mean . . .! And he wasn't going to believe either, he added manfully, that the whole story of the stolen money was made up.

Some, including Stewart and Biddy, thought this well done of Morgan, showing a nice, forgiving spirit. Some did not. Alec remarked cynically that it was a real break for Morgan and he was making the most of it. There's no surer, safer way of getting back at anybody, he pointed out, than to go round saying you don't believe they took the baby's rattle. Lawrence agreed and kept out of Morgan's way. He was very sorry for Anthea about the money—even more for the unpleasantness than the loss—and, like the others, he regarded the commotion about the letter as nothing more than a prestige flap.

In the Tully, however, as he and the dog waited in the kitchen for the McNaughtons to go away, he listened to the sound of the three voices—Mrs. McNaughton's high, sweet and agitated, Anthea's lower and rounder in tone, the Minister's dry and deliberate as usual—and wondered how serious it all was. They sounded serious enough and the McNaughtons had certainly looked it. His eyes met Dan's. Dan was also serious, and as they stared at each other he made one small movement of his drooping tail. "No," said

Lawrence. "I don't get it either. . . . May as well put the kettle on."

When the McNaughtons drove away the two emerged from the kitchen with relieved faces—tails up again—and a tray of tea.

"We thought you'd need it," said Lawrence. He gave Anthea a cup, looking at her sympathetically, and remarked that though Mrs. McNaughton was sweet, the Minister was the most uncomfortable chap he'd ever known. "I feel ten years old and full of sin if I even see him in the distance."

Anthea seemed pretty fed up. She said, "Well, it happens I *am* full of sin. I've been careless about money and got into trouble with the police. He wasn't really so hard on me, considering everything."

"Biscuit?" said Lawrence. "Cigarette, then." He lit one for her. "I don't see why anybody should be hard on you at all. You couldn't help having a burglar and you're not responsible for Cleever's correspondence."

"No, but if his correspondence doesn't turn up, what's happened to it? Somebody must have swiped it."

There was a slight pause and then Lawrence said, "If anybody seriously thinks you could be mixed up in that sort of ploy, Anthea, they must be nuts."

Anthea was annoyed with herself. It is almost always better to say nothing at all. Lightening her face and voice she told him you can't go by appearances. "I should think that's rule one in the policeman's primer. They say murderers—and not only the accidental kind—are perfectly ordinary people in civil life. Full of charm as often as not."

"So they say." He was scornful. "You have to be pretty thick, in my view, if you can't tell when there's a *possibility* and when there isn't."

"One likes to think that's true. I believe myself that there are people you just know are incapable of crime—dishonesty. My uncomfortable Cousin Walter is one, incidentally. But circumstantial evidence has to be looked at. You warned me yourself, you may remember, the day I arrived that I needed a better cover story than I'd got."

Lawrence said that was a precaution against a charge of eccentricity, not crime. He ate a few biscuits while she smoked and drank her tea, and then, since the subject had come up, said, "I simply don't believe that anybody deliberately swiped that letter, but what happens if it just stays lost?"

"I don't know," said Anthea. "Just one more unsolved mystery."

They had finished their tea when Jock arrived to take them back to the House. To Lawrence his face looked as it always did, but Anthea, knowing it better, felt a slight chill.

"Is there something new?" she asked.

"Something," he replied laconically. Lawrence leaned back in the car but his tact was wasted. Nothing more was said.

As they drove into the yard after a silent journey Jock told Lawrence over his shoulder that the police wanted to see him. "Time check," he said.

"Look here," protested Lawrence, leaning forward, "they can't think old Cleever's stupid letter has been swiped. It's too—"

"Never mind what they think," said Jock. "Just answer their questions and otherwise keep your mouth shut. Nobody's going to ask for your views."

Lawrence said, "More fools they," and looked, as the car pulled up, at a dejected figure which appeared at the door of the kennels: Ian McNaughton in the wet clothes he had worn on the moors, his fair hair dark and curly, his face miserable.

He approached uncertainly and Jock watched him come. "Hallo," he said. "Got something on your mind?" Ian nodded, and he turned to his passengers. "You go straight in," he said to Lawrence, and to Anthea, "do you mind waiting? They won't be many minutes."

"Hell!" grumbled Lawrence, getting out of the car, and muttering crossly he went into the house while Anthea followed slowly.

She was puzzled. Jock's silence was unlike him and Lawrence's presence could not altogether explain it. There was something new, he wasn't telling her what it was, and she felt as indignant, ill-used, as an invalid who suspects that the worst is being kept from him and is thereby deprived of his adult status.

He said, "Wait," to Ian and caught her up. In a tone which apologised to her puzzled face he said, "There is something new and I promised I wouldn't give it to you in advance. You can see I have to be careful to play fair— they're being pretty good and unorthodox. Don't worry. I'll come in a minute, but I must just see if Ian's got anything."

He turned back to the drooping Ian, and she went in and along the passage, where she waited for a moment till Lawrence came out of the housekeeper's room. He was rather flushed and indignant and she asked, "Have you been grilled?"

"Well, not exactly. They were damned keen, though, I must say. *When* I met you, *when* I took the sherry to you . . . how I knew it was after half past seven when I met you coming in—"

"How did you?"

"Because I listened to Cricket Scoreboard, writing it all down. I wouldn't have known ordinarily." He looked at her. "Are you going in now? Give them hell."

"I'll do my best," said Anthea and knocked at the door.

At the table sat Mr. Peachey and Superintendent Wilkie, with Sergeant McNab and a young man in plain clothes in the background and Sir Andrew coming forward to meet her. They all got to their feet as she went in and the sergeant placed a chair for her. She slipped off Lawrence's coat and sat down.

"We have the statement here that you made this morning, Miss Logan," Wilkie began. "Would you mind reading through it?" He handed her a sheet of typescript. "It's the part concerning your movements yesterday afternoon I would like you to check."

She read it and said, "This is correct."

"You don't, after thinking it over, wish to alter anything?"

"No. It's as accurate as I can make it. I don't remember exact times, I'm afraid, except that I left the harbour to go to the Manse at a quarter past four."

"It's a bit more radical than that," Wilkie said. He picked up another paper from the table. "We have a statement here from Mrs. Vida Carruthers. She says that she and her husband, Mr. Bryce Carruthers, drove in to the village just behind you—about half past three, she reckons —and saw you parting from a man who had just got out of your car. He was shutting the door, and they had caught sight of him in your car earlier, on the road."

Anthea, remembering her blushing passenger, gave a laugh. "I'd clean forgotten about him! I gave him a lift. I've no idea who he was."

"Do you often give lifts?" asked Mr. Peachey. "I mean, most women hesitate to pick up a stranger when they're alone."

"I don't usually do it on big roads," she said, "but here everybody gives lifts—there are so few buses—and he couldn't have looked more harmless."

"Can you describe him?"

"Well—not in detail. He was so bashful I didn't look at

205

him much, and it wasn't many minutes." She paused to recall the youth. "He was squarish and fair and he blushed a lot. . . . I think he had on one of those leathery jackets and—oh yes, he had a small suitcase."

"You don't know where he went—or where he was going?" asked Wilkie.

She shook her head. "No, I didn't notice, and he didn't tell me anything. We really didn't talk at all." She looked at Wilkie. "I'm sorry—I should have mentioned him, of course, but I really had forgotten. What made Mrs. Carruthers—I told her he was just a boy who'd hitched a ride."

Wilkie said, "Mrs. Carruthers thought it right to come forward for two reasons. She saw the man again—she described him much as you've done, except that she seemed to think of him as older. When she and Mr. Carruthers came back here after leaving you at the harbour he was walking up the drive and dodged off among the trees when he heard the car."

"Good gracious!" cried Anthea. "But she couldn't think . . . He really was just a boy, and terribly simple. I thought he'd probably got his first job away from home and was coming back for the week-end—something like that. Wouldn't he be a keeper's son?"

"No, he doesn't fit anywhere here," said Wilkie, and Sergeant McNab wagged his head in gloomy corroboration.

"He doesn't fit a daughter either—in a courting way?" she asked. It seemed that he did not and she went back to Vida. "You said she had two reasons for coming forward . . .?"

"Yes," Wilkie said watching her. "Mrs. Carruthers wouldn't likely have taken much notice of the man—boy—but for your manner. Down at the harbour you seemed upset, she said. You seemed to resent it when she and her husband spoke about this man and you were—" he glanced at the paper he held—"she says you were quite hostile: very abrupt, she says, and seemed anxious to get rid of them. Then again, you were late for dinner and when you did come down she thought you were unlike yourself. Of course, you've told us yourself you were troubled. There's nothing definite you can say?"

Anthea looked down at her hands lying quietly in her lap. She was in danger of losing her temper. Why in the name of anything imaginable should Vida come barging in with a blown-up story to add confusion to a situation already confused enough? Malice? Longing for sensation? Or just plain self-importance? She lifted her head and with a small gesture, a minimum apology, addressed the superintendent.

"Mr. Peachey will have to excuse me," she said. "Normally I am quite polite, but the truth is, Mrs. Carruthers has been a nuisance. She bores me very much and I think she demands a lot from her friends. I had a lot to think about. I went to Carse to get away from her, and when they followed me down to the harbour, I could—I could cheerfully have pushed her in."

Sir Andrew smiled. Mr. Peachey, who was getting very tired of the fence on which he necessarily sat, raised his eyebrows and his shoulders in what might have been tacit admission that his friend Vida—and even his friend Bryce—might at times become tedious. Or it might, Anthea thought, merely signify, "Well, that's your story." Superintendent Wilkie passed on, without comment, to the footprints in the thicket.

Anthea had seen nobody, heard nothing, on her way back to the house from the garden. Wilkie asked what shoes she had been wearing and she held up a foot in a casual walking shoe. "These," she said, and then corrected herself. "No. I had put a skirt on because I was going to the Manse. I had on a pair with more heel," but as she spoke she saw

207

that shoes of hers had already been compared with the prints. Whether they fitted or were ten sizes out she was not informed.

"Now," said Wilkie, "the time after you came in from the garden. Mr. Vine says he took the glass of sherry to you soon after half past seven. You weren't down till fifteen or twenty minutes past eight. You saw nobody? The maids turn down the beds and so on about that time, don't they?"

"They do," she said, "but nobody came while I was in the room."

"Thank you," said Wilkie. He glanced at Mr. Peachey and Sir Andrew. "Have you anything . . .? Then I don't think we need keep you any longer, Miss Logan."

As they rose from their chairs there were sounds of voices in the passage, a sharp knock and the door opened. Three people entered: Jock Gregorson and the two young McNaughtons. Ness was scarlet and furious, Ian scarlet but determined, and Jock was in charge—within limits.

"Forgive me," he said. "I have some information which I think you should have at once." He introduced his companions to Wilkie. "Ness and Ian McNaughton, both employed in the hotel."

Wilkie nodded and sat down again. Anthea wondered if she was meant to leave the room, but she didn't want to and withdrew unobtrusively to the background where she might be overlooked. Chairs were indicated to the newcomers but nobody followed Wilkie's example and sat down, because Ness, standing with her eyes fixed on the police caps placed by Wilkie and McNab on a side table, was dissociating herself from the scene with all the obstinacy at her command.

Jock ignored the demonstration. "Go on, Ian," he said.

"It's about the money that was stolen from my cousin — that is, Miss Logan," said Ian in his soft uncertain voice.

"There's something—" he gulped unhappily—"it probably has nothing to do with it, but Greg—Mr. Gregorson—said look out for anything unusual and this was a bit queer."

It was last night, he went on, when he was going to the party at the Tully. As he was leaving the house he met Ness going in. She was carrying a parcel. "I asked what it was and she said it was none of my business and we had a—a scuffle." He blushed. "The girls get boxes of chocolates given them sometimes and I thought—well, I made a grab at it. It wasn't a box. And then Ness said it was something Morgan had given her to keep for him, so of course I gave it back. But when I heard about Anthea's —Miss Logan's—money I began to wonder why Morgan should give her something to keep at the Manse, so I—"

"Why didn't you report this before?" Wilkie asked sharply.

Jock explained. "He's been out with the guns. He came to me as soon as he got back to ask if I thought it worth mentioning. I did think so."

The superintendent looked at the sodden garments and unhappy face and regretted his sharpness. He gave Ian a nod and spoke soothingly, rather broadly. "Aye, jist as well. Anything a wee bit out of the usual needs to be cleared up in a case like this." He turned deliberately and addressed Ness's back. "You and this lad—Morgan, did you say his name is?—you'll jist explain and then we'll know. Now what was this you were to keep safe?"

There was no reply. Ness stared at the caps as though her life depended on accurate counting of the checks on their bands.

"Ness," said Jock with most lively exasperation, "don't be silly." He took a step forward and putting his hands on her shoulders turned her round to face Wilkie. "You know this is serious," he said holding her. "It's not the time to behave like a child."

There was still no response. Anthea caught her lip between her teeth, Mr. Peachey and Wilkie opened their mouths, but before they could speak there was a rumbling and a surging in a hitherto passive quarter and Sergeant McNab, the Balgarvie policeman, took over the Balgarvie problem.

"Now look here see, Ness," he said in broad calm Scots with a not uncomfortable note of authority, "this'll no do, ye ken. Here's this lady—yer mother's cousin—lost a terrible lot o' money, and there's this letter belongin' to the American gentleman forbye. We canna jist let them go. D'ye think this lad Morgan's a thief?"

"No," snapped Ness. "Of course not. I know he isn't."

"Well then," pursued the sergeant, "what are ye feared for?"

She turned on him angrily. "I'm not frightened, Mr. McNab. Morgan gave me something to look after for him because he's got nothing in his room *here* that can be locked. He trusted me. Ian had no right to talk about it. It had nothing to do with the money or the letter."

Sergeant McNab was a stolid man, red, healthy and slow of speech, and when he had set his course he stuck to it. "What like a parcel is't?" he asked, ignoring all else. "A book mebbe?"

"I won't say anything."

"I think it was papers," Ian said. "Quite a big bundle of papers it felt like."

"Mebbe," hazarded the sergeant, "something he's been writing. Vairses even. But there's nae herm in that." He had seen some queer things in his time and grown tolerant. "He wouldna want the other lads tae get a hold o' them but he'll no mind me or Mr. Wilkie takin' a wee look jist tae prove it. It's at the Manse, ye say? Ian'll jist rin doon on his bike and get it and then we'll hae Morgan in here and see what's what."

Ness was stubborn but there was too much weight against her. "It's locked up," she said. "I'll go myself—"

"Where is it?" asked Ian, who knew exactly which bits of the Manse furniture would lock.

"You don't—I don't want you—"

"Likely," said Sergeant McNab helpfully, "the Minister'll hae a key."

"*Here's* the key," snapped Ness and took it from her pocket. "But I'd rather go myself. It—the parcel—is not to be opened except by Morgan. Nobody has any right—"

"I'll run you down, Ian," said Jock.

They left the room and there was a short, exhausted silence. Sergeant McNab received a nod of commendation from his superior and settled back.

"I'm supposed to be on duty, in case you're interested," said Ness in a high, tart voice. "And Morgan's very busy. I don't see how he can drop everything."

"They'll have to manage without you both for a wee while," said Wilkie.

"I'd better at least *tell* Mr. Saunders then"—but she was not allowed to leave the room. Sergeant McNab went to find the manager and arrange for Morgan to be released from duty.

"I think," Mr. Peachey said, glancing at Wilkie and Sir Andrew, "that Senator Cleever should perhaps be here in case there is anything. . . . Do you think so? And Miss Logan? Yes . . . I'll go."

"Aren't you going rather fast?" demanded Ness, her voice still high. "The parcel Morgan gave me has nothing to do with these things you think you're going to identify. If he had stolen them, what on earth would he have given them to me for? You're simply looking for a victim."

The rigid figure in its black-and-white uniform was the embodiment of the spirit which defies law and order and demonstrates its belief in the corruptness of authority by sitting on pavements. Mr. Peachey smiled faintly as he left the room, and Wilkie with unruffled calm said, "You know fine there's no question of looking for a victim. We're looking for a criminal—mebbe more than one. If this lad's innocent he'll be cleared in minutes."

He returned to his papers but Ness had not finished. "That's all very well," she said. "It sounds fine but it isn't true, you know. It's not justice the police are interested in." Wilkie looked up, and under his steady eyes a wave of colour swept over her face and drained away. Anthea got up and she and Sir Andrew converged upon her.

"Ness, do be sensible," said Anthea. "Just help to get this horrible business cleared up. Nobody's gunning for Morgan—or anybody else. We have to find out the truth."

"Sit down, my dear child," Sir Andrew commanded. "Your cousin has lost a great deal of money, she is undergoing a severe ordeal and she, as you see, is making no fuss. Sit down and think what it is we are trying to do." Ness sat down in the chair he indicated and he seated himself beside her. "You must know," he went on, "that this is a very serious matter. A theft of money means loss and perhaps distress for one person, but if somebody has deliberately stolen Senator Cleever's letter it is the sort of crime that may affect thousands, millions of people. It is your duty, as it is everyone's duty, to give the police all the help you can. And you might perhaps remember that these things have happened to visitors to Scotland. That's not a very nice thing for us to think."

She stared at him. "But—what sort of letter is it, then, Sir Andrew? I don't understand—"

The door opened and Morgan in his white coat came in with Sergeant McNab and Mr. Saunders, who looked more than ever distracted and pallid. Morgan's expression of puzzled willingness to help sharpened to genuine surprise when he saw Ness, and she gave him a wavering smile of reassurance.

Before anything was said Mr. Peachey ushered in the three Americans and there was a period of movement and confusion. Ness, automatically remembering her position in the hotel, got up and was gently shepherded away from Morgan by Sir Andrew. Then those who were seated and those who remained standing were still, and Superintendent Wilkie began.

"You know," he said to Morgan, "that we are investigating a theft of money and the loss, which may be a theft, of a letter. You can maybe help us. Last night you gave a parcel to Miss McNaughton for safe keeping. What's in it?"

"Parcel?" said Morgan. He looked at Ness and back to the police officer. "I don't understand."

The room tightened. Eyes became alert and the bulging figure of Sergeant McNab was suddenly more compact.

"Morgan," said Ness, staring at him with anxious apology. "I couldn't help it—honestly. But it hasn't been opened. It's just as you gave it to me and I don't think it's— I mean I'm sure—"

"But what parcel?" he asked again. "I'm afraid I'm just not with you."

Again the door opened. Jock and Ian came in accompanied by the Minister, who carried a flattish parcel in his hands. It was as a Justice of the Peace, a knowledgeable as well as a scrupulous citizen, that Mr. McNaughton now acted. He went straight across the room to Superintendent Wilkie, looking neither to left nor right, and placed the parcel on the table before him.

"This package, which I understand you wish to examine," he stated, "was taken by me from a locked drawer in my daughter's room in the presence of Mr. Gregorson and my son. It has not been out of my hands since."

The superintendent said he was much obliged. Mr. McNaughton greeted Sir Andrew, bowed to Anthea and in the general direction of Senator Cleever, glanced at Ness and retired to a ring-side stand.

Ness was formally asked by Wilkie if she identified the parcel as the one given her by Morgan last night. "Yes, of course that's it," she said, "but—"

The official eyes moved on to Morgan. "Do you recognise this as your property?"

"No," said Morgan bewildered. "I never saw it before. I don't know what all this is about—I never gave Ness anything last night. Or any time."

There was a McNaughton uproar. "But Morgan!" cried Ness. "Here!" shouted Ian. "Are you denying that this is your property?" demanded their father.

"Yes, sir." The young man looked from one face to another. "I don't know what's going on—why you're asking—I'm very sorry, Ness, but I've got to defend myself, haven't I? It's not mine and I never saw it before."

"This is an extraordinary thing," said Senator Cleever severely. He turned to Wilkie. "Let me recommend you to open up this package without further delay. Very likely it may tell us—"

Wilkie said, "In a minute, sir," and looked at Ian. "Will you repeat what you told us about meeting your sister with this in her hands last night?" Ian did so and Ness was asked, "Do you agree that this is what took place between your brother and yourself?"

Ness's fair-skin face, which flushed so easily, was white and her eyes were wide and frightened. "Yes, *yes*," she cried. "I've told you. But—Morgan! Have you had a blackout or something? You can't have forgotten giving me this—"

Morgan made a gesture of hopelessness. "I just don't know what you're talking about."

"Oh gosh!" burst from Ness. "This is—I don't understand anything. Have I gone nuts? Daddy—"

The Minister, though rather a cheerless parent, was reliable. He made no move to receive Ness but he allowed her to cling to his arm and dealt firmly, as he always did, with emotion. "Now, now," he said. "There's nothing the matter with you. The superintendent is waiting to ask you a question. Pay attention."

"What do you believe is in the parcel?" was the question and it was followed by dead silence. There was no further symptom of hysteria in Ness; she was merely dumb and unmistakably frightened, and before the silence could declare itself as either a refusal or inability to reply, Jock broke it.

"Ness," he said and waited till she looked at him. "We are *only* concerned with these two matters. Nothing else." Ness opened her mouth and shut it again and he raised an eyebrow at Wilkie and went on deliberately, "If you think the papers in this parcel have any connection with nuclear disarmament demonstrations we're not interested. Is that it?"

She nodded and gulped nervously, withdrawing herself from her father who was staring at her sternly, and the Superintendent's question was answered. It left him looking bored but he made no comment. He asked how Morgan had been appointed to the hotel staff.

"It was me," said Ness. "He wanted a job and I told Mr. Saunders about him."

"Did you take up references?" the manager was asked.

"Er—no," said Saunders uncomfortably. "It hardly seemed necessary. When a student who has been satisfactory recommends a friend it has always been all right, and membership of a university is usually acceptable as a guarantee."

The Minister's lips tightened. Wilkie said, "Well we'll check—Edinburgh, you said?" and Morgan exploded.

215

"What do you think you're getting at?" he shouted. "It's a frame-up—"

"Whisht m'n," said Sergeant McNab and got to his feet. "Quiet."

Morgan pointed at Anthea. "Check up on *her*. Ask *her* what she's doing here—where the letter is—" He made a dash for the door, but there was no pause and no scuffle before he was firmly held by the Law in the person of Sergeant McNab.

Wilkie opened the parcel. It was wrapped in brown paper which had been used several times before and its appearance suggested a small quantity of personal laundry more than anything else. But it was more liberally sealed with gummed strips than a bundle of washing usually is, and as the superintendent attacked it with his pocket-knife Morgan flung up his head as if his moment of panic was over.

"You will find," he said, deliberately though a trifle breathlessly, "Miss Anthea Logan's money and Mr. Cleever's letter safely wrapped in newspaper in that parcel. You'll have to ask Miss Logan herself how the letter came to be in her possession."

CHAPTER 16

IF Senator Cleever with his letter in his hand had a nice moment of pure relief, when it seemed that all the troubles connected with it were over, Anthea felt no such pleasure. Her money was on the table before her. Presently she would be glad to have it back, to have no need to borrow from Jock, to leave her little capital untouched and be able to think again about finding a cheap place where she could write undisturbed by clocks and bosses. In the meantime, unless Morgan could be brought to confess how he had got the letter, she was by no means out of the wood.

Morgan could not be brought to confess it. He became very grand under questioning, and his story was one of pure patriotism. Nobody believed it. On the other hand he was not to be shaken and there was no other story.

He had had suspicions of Miss Logan from the first and had been keeping unobtrusive watch on her movements. Her money he had taken in order to foil any attempt at a moonlight flitting when he found the Senator's lost letter in her locked, hidden case after she had gone to the Tully last night. How did he know it was the Senator's lost letter? The Senator himself didn't know it was lost until morning. Morgan blinked, but he was equal to it. The address had told him that it had no business to be where he found it.

"What did you think you were going to do about it?" Wilkie asked, and he smiled and gave Mr. Saunders a condescending glance.

"Well—it's not quite the sort of thing one reports to the hotel manager," he said. "Quite honestly, I don't know: brought it to you, possibly. I had to think about it. I gave Ness the parcel and she promised—"

"Are you implying," said Mr. McNaughton loudly, "that my daughter is your accomplice?" He turned on Ness. "Did you know what was in the parcel?"

"No!" cried Ness. "Of course I didn't. I thought it was C.N.D. stuff."

Wilkie regarded her without enthusiasm. "If what he says is true, it wasn't that far off C.N.D. stuff, was it? Did he not speak to you about these suspicions of his?"

"No, of course not," Ness said again. "You don't think I'd have stood for nonsense like that about my cousin, do you?"

Morgan laughed. "Well well!" he said. "This is a change."

"Ach!" Wilkie said disgustedly. "Take him away." He got up from his chair and watched Sergeant McNab lean on his protesting charge and bear him away, and then, rather abruptly, thanked the company for their assistance and said he would not keep them any longer.

Some of the company were not very willing to go. It took all Mr Peachey's urbanity to persuade the Senator to accept dismissal, to leave his letter for finger-printing and leave the case itself, so far from clarified, to the police. And the Minister lingered. He was not yet certain how far his daughter might be implicated. For a night and most of a day stolen property had lain hidden in the Manse, and worse—far worse—his child had been afraid of the police. He did not suspect for a moment that she had had anything to do with the thefts—she was incapable of it—and he was convinced that she had not known what the parcel contained: but it appeared that her part in the campaign for nuclear disarmament had been more aggressive than he had imagined. He was shaken and very glum. Anthea was standing by herself a little apart, and he went up to her. "Anthea," he said, speaking stiffly because it was impossible for him to speak otherwise, "would you not be more comfortable at the Manse? Your Cousin Maud and I would both be easier in our minds if you were with us, and I would have thought that in the circumstances you would prefer more privacy than you can have here."

"Thank you, Cousin Walter," she said, "but I really do feel I must stay till this is over. I can't quite explain—I think it's because I don't want to be sheltered. This is part of the aftermath of—of Randal, and I don't want even to look as if I was trying to dodge it or hide."

There was a slight pause and then he said, "Very well. You may be right. I would certainly never advise you to hide or dodge, as you put it, or be less courageous than your nature enables you to be. Call on me at any time if you should feel you need me. What will you do about church?" She said she would like to go to church if she was free. "Very well," he said again. "Come to us afterwards. May God bless you and bring you safely through this trial," and he went away with Ian.

Ness and Mr. Saunders had disappeared, Mr. Peachey had personally shepherded his recalcitrant little flock away from the operational zone, and only Jock, Sir Andrew and the police officers were left in the room. Anthea wondered if she was meant to go or stay. Superintendent Wilkie almost seemed to have forgotten about her—or at least he had taken no notice of her since Jock burst into the room with Ness and Ian.

He was talking now with Jock and Sir Andrew, all three bent over the papers which lay on the table, and she went up to them.

"Superintendent Wilkie," she said, "can you tell me at all where I am?" They all straightened and he looked at her inquiringly. "I mean—what do I do now?"

She had not been charged or even cautioned, but Wilkie's faint amusement at her ignorance did not appear. The possibility of a charge could not be ruled out. "We couldn't let you leave the district at present," he told her, "and if you were going to be away from the hotel it would be convenient to know where you could be found. That's all. By all means go out—just do what you'd do in the ordinary way. We'll find you if we have anything to tell you."

Jock beside him held the paper they had been reading and drew attention to it. "Do you think . . .?" he said.

"Aye, no harm," said Wilkie taking it from him. "We asked for information about your brother, Miss Logan, and this has just come through." He neither showed her what had come nor read it out to her, but told her briefly that it confirmed her statement. Her brother had left the country two days after he had visited her at Flatford-on-Sea and the facts about her job and her residence were established.

"Yes," said Anthea. "It doesn't really get you much further, does it?"

"It doesn't tell us a great deal," he agreed. "But then, if folk just live in a very quiet way there's not that much to tell."

She sighed. "Well, I don't know," she said. "Mrs. Carruthers says one thing and I say another; Morgan says one thing and I say another. . . . It's no good going *on* saying it." She looked at Wilkie. "You'll have to sort it out."

"We hope to do it," he said. Though a policeman can't afford to let instinct ride him, a man can't rule it out—not if he's good at his job. He would almost bet his career on this girl's honesty, but there was clearing up to be done and all he allowed himself to say was, "We don't make mistakes very often, you know."

"I'm banking on that," said Anthea.

"I was wondering," Sir Andrew said to her, "if you would care to dine with me this evening?" He turned to the superintendent. "Miss Logan is very brave, very good, but I believe she would eat a better dinner if she had company."

"The very ticket," said the superintendent. "I wouldn't wonder if you ate a better dinner yourself for it, sir."

Sir Andrew said, "Oh there's no doubt about that," and Anthea accepted with gratitude and thought, as they looked kindly at her, that she'd better get out quickly before she burst into tears on the nearest—Wilkie's—manly bosom.

"It must be a painful thing for a cop," remarked Jock walking along the passage with her, "when he finds himself half in love with the chief suspect."

"That's a scurrilous suggestion."

"No. I don't suggest that he'd let it affect his judgment or his loyalty to Mrs. Wilkie. It's rather a noble sentiment, as a matter of fact; shows the age of chivalry is not dead. And you'd be grateful if you knew how scrupulously and with what wiliness he's protected you from the impulsive types."

"I am grateful," she said soberly. "It's so convincing. I've almost been convinced myself more than once. Vida Carruthers—honestly, Jock, if you'd seen that blushing boy! — and yet how sinister! I wonder who he was—is."

"Yes," said Jock. "It would be nice to know. We just want a couple of facts—quite small—and I think we'll get them." They had reached the hall and he asked, "What are you going to do now? Would you like a drink?"

Nearly everybody had come in early because of the rain and the hall was full of people. She shook her head. "No, I'll go straight up."

He had seen her look round the hall, and as they left it he said, "But you're to come down and eat your dinner, mind. It's no good staying to see the thing through if you're going to cower in your room."

"I'm going to cower till dinner time and nothing shall stop me," she said firmly.

"Well, that's not unreasonable," he allowed. "Could you cut it by, say, a quarter of an hour? I'm going to ring

William at six—by appointment—and then there's going to be an evidence-sifting session that I want to be in on. Can I come up to your room or see you in some other quiet spot after that?"

She said, "Yes, come up. I don't see, you know, that William's snoopers could get anything more than the police have already. What is there to *get*? Nobody can prove I didn't spend my evenings and week-ends doing a correspondence course in spymanship."

"So they can't," said Jock. "But William will be useful all the same." They were at the end of the tunnel and he stopped and put a hand on her shoulder. "Go and have a rest," he said. "You've nothing to worry about. And you have great reason to be proud."

"Proud?" she exclaimed. "What of, for heaven's sake?"

He laughed and tweaked her lock of hair. "Think it out," he said.

He went home to the privacy of the Tully to make his telephone call, but he returned to the hotel immediately, and in the yard found Mr. Peachey, who remarked that the rain had stopped. "I haven't been outside the house all day," he said discontentedly. "Shall we take a turn? Wilkie and his minions are still engaged on technicalities."

They strolled past the kennels and through an archway which brought them to the path along which Anthea and Chet had walked the evening before. Jock looked, on the whole, rather contented; Mr. Peachey the reverse. His day had been devoted to a task which by its nature was not only thankless but inevitably misconstrued by all sides. And he felt obscurely shaken in his confidence: as though he had lost ground not so much with other people as with himself—a dissatisfied, gritty sensation.

"This really is an *intolerable* affair," burst from him with more passion than he intended.

"Cleever and Scudamore are beefing, are they?" asked Jock with moderate sympathy.

"Yes of course they are. And you really can't blame them. They feel the hotel has been lax—which it has. With the people we get here, Saunders is a criminal fool not to take ordinary precautions about the staff."

Jock said that it would be difficult to check the political opinions of the temporary staff and he thought hardly worth it. "Their views change so rapidly. And though they may be politically savage against foreigners or the rich, they serve individual specimens with perfectly good will. Morgan, I grant, is a misfortune, but I don't know that Saunders can be blamed. Ness was the mug. And even he would probably have been harmless without this particular blend of circumstances."

"Unfortunately," said Mr. Peachey, "the particular blend occurred, and Ness, a self-confessed banner-wagger, will be in the dining-room to-night as usual."

"She won't do Cleever any harm."

"It's what Cleever feels about it that does harm," was the retort.

They walked slowly on. Mr. Peachey gave a gusty sigh and lit a cigarette. Jock waited for what was coming, and as they went through the gate into the garden it came.

"If this case remains unsolved—and that is how it looks as of now—it's going to be the very devil, Gregorson. You must see it. Morgan will be tried and so on, presumably, but nobody is ever going to believe that he was responsible for the letter *originally*. Well, who was? As they see it—Cleever and Scudamore—the letter was stolen and there is a strong case against Anthea Logan. They feel, frankly, that the local police are not the people to deal with it. Too easy-going and too liable—you must excuse my saying this; I only repeat what is being said—to be influenced by you and Mc-

Naughton. Nobody could be more anxious than I am to see her cleared," said Mr. Peachey, not quite accurately, "but I confess I am not happy about her. The brother, the very odd life she has led since his conviction, coming here as she did . . . Then Vida Carruthers—she isn't an intelligent woman, but she reported *facts*; and Morgan's story at least gives an explanation. Against that, what have you? The Flatford-on-Sea police told us nothing except that she lived there."

"We have a bit more than that," said Jock. "And if it makes you happier, I will promise you that the case won't be left unsolved."

"What do you mean?" Mr. Peachey looked round, but with more nervousness than joy, and Jock smiled slightly.

"I'm not too worried about questions that may be asked about negligence," he said. "Whatever Cleever may think, the case against Anthea wouldn't hold and the questions would more likely be about victimisation. But she must be cleared. I won't stop till she is, and William Humbolt—"

There was a sharp cry. "*Humbolt*? You mean the *Trumpeter* . . ." Mr. Peachey stopped dead and surrounded by vegetables and raspberry canes stared in utter horror at Fleet Street. "Gregorson—for God's sake—you're not going to bring the Press—you really *can't* make a stink—"

"*I'm* not," said Jock. "Nor is Humbolt. A stink is the last thing we want, but Cleever is more likely to stir it up than we are. If he goes grumbling in high places," he added with some relish, "he can hardly fail." There was a loud groan from Mr. Peachey and he laughed heartlessly and then relented. "I hope he won't do it."

Mr. Peachey thought that after all he had held the balance pretty creditably. Sitting on his fence—never a comfortable position for long—soothing the Senator, supporting the police, showing no bias and being shot at from both sides. "Why is Humbolt taking it big?" he asked fretfully.

They walked on round the garden and Jock told him. "He thought a lot of Anthea," he said. "She was a very bright kid. He was all ready to carry her through the scandal when her brother was arrested, but she wouldn't have it." He paused; but wondering whether Anthea could have stayed and weathered the Randal storm if she had not, simultaneously, been knocked down by himself was an old and unprofitable exercise, and the pause was very brief. William Humbolt, he said, had been offended when she refused his help and chose, as he put it, to go out into the wilderness, but he had got over that and he had never forgotten her. "And he finds it—as I do—intolerable that she should be endangered again—incriminated by her brother's record."

"It's unthinkable," said Desmond Peachey. "One couldn't, I'm sure you must agree, ignore it, but I myself have tried, I assure you, not to—"

"Oh, of course," Jock broke in. "It had to be thought of—that and all the rest. There's enough to give us a hell of a lot of trouble unless we find that damned boy and how Morgan got hold of the letter."

"Yes." Mr. Peachey's tone was more natural. "And both, as Sir Andrew says, may be under our noses. . . . What is Humbolt doing?"

William Humbolt's main function had perhaps been fulfilled already in the garden of Balgarvie House. His name and his interest, the power of the Press behind him, had ensured that the efforts of the Foreign Office representative would not flag in reminding all concerned that questions of an undesirable kind might come from more than one direction. But Jock said peaceably that a chap had been in Flatford—he hadn't got a great deal more than the police—and William himself had been telephoning.

"He found the publishers who have got Anthea's book," he said.

"Oh?" said Mr. Peachey. "Are they? You look rather elated."

Jock smiled. "I am," he said. "They're very pleased with it."

Anthea went to the turret window as soon as she reached her room and stood looking out at the wet landscape and the sea. The clouds were higher than they had been all day and there were curious silvery shafts of light which caught and lit up peaks or slopes of the hills. The familiar changeful loveliness of Balgarvie had been so much a part of her life that even in the worst days—in the smelly flat with her poor, defeated mother; struggling to get control of her un-congenial job—she could look inward and see it: a private treasure which refreshed her spirit, and a kind of promise. Looking at it now, though she was there, watching the changes of colour, breathing the fresh, damp air, she felt as remote as she had felt in Flatford; as if she looked at it across a gulf, a chasm worn by the events of the day.

Alone and able to think about it quietly, she went through it all, wondering where it had really begun. From the moment Senator Cleever's letter was lost—and that, per-haps, only happened because she had inadvertently taken Chet's mind off it—she must have come under suspicion. Apart from improvidence, nothing could be proved against her, and she did not now think that she was in danger of ar-rest; but unless proof of her innocence was forthcoming she was in danger of being left in a very unpleasant position, stig-matised by what was virtually a verdict of "not proven." And she, as well as Jock or Mr. Peachey or the superintendent, dreaded the effects of a dissatisfied Senator Cleever pushing his grievance on and up till they were all writhing in the glare of publicity, the prey of sensation-mongers.

It was when she began to think about changing for dinner that she remembered that her room had been subjected to the eyes and hands of the police and before them of Morgan.

It was a disturbing thought. Her things had been replaced exactly in the order she had assigned to them, or if not that—she was not naturally very tidy—in the positions in which they had been found, but she felt absurdly uneasy. It seemed necessary to go round formally taking possession of her belongings, getting back, so to speak, on the old intimate terms.

She had a bath and was half dressed when there was a knock at the door and she called, "Wait," as she huddled on her dressing-gown.

"It's only me," said a subdued voice and Ness appeared. "I came," she said, "to apologise."

"Oh, Ness!" said Anthea and gazed at her rather helplessly. Ness was pale but she was, if anything, even less approachable than usual. "There's nothing you have to apologise for," she said lamely. "It was a miserable shock. Worse for you than for me, really."

"Oh, I'm not apologising for Morgan," Ness said with a touch of scorn. "I suppose I was a fool to be taken in, but how are you to know? You can't go round thinking everybody's lying to you."

It was Anthea's opinion that she had been too ready to believe that only Morgan told the truth, but she said, "No, of course you can't. Have you known him long?"

"Quite a long time. At least—it was last winter."

"Is he—was he a boy-friend?"

Ness stiffened. "No. I don't go in for that sort of thing. We were friends because we were both working for—something." She glanced at Anthea. "Young people don't *all* think of nothing but petting, you know. Some of us think the world can be a better place if we're prepared to take action—and even risks." This was said rather grandly and Anthea could not quite let it pass.

In a meek, quavering voice she said her own youth was so remote that of course she had forgotten what it felt like

227

and what she thought about. A startled, rather indignant face came round and she laughed at it. " 'Young people'— quote," she said, "always think they can reform the world. When— and *if*—they grow up they find it isn't so simple so they talk about it less. However, if they lose the illusion they're not so apt to be taken in by the Morgans. Be comforted."

"I still feel Morgan's had a hell of a time somehow," said Ness, too gloomy to argue. "To sort of warp him. I mean there seemed to be so much that was valuable in him. Idealistic."

"There is good in all of us," said Anthea and looked at her watch. "Ness—don't go, but do you mind if I press on? I'm having dinner with Sir Andrew, and Jock—Greg —will be here in a few minutes. Also the police have been in here doing a search so I don't feel I know where things are."

"Good lord!" Ness was aghast and her eyes went round the room in a search of her own. "Did you have time to—did they go through *everything*?" She began collecting and folding Anthea's discarded garments as if a police searcher might burst in again at any moment. "What are you laughing at?"

"Nothing," said Anthea. "I'm sure they went through everything but I don't suppose they have much modesty. I was only thankful they didn't search *me*. You'll find hangers in there. . . ."

"What I *am* apologising for," Ness resumed, at the same time clipping a skirt into its hanger, "is being so foully rude and unbelieving to you. I really am sorry now. And of course all that stuff of Morgan's about suspecting you was rot." She paused. "All this about Mr. Cleever's letter—is it serious? It seems so silly."

Anthea said, "It's both silly and serious. I hope it will be cleared up. I think so, but I don't know how." She had put her dress on, and as she turned to the mirror she met Ness's eyes in it, puzzled and anxious.

228

"Why on earth do they think *you* had anything to do with it?" she asked.

The well-known secondary reasons had been enough for Vida and for Morgan, but Anthea left them. If someone in one's family has a criminal record it is better to know. " A major reason," she said, "is that my brother Randal was in prison for selling secret information. You wouldn't have been told, but I'm telling you now and you tell Ian. So you see they think that being pretty hard up and a bit shaken I might have got into strange company and might not be very scrupulous."

"Oh gosh!" Ness whispered. She sank on to the bed where she sat with a flushed face, staring at the frocks hanging in the open wardrobe.

Anthea did her hair and went on explaining her circumstances. "Of course I haven't got much money. But—"she frowned at her reflection—"I was so *sick* of being poor and dim. This—coming to the House and things—was just one good burst to sort of set me up, so that I could feel like a person again. *Not* an unqualified success damn it."

She put her comb down and picked up her powder. Ness, not letting her left hand know what her right hand did, groped for her handkerchief and blew her nose cruelly. "I suppose," she said in a thickened voice, "Greg knew all this." Anthea looked at her inquiringly and she explained. "He blew me up. He asked how much I knew about you and if I didn't admire the kind of courage that keeps its troubles to itself."

"Did he say that?" said Anthea.

"Yes, but of course I didn't know what he was talking about. I wish you'd said—I mean about the burst."

Anthea, dealing with surplus powder, said she thought they—the McNaughtons—would know, at least enough, without being told.

"They may have," Ness said morosely. "The parents, I mean. They didn't think of telling me—they never do tell you the things that matter. Of course Ian never thinks about that kind of thing."

"What kind of thing?"

"Well—the way people live."

"Why should he?" asked Anthea.

Ness looked at her. "Meaning?"

The clock in the yard struck seven. "Think it out," said Anthea, and as Ness got hurriedly to her feet, reminded of duties awaiting her in the dining-room, she took her by the shoulder and inflicted a brief kiss on an unresponsive cheek. "Cheer up," she said.

"I feel such a fool," said Ness. "Can you see I've been crying?"

Anthea said, "A little." She gravely applied powder to conceal the pinkness and then watched her young cousin straighten her shoulders and go away to carry out her duty to her employer.

CHAPTER 17

AT A quarter past seven Jock arrived. He announced himself by giving the door a kick instead of a knock and shouting through it that he had no hands. Anthea opened it and he came in carrying two full glasses.

"Welcome," she said. "A small tray or salver is the answer."

"Didn't think of it," he said, putting the glasses down carefully. He straightened and turned to look at her, his eyes, his whole dark face, alight . . . grinning.

"What—"Anthea began, but she got no further. He swooped and she was caught up in a bear-like hug. Jock had been noted in the *Trumpeter* days for sudden outbursts of lunacy, when he would seize the nearest girl and at the top of a moderately tuneful baritone bid everybody see him dance the polka. This was a lunatic hug: a rough, back-thumping, reeling-round-the-room hug of jubilation. "Hey!" she protested when she could. "What's the *matter* with you? Have they—"

"See me cover the ground," sang Jock. "See my coat-tails flying—"

"*Stop* it!"

He stopped it—partially. He kept his grip but held her off so that they could look at each other. "Why didn't you tell me about your book?"

She gaped at him. "I did tell you about it."

"No you didn't—not the half of it." She was seized again and lifted off her feet. "Oh God, Anthea! I'm so *pleased*. . ."

Anthea put her hands on his chest and pushed. "Calm," she begged. "Could we have calm? . . . I'm just not with you—who said that some time to-day? Morgan?"

"Never mind Morgan," said Jock. She was probably not aware of it, he said as he put her back on her feet, but as

231

they talked at lunch she had indirectly told him who were her publishers. William, who had friends everywhere, had successfully Telephoned Up. "Did you know," he asked, "how pleased they are with the book?"

To his delight she blushed. "Oh well . . . they were nice about it," she said.

"Nice enough to give you a good contract and encourage you to go ahead?"

"Yes—but . . . it's only one and not even published yet," Anthea said, almost with distress. "I've been so careful *not* to do any counting or rejoicing."

Jock gave her another hug, a gentler one. "My dear clever girl," he said, "you can take it from me—and William—that a little sober rejoicing is quite in order. We *knew*, we told each other on the phone, that you'd got it in you, and you're on your way. Publishers don't enthuse easily and William's no optimist." He patted her shoulder and handed her a glass. "Neither am I, actually," he added picking up the other glass, "but I drink to your success with reasonable hope. . . . William wants you back, by the way."

"Does he?" said Anthea doubtfully.

"Think about it later," he said. "There might be something in it—at least for a while—but now, let me tell you where we are in this damned inconclusive case."

There was not much to tell. The only thing that was new in the conference from which he had just come was the change in Anthea's position—her status—brought about by William Humbolt's participation. Backed by the encouragement of a well-known publisher, the giving up of an indifferent, too taxing job, searching for a place and a way of living which would allow her to devote herself to writing, looked neither silly nor sinister; and there was William himself as a force to be reckoned with. If the mysteries of the letter's journey from Chet's pocket to Morgan's parcel and the stranger, the blushing boy, in the grounds were to remain unsolved, there was no longer, Jock thought, much danger of the case being taken further.

"The risk of a stink," he said, "just isn't worth it. Scudamore will never forgive nor Cleever forget: it'll nark Peachey for the rest of his life and old Wilkie will go on investigating it for the rest of his—"

"And I," said Anthea, "will be under a cloud for the rest of mine. The very thought of a stink makes me feel sick, but I'm not sure it wouldn't be better to have it and have done."

Jock said, "Well—if there was any guarantee that you would have done, but is there? If Morgan's was the only crime and the rest accident, as I believe, there isn't much to work on. However—I hope we'll solve it."

It was time to go down and join Sir Andrew. Anthea went to tidy her hair after the rough handling she had suffered in the earlier part of Jock's call, but the tone of the last remark made her turn to look at him.

"Do you think—are you on to something?"

He shook his head. "I have nothing more to tell you at present."

She scowled at him. "I believe you are," she said crossly. "And I'm damned if I see what right *you've* got to mount a cagey, official high horse."

He met the scowl blandly and she turned back to the mirror, ignoring the dark face reflected behind hers.

"You've still got a bit flopping over the left eye," Jock pointed out as she put the comb down.

"It lives there," she said coldly and picked up her handbag. "You might bring those glasses. I don't want any suggestion of drunken orgies left about my bedroom."

"Blandishment," said Jock, forking the stems of the glasses between the fingers of his left hand, "wouldn't have got you anywhere but it would have been pleasanter. More feminine."

"The last thing your masculine ego needs is encouragement," Anthea retorted. She made for the door and he, arriving with her, put his hand over hers on the handle and displayed his teeth in a very genial, patronising smile.

"Happily," he said, "the masculine ego has plenty in reserve. Take care, my proud beauty."

"Huh!" said Anthea, and they went downstairs to the hall, where Sir Andrew Gibb was waiting for her.

Jock placed the glasses on the nearest table, refused Sir Andrew's invitation to dinner, winked at Alec, who was in Morgan's place behind the bar, and went out. He got into his car, glancing at the petrol gauge as he switched on his engine, and at the gates, instead of turning left to the village and the Tully, turned right and drove along the road by which Anthea had come less than a week ago. After ten miles or so he left the road and proceeded cautiously along a track whose surface presented alternating hazards of boulders and canyons, and at the end of it he drew up at a small tidy croft. A small tidy girl of about twenty appeared at the door, drawn by the unexpected sound of a motor vehicle, and gaped at him with dropped jaw.

"Hallo, Peggy," said Jock.

Sir Andrew enjoyed his dinner. The only way in which Anthea could repay the kind courtesy which gave her countenance and comfort was to put aside all thought of trouble. She was composed and beautiful, charmingly companionable, and her cream-coloured frock and shining hair were far removed from any suggestion of sackcloth and ashes. In a quiet way they were undoubtedly the gayest diners in the room, and Louisa, who waited on them in place of Alec, who was taking the place of Morgan, beamed upon them with warm approval.

The three Americans did not linger over their meal and got up to leave the dining-room as soon as they had finished. Senator Cleever was anxious that his blameless fellow-guests should not feel that he regarded them with hostility. Though it was true that he had suffered outrage on Scottish soil, nobody knew better than he that guilt must not be allowed to touch the innocent and that signs of tension are unbecoming in social life. He was going straight upstairs and having them bring coffee to his room, but he took care not to hurry and greeted everyone within reach as he went, even veering from his direct route sufficiently to tell Anthea he was glad to see she had pleasant company for dinner and to urge her earnestly to have a good night's rest. Mr. Scudamore followed the Senator. Chet followed Mr. Scudamore, but choosing a suitable moment he doubled back and rather diffidently approached Sir Andrew's table.

"Good evening, Miss Logan. Good evening, sir." He greeted them with two formal little bows and he looked so unhappy, so much as if in one day he had left his youth behind, that Anthea's heart ached.

"Chet, I'm so glad to see you," she said. "I've been thinking about you and wanting to talk to you all day."

"You have?" he said. "Well, that's mighty . . . I'd have thought you had plenty to do thinking about yourself and you wouldn't be liking me very much. I wondered could we have a little talk, but—" he turned to Sir Andrew—"I don't feel, sir, Miss Logan and I should be alone at all. Would you . . .?"

Sir Andrew glanced at Anthea and got up. "Miss Logan and I are going to have our coffee in the lounge," he said. "Will you join us?"

"Thank you, sir," said Chet with his bow. "I'd be glad to."

Saturday evenings were a little depressing at Balgarvie. Absolutely nothing happened on Sunday, and a day so blank was apt to cast its shadow before. In his early days Mr. Saunders had suggested films but the experiment was a failure, most of the guests regarding it as an officious attack on the liberty of the subject and preferring to sleep under newspapers or blink drowsily at television. Tonight TV drew a crowded house. While the peace of Balgarvie was disturbed by crime and rumours of crime it at least provided an object on which the eye could rest without embarrassment. There were very few people in the lounge, therefore, but Sir Francis and Lady Vine were there, both reading; and, near enough to exchange remarks, were the Carruthers, at a loose end. Mr. Peachey had disappeared immediately after dinner, and Bryce and Vida, smoking and looking scornfully at *Tatlers*, seemed lost without him.

They raised their heads as Sir Andrew led his little party in and Anthea, with a slight heightening of colour, received a long cold stare from Bryce and from Vida an agonised smile. "This is hell, darling," it said, "but what could I do?"

"Do you know about that one?" Anthea looked at Chet as they sat down, with a tiny inclination of her head towards the remains of the smile. "Yes," he said gloomily, he had heard about it. "It adds confusion, doesn't it," she said.

Chet sighed and passed her his packet of Luckies, while the head waiter—more active this evening than he liked—served their coffee. "You know," he said when the man had left them, "I can't believe any of this is happening. I just *know*, all it was, I took my eye off the ball and dropped that letter someplace. What it should have done was just turn up this morning a bit soggy and muddy, maybe, so I had to type it again. How in hell it got this way—bringing trouble on you, passing *via* that dope Morgan to the Manse, raising an unknown guy and unidentified footprints in the grounds . . ." He made a despairing gesture. "It beats me. It's not real."

Sir Andrew had been dealing tenderly with the one very

good cigar he allowed himself after dinner and it was now alight and smoking beautifully. "I agree that it is unreal in so far as it has pointed to an organised plot," he said. "But I do still wonder if Morgan may not have taken it in the first place—just supposing that you didn't put it in your pocket but left it in your room. It seems he has been able to prowl about the house freely enough, and as they say nowadays, he's politically conscious."

"But what would he do with it?" asked Chet.

"Well, he might not consider that very clearly." Sir Andrew smiled slightly. "He no doubt thought, however he got it, that he would be able to make some very clever use of it."

"No doubt," said Chet. He shook his head. "But I still don't believe it was stolen—not at first. I just know I lost it." He looked miserably at Anthea. "And I can't tell you what I feel about it."

"Chet, if you lost it, it was sheer accident," she said. "Perhaps partly because I was off-course and worrying you with my troubles. He was very, very good to me yesterday evening," she told Sir Andrew.

Sir Andrew could well believe it. Chet muttered that she had plenty on her plate without him adding to-day's trouble, and then, more articulately, added that he hoped she wouldn't think too badly of Senator Cleever. "It's quite true," he said, "they're really worried all the time about security. They're kind of conditioned so it's the first thing they think about."

"One of the features of the case to-day," said Sir Andrew, "has been the leading suspect's readiness to see the reasonableness of the investigation."

Anthea thought that though the Senator was self-important and basically obtuse—thick, as Lawrence would say—he had kept his human feelings as he bumbled his way up. She bore him no grudge, but she felt a good deal less cordial towards Mr. Scudamore, who, she was sure, had abandoned human feelings long ago, and she was worried about Chet.

"How does this affect you?" she asked him.

He shrugged his shoulders. "Well—it's a black. I guess what happens depends on how it comes out. But I don't know if I'll wait to be fired. I told you there's the business at home, and right now it looks pretty good. You've got to take root some time."

To take root, marry a wife and raise a family was what Chet was designed to do, Anthea thought, but the theme could hardly be developed in the presence of a third person, and before she could find something sufficiently non-committal and encouraging to say, he turned to her with a lightening of his gloom.

"You never told me I was talking to a writer," he said. "Why'n't you give me that publisher's address instead of a bank with nothing in it?"

Anthea said, "It would have been like giving you the address of a house I *might* live in some day," but they were still, all three, talking about her book and its future when, a few minutes later, the door opened and Mr. Peachey came in carrying a generous tumbler of whisky and soda. He looked with faint surprise at Sir Andrew's cheerful little party and smiled at them collectively as he went across to the Carruthers.

"Are you *still* at it?" asked Vida in her drawling voice.

"Well, yes and no," he replied. "Not *en masse*. The police have gone to headquarters—to confer with their deity, the chief constable, I believe—and Gregorson has vanished without trace, but they're all supposed to be coming back."

Bryce Carruthers was heard to begin a sourly funny speech to the effect that he could more easily believe that the local police were slow than that they were sure. By this time everything imaginable must have been said again and again and again. . . .

His voice as usual was loud, and Anthea suddenly felt that she could stand no more of this day. She excused herself, saying truly that she was tired, and got up, thanking Sir Andrew and giving Chet a friendly pat on the arm. "Good night," she said smiling at both of them, and with a general "Good night" in the direction of the others she went composedly out of the room.

Everybody, more or less openly, watched her go, and a little silence was broken by Vida. "Oh God!" she said in her deepest tones. "We laugh and talk, and all the time— I simply never stop thinking about Anthea. I mean she keeps up marvellously but—"

Mr. Peachey for once was awkward. "Oh," he said, "I don't think we need take too gloomy a—"

"I feel so absolutely awful about that evidence of mine. I mean I had to—I *couldn't* not tell them, and yet—"

"Will you excuse me, sir?" said Chet to Sir Andrew. He was already on his feet and Sir Andrew put his hands on the arms of his chair to hoist himself up. "Yes," he said, "I think I'll—Yes, Alec?"

Alec, who had materialised quietly beside him, put an unobtrusive hand under his elbow and assisted with the hoist while he murmured, "Superintendent Wilkie's compliments, sir. He would be obliged if you could spare him a few minutes."

"Certainly," said Sir Andrew. "Thank you."

"I think you too, Mr. Hart," said Alec and went on to murmur the same message in the ear of Mr. Peachey, who was already alert and waiting for it.

The three men went out and Lady Vine glanced at her husband. They also left the room before the speculation in the Carruthers's eyes could be uttered.

Lawrence, off-stage since dinner, had spent the time agreeably in the wings, helping Louisa, who was on late duty, and hobnobbing with Alec in the bar. The bar had access to the pantry, which was convenient, and business was slack. It also had a comprehensive view of the hall. The student staff had been shaken and felt solemn when they heard that one of their number, even Morgan whom they could not like, was actually in the hands of the police, but in a way they were rather enjoying what Alec called the crime wave. Nobody could take Senator Cleever's bits of paper very seriously, and though there was a flap on about Miss Logan she was so obviously cast for the role of heroine that they had no doubt she would come through triumphantly—probably to the sound of wedding bells.

"I'm glad I came," said Louisa. "It's really a splendid crime. No blood or bodies but—"

"Neat but not gory," said Alec and produced his smug laugh. "*Huh*, huh, huh!"

"Huh," Lawrence and Louisa responded politely, and Lawrence said, "But if kicks are what you go for, Louisa, you'd better try elsewhere next year. I've been coming to Balgarvie for more years than I care to remember and this is the first time anything's happened at all."

"Oh, I don't know," said Alec. "There was the goon last year who sprayed Tom Robertson and the dog with shot. Tom had six pellets in his leg. Still—it wasn't technically a crime, of course. Who dunnit, Lawrence? Have they any clue yet?"

Lawrence didn't think anybody had dunnit—on purpose, but Louisa rejected so dull a theory. "It was Morgan and Ness," she said confidently. "Morgan for sordid motives—blackmail? Ness seeking martyrdom."

"No," said Lawrence and Alec.

"No? They were both arrested for sitting down somewhere, you know. They're very dedicated. At least Ness is. Actually I wouldn't be surprised if Morgan veered, after this. He's just the type for those Nazi people."

Lawrence remarked that Morgan would probably have little opportunity to veer effectively for some time. "I don't know who dunnit," he went on. "Not Ness, though. I know she's an ass, but she just wouldn't touch anything remotely like stealing for any cause."

"An ass but an honest ass," said Alec. "And Presbyterian to boot. All the same you may have something, Louisa. Morgan isn't hampered by principles and—"

He broke off and with practised ease rearranged his face while Lawrence and Louisa faded into the pantry. "Good evening, sir," he said to Mr. Peachey, observing that he looked a bit rubbed round the edges. "What can I get you?"

Mr. Peachey was worn but he was still awake. He said, "Double whisky, please, Alec," and glanced blandly towards the pantry. "Getting anywhere?"

"No, sir, not noticeably." Alec, measuring the whisky, was equally bland. "Soda, sir? But of course"—he was frank and reasonable—"we're all trying."

"Yes," said Mr. Peachey with a sigh. "I'm sure you are. Well—keep at it. You never know." He leant his elbow on the bar and nodded to Louisa and Lawrence, who drifted forward again. "I suppose you've heard about the fellow in the grounds," he said. "All the staff *have* been checked— questioned, haven't they? Nobody away or anything?"

"Only Peggy," said Louisa. "The little one. She's gone home for the week-end and we all forgot about her. I only remembered when Mr. Gregorson was sort of going through everybody again before dinner, but actually she went off too early. She was off duty before six."

Mr. Peachey nodded and taking his elbow off the bar went away.

"He's not interested in poor Peggy, is he?" observed Louisa. "Greg paid more attention to her."

"Can't think why," said Alec. "If she found a masked man with a gun in one of the rooms she'd merely say 'pardon' and scuttle away."

"Well, what would you do?" Louisa asked reasonably. "Of course she'd scuttle, but if you asked her three months later she'd describe the man to the last notch in his gun."

"Dah!" said Alec. "She never utters. The ultimate rabbit."

"I'm not so sure," said Louisa. "I think she's a dark horse—or a dark rabbit perhaps. Nobody ever sees her, but I suspect hidden depths in Peggy."

A few minutes later Anthea, in her cream-coloured dress, came across the hall, her walk upright and graceful as usual but her head drooping a little.

"Hi!" said Lawrence and ducked under the flap of the bar. "Come and have a drink."

"Hi to you." She smiled at him and Alec, and a more distant view of black-and-white uniform and shining blonde hair. "No drink, thank you. You overestimate my capacity. What are you all doing?"

Louisa, emerging from the pantry, said they were helping Alec—"He's rather lost, poor thing"—while her bright eyes took in Anthea's appearance with the comprehensive accuracy which she had attributed to the absent Peggy. If she felt as the heroine of the Balgarvie drama looked, a drink would make her sick. "Miss Logan," she said in her sweet high voice, "it's such a miserable chilly sort of night, would you like a flask of hot milk or something? I've got everything here—Ovaltine, Horlicks . . .?"

"Louisa," said Anthea, "you're an angel. Horlicks in bed—heaven!"

"I'll bring it up," said Louisa.

"Have you plenty of cigarettes?" said Alec.

"I'll come up with you in case of Communists," said Lawrence.

"Three angels," she said, taking a packet of cigarettes from Alec.

They smiled at her and then looked suddenly alert at the sound of the rapid steps in the passage leading from the yard door.

It was Jock who emerged from the twilight of the back regions, and seeing the group by the bar he made a spacious gesture of greeting and came straight over.

"Louisa, you got it," he said, and, putting both hands on the bar, leaned over and planted a smacking kiss on her cheek.

Louisa smiled radiantly. "She did—?"

"She did. Why the hell you didn't think of it before—but never mind. She went off duty at six, but her boy was hanging about from half past three or so and they had to wait for her father to fetch them, which he didn't do till after half past seven." He turned to Anthea and took her hand. "Anthea—we have the facts—"

Her lip was caught between her teeth and he broke off.

"Come and I'll tell you about it," he said, taking her arm. "Alec, will you find Sir Andrew, Mr. Peachey and the Yanks and tell them the Superintendent wants them?"

"Right," said Alec. "Watch the bar, will you, Lawrence. . . .?"

In one of the gun-rooms, which Colonel Garvie had sketchily furnished as his office, Jock told Anthea his story. Acting on the conviction, shared by most of those concerned with the case, that the facts they needed were perfectly simple and probably under their noses, he had gone to the pantry between the evening conference and his talk with her and begged his friends there to exert their wits and their memories as never before. He had described the

243

stranger, Anthea's blushing boy, and it was as they went through the list of staff with him in mind that Peggy had come to light.

"But the times are wrong," said Biddy. "You say this boy was seen at half past three or four and Peggy was on duty till six. But she did go off then and that's too early for the letter, isn't it?"

Jock agreed. He went away, rather dispirited, and Louisa ran after him.

"Greg," she said, rather pink and breathless, "I didn't want to say anything before the others and *please* don't make too much of it—it may be nonsense—but I do think Peggy was up to something yesterday. She was excited and sort of scatty. She's paralytically shy—she hardly ever speaks—but I think she's got a boy: you can tell, somehow. And if he's anything like her he might lurk about for hours waiting for her."

"So I went to see," Jock told Anthea in the gun-room, "and there they both were—both blushing—and that's just what he'd done. They found the letter on the path and knew Hart must have dropped it because they saw him come out of the garden. The rule is that anything found is taken to Saunders, but Peggy was not very keen to see Saunders. She had told him her father was coming to fetch her at six, when he wasn't in fact due till half past seven. So she sneaked in and gave the letter to the first pal she met, Morgan, who obligingly promised not to give her away."

"But," said Anthea, irrelevantly worried, "what did the boy *do* all that time? It wasn't more than half past three when I dropped him."

Jock laughed. "They're getting engaged this week-end. He'd come off his ship at Carse and had nothing else to do. He just waited. Peggy nipped out from time to time when she could and joined him finally when she was free. They were perfectly happy—sustained by love and chocolate bars; but they had to make a quick getaway when you and Hart loomed up, heading for their nice, secluded bench."

Peggy. Anthea visualised the pretty, shrinking little person of her chambermaid and the bashful, patient boy. Peggy had told a fib and daren't face Mr. Saunders. . . . Morgan was vindictive. . . . But it was only if you were yourself vulnerable that such chances were dangerous. . . .

She had put her hands up to her face and stood staring at the ground, pale, unemotional and remote. Jock felt she was miles away. Her stillness frightened him a little. He put his arms round her and held her, pressing her head against him.

"It's over, girl," he said. "You've been so good—I'm so bloody proud of you. . . . Anthea, it's over. Randal, everything. Now you have the future—your writing, friends . . . love, darling."

Anthea put up her hands and drew his face down. She held his cheek against hers and then kissed it. "Dear Jock," she said. "Thank you. You're the very best," and before he could move to stop her she was gone.

CHAPTER 18

As Anthea remembered from her last visit, the McNaughtons were good in church. Mrs. McNaughton and Ian were already in the Manse pew when she went in. Ian, who was at the end, stepped out to let her pass with no modification of his weekday grin, and his mother merely gave her a brief smile, moved along a bit and let her be. The Minister, too, was better in church than out of it. He entered the pulpit to praise God and shame the devil and he did so with dignity and uncompromising conviction: if his vision in mundane matters was narrow it was clear and penetrating here.

But Anthea did not hear much of his sermon. Besides the cousins there were more "kent faces," as Balgarvie would call them, in this stark little church than she would have seen in any other church in the world. Jock was there, sitting with his head thrown back in an attitude she remembered—it could mean that he was listening or that his mind was miles away—and Tom, the young underkeeper, sang in the choir. Sir Andrew sat serenely still, Colonel Garvie—driven to worship, perhaps, by the alarms and excursions of yesterday—fidgeted. The doctor and his wife were a solid, reassuring couple and Stewart and Biddy sat together very peacefully in the gallery. She felt peaceful herself: soothed and unmolested. It was a pity—it was very sad—that she had to leave this place and these people, but yesterday had underlined what she already knew to be true: you can put up with almost anything if you have to. Go ahead, a step at a time, without thinking too much about it and "as thy days so shall thy strength be."

Lunch after the service was eased by the presence of Ian. His kindly, unassertive nature was easier to live with than

Ness's fervours, and though he never thought of managing anybody he managed his parents with some skill. He had got over his shyness with his cousin Anthea and liked her very much. Also, in spite of his dislike of what he had heard of him, he could not help feeling that his cousin Randal was an interesting variant on the usual run of relations and regretting that he had never even seen him.

It did not occur to him in this family party to avoid delicate subjects. Interested and unembarrassed he talked and asked questions about the progress of yesterday's mystery, displaying, to the scandalisation of his parents, some disappointment that it had ended so tamely. Not, he assured Anthea, that he would have liked to see her in chains, but given the *right* criminal . . .

"Who do you favour?" she asked him. "Jock—Greg—chose Mr. Scudamore."

No, Ian thought not Mr. Scudamore. A bit too obvious He preferred Mr. Carruthers. Mr. Carruthers was the rudest man he had ever ghillied for, and then you could tack on Mrs. as an accomplice, and even—stretching it—Mr. Peachey. He smiled at Anthea and asked what she thought Randal would be doing. "Do you know where he went?"

Mr. and Mrs. McNaughton shied visibly. Though they had come to feel that they had done wrong in avoiding it, they had intended to broach the subject of Randal on some private occasion, leading up to it gradually and with care. But as Anthea replied to Ian, telling him about the job Randal had been doing before his arrest and what she imagined he might be doing now, they gradually relaxed and the atmosphere became more comfortable than at any time since she came.

It was not entirely without awkwardness. As the cold beef and salad were removed Cousin Walter spoke of his regret that they, he and his wife, had lost touch with her, that they had not gone to her "in her trouble," and Cousin Maud was emotional as she helped the home-grown raspberries.

"At the time," said Mr. McNaughton, "it was difficult to see what we could have done, and the expense, of course, was a consideration. You had our prayers."

"Yes," said Anthea. "There wasn't anything to be done, and—perhaps we were wrong—all we wanted was to get away and . . ." She hesitated and then concluded abruptly, "It's the sort of thing one has to cope with oneself."

"With God's help," said Mr. NcNaughton. "But it is painful to us now to know how much alone you were. If we had realised how completely your mother had broken down . . . However, that is past." It was good news, he went on, that she had discovered in herself this talent for writing. It was an outlet, an interest which would be of particular value to her since she had not married.

"It was perhaps hardly to be expected that you would," he continued calmly. Cousin Maud made a small protesting sound and Ian looked surprised, but he passed on, feeling, apparently, that enough had been said under that head. "Nevertheless I am convinced that within a very few months you will return to teaching. That is a career of real usefulness and you would have time enough for your writing. In my opinion the discipline of regular professional work can do nothing but good." He held up his hand in a pulpit gesture. "It is a basis on which the freer work of a writer may most safely—I do not use the word purely in an economic sense—may most safely be built."

But, Cousin Maud said quickly, there was no *hurry* to find another teaching post. Anthea must stay at the Manse. "As long as you like, dear, and you can write to your heart's content. You could have a fire in your bedroom or—" a better idea struck her—"you could work in here, perhaps. We only use it for meals."

"I don't," Anthea began, and as she paused, searching for words, she met the dancing eyes of Ian.

"Greg," he said, addressing them all cheerfully and factually, "sometimes works all night and then sleeps all day. Sometimes he eats ordinary meals and sometimes he lives on coffee and tobacco—oh, and dates. He says it's quite true you can get along for ages on dates and brown bread. It sounds a bit daft to other people but that's the way books get written, I suppose."

Anthea saw "health" in Cousin Maud's eye and "self-discipline" in Cousin Walter's. So did Ian.

"You'd never stand it, you know," he told them. "Mum would keep ringing the dinner bell and Dad would say, 'Isn't that girl in bed *yet*?'"

Even the Minister smiled at a very fair imitation of his severe voice and Mrs. McNaughton looked fondly at her son. "I suppose we do fuss," she confessed. "Though there seems quite a lot of fussing we don't do."

"Oh, you're not so bad," Ian said kindly. "But it would never do for Anthea. I wouldn't think she'd want to live with anybody. Greg doesn't."

If Anthea could not be wholly delighted by his view of writing as essentially a solitary, unlivable-with occupation she thought it was a true one, at least for many writers, and she was grateful for his help. She said she didn't think she would go back to teaching—"I'm not really good at it" — but she had heard that there was an opening for her, or a re-opening with the *Trumpeter*. "I think I'll take it," she said and was suddenly, as she spoke, convinced that it was the obvious, the right, thing to do.

"I have never been to London," said Ian hopefully.

"Just as soon as I have a flat and one of those put-you-up sofa things," said Anthea, "I'll invite you and we'll do the town."

When she left the Manse she had accepted a renewed invitation to remove herself to it from the hotel. Even for the one night or two that she meant to stay in Balgarvie the thought of the hotel—Mr. Peachey, the Carruthers, Mr. Saunders—was intolerable. But the Manse, too, had drawbacks. "So long as you are at home, you will conform to the ways of the house," she remembered Cousin Walter telling Ness, and as she got into her car she was reflecting that independence was death to adaptability. There was nothing she wanted less than to conform to anybody's ways: which, she reminded herself, fitted quite well in her circumstances.

She did not drive far. Once more she drew up at the head of the Water Wynd, and leaving her church-going hat in the car began a leisurely descent of steps and path. On his way up was a sturdy figure dressed in Sunday trousers, navy-blue jersey and cloth cap, the fisherman's Sunday-afternoon uniform. It was Ecky Soutar, the skipper of *Lea-Rig*, and as they approached each other it became clear that she was to be greeted.

"Aye," he said with the sideways nod she had seen accorded to others. "Braw day." She agreed that it was fine and found that the conversation was to continue. Mr. Soutar had stopped and turned round as if it was customary to talk facing the sea.

"I hear tell ye had some on-goin's up at the Hoose yesterday," he said unexpectedly. "Wis that ane o' thae Americans ye had doon here a twa-three days back?"

Anthea said it was. Ecky said regretfully that if he'd known, he would have taken a better look at him.

"That was the day *Lea-Rig*'s shaft broke," Anthea reminded him. "Is it mended?"

"Oh aye," he said. "We'll be oot the nicht." He gave her a sudden gap-toothed grin, brief and slanting. "I mind ye fine, bidin' at the Manse when ye were a lassie. I minded ye

250

as sune as I saw ye, but I never heard yer name. Queer thing." He jerked his head in the direction of the Tully. "Greg there, first day he cam' tae Balgarvie he asked at me did I ken onybody the name o' Logan. There was a Logan kept the draper's, but that was long back. Then there was a Mistress McCleish took in visitors for a while, she micht a' had Logans bidin', but she dee'd. I never thocht o' you."

"No, you wouldn't," said Anthea.

They talked for a minute or two about the fishing and the harbour and he asked if she had ever been out in one of the boats. She never had, she said. She had never seen Balgarvie from the sea.

"Is that a fact?" he said with condescending surprise. "Ye'll need tae get a sail ane o' thae days," he added affably and prepared to move on; remarking that she would have been at the Manse to her dinner and concluding, "Greg's doon there at his boat. Cheerio."

"Cheerio," said Anthea and went on down, with her ideas about the harbour's indifference to strangers somewhat disrupted.

The sun was shining and Balgarvie Harbour was wrapped in Sabbath peace. The children were in Sunday School or otherwise disposed of, and on such a day as this, when the tide decreed that the boats went out as soon as it was Monday morning, most of those concerned were asleep. Anthea walked round quietly, looking with love and a conscious storing up of what she saw: at the boats filling the basins, their masts just moving; at the gulls, as peaceable now as the men too old to go to sea who sat on the benches gazing at the water.

When she reached the angle where the small boats lay, the dog Dan got up from the warm stones to welcome her and Jock appeared, unfolding his length from *Skua*'s cabin as he had done less than a week ago. But to-day he too was

251

Sundayfied, less piratical. He no longer wore the suit she had seen in church but he had kept his tie on and his flannels were comparatively clean.

"Want to come aboard?" he said, and then shook his head at her smart suit. "No, we're not up to it. Willie does a good job but there's no use kidding ourselves we're a yacht."

He climbed up neatly on to the pier beside her and they strolled on.

"I thought you'd be working," Anthea said, "after losing the whole of yesterday. What about the output schedule?"

Jock said, "The hell with the output schedule. I'm suffering from—quite enjoying, really—reaction, profound lassitude. Are you?" He looked round at her. "You look very calm."

"Oh I am. . . . I've just had a unique experience."

"What was that?"

"I've held converse with a fisherman. Skipper Soutar, no less. I didn't know they ever noticed strangers. I know better now but I'm still sort of awed. As if I'd been spoken to by Margot Fonteyn or Ted Dexter."

"What did you talk about?"

She told him. "It's nice of him to be apologetic because he couldn't tell you my name six years ago," she said, "but I don't know why he's so matey *now* when he never even looked at me before."

"Ah," said Jock. "Ecky's romantic."

"Oh, that's it, is it? I find it upsetting, I must say. It was so comfortable to feel invisible."

"Well, you can give them credit for allowing you to feel it," he pointed out. "They don't miss anything—at Balgarvie you have to make the most of whatever God sends in the way of novelty—but their scrutiny isn't ill-natured as a rule. And it's quite frank. 'Whatna lassie was yon ye were speakin' tae on the pier?' asked everybody after you cropped up on Tuesday. Which suggests the thought that we've provided enough sensation for one afternoon. Come to the Tully and you can make the tea."

"Wouldn't they suspect the worst?" asked Anthea.

"Oh no," he said. "They know I'm respectable."

They walked up the path, Dan padding ahead, stopping now and again to make sure they were following all right; and in the Tully they made tea—a simple repast with cake left over from Friday's party and biscuits in a tin.

It was characteristic of the way in which their minds marched that almost nothing was said about the crisis of yesterday. There was no need for spoken agreement: to both of them it was a thing past and best forgotten—as far as possible. But when, as they were drinking last cups, Jock went back to Friday night he did so with an assumption that the day between had brought about some change, not, perhaps, in Anthea's own position, but in their joint position. After yesterday any pretence that they were not at least intimate friends was impossible.

"What are you going to do?" he asked, lying back in his chair, his long legs stretched out. "Are you still in residence at the House?"

Anthea shuddered. "No. At least I haven't left officially. I'm going along now to pack and pay and collect the cash from the safe—if it's still there. I'm going to the Manse for a night or two."

"And then?" said Jock, watching the smoke rising from his cigarette.

"Well, I've told the McNaughtons I'm going to London." She gave an involuntary laugh. "They had a splendid idea. I should stay at the Manse and do my writing—in the dining-room, Cousin Maud thought, between meals. I had to say something—But in fact I think—did William really mean it when he said he wanted me back or was he just having an emotional moment?"

Jock said that William had certainly meant it. "I don't know what he had in mind. I don't suppose he had anything specific, but he'll undoubtedly give you a job—if you want it."

"Yes, well I think I do," said Anthea. She drew on her cigarette, frowning a little, and went on with a firmness which suggested that she was forestalling opposition, "It seems sort of meant . . . it fits. And I've been out of the world so long I think it would be a good thing to be in London working with people again. And of course it solves the financial problem."

"All good, well-thought-out reasons," said Jock politely. "It was fascinating to watch them occur one by one. Would you like any more? I could produce a few—but I dare say you have enough." Her mouth opened, but before she could speak he sat up and launched a new and apparently irrelevant topic. "Anthea, you're sitting on your bench on the pier. You know the little row of cottages on the left, nearest here?" Blinking at his sudden swerve she said she did. "One of them is empty. It belongs to Ecky Soutar. His mother lived in it but she died, full of years, a few months ago and Ecky wants a tenant. Two rooms and a scullery so the rent's not high. Five bob a week in fact."

Anthea got up and walked straight out of the house and across the grass. By the low wall she stood and stared down the hill at the meek little row of cottage roofs, red like the Tully, which made a diminishing tail to the harbour buildings.

Ten minutes later she went slowly back to the house. Jock was still spread out in his chair. "You would observe the privy," he said. "Outside, but W. What do you think?"

She shook her head. "No. I'm afraid not."

"Why not? It's tiny and without cons, mod. or otherwise, but that wouldn't put you off."

"No," said Anthea again. "It's not that. . . ." Of course it was perfect, that cottage. Exactly what she wanted—everything she wanted. Looking at it she had wondered if it was possible that she could live in it, even for a few months, with Jock up here and the McNaughtons at the Manse: the harbour at her door. . . .

But it was not possible. If she lived in that cottage she would be looking out for Jock's tall figure and black head all day, thinking about him all night. "I don't think Balgarvie's the place for me," she said. "I did wonder about it, but . . ."

"But?" said Jock.

She glanced at him nervously. "*But* I think I'd do better to go back to London. I think I can do a job for William— not a big one—and have enough left for my own—"

"Boloney!" said Jock. "You *know* what you want to do. You've enough money to risk it—why give up?" She had not sat down, and he got up and took her by the shoulders. "Anthea, what's the *matter* with you?" He gave her an impatient shake. "If you want to be on your own—to concentrate everything on your work—that's understandable; but why the hell should you cut yourself off from the place you like and your friends and your perfectly good plan? What are you jibbing at?"

"I'm *not* jibbing," cried Anthea. "I'm—"

"Ass!" said Jock. One arm went tightly round her, the other hand took her, not too gently, by the chin and he kissed her, not a kindly or amicable kiss but the kiss of a man in love who has been pushed rather far. Her hands went up to resist but having no effect went on to his shoulders and round his neck.

"*There* you are, you see," she said a few minutes later, shaken, breathless and cross. "We want to kiss—to love each other. How much work would I do down in that cottage with you up here? How much would you do?"

"Easy," said Jock. "Live up here with me and—after a lit-tle—we'll both be able to work. My darling Anthea, you've said it—we love each other, we're deep in love. Let's be married as soon as McNaughton can lay it on."

There was no use trying to deny that they were in love and she didn't try. "But you can be in love," she cried, "and yet know that marriage would be wrong. It's only very young people who assume that it inevitably follows." She saw his face change and with a sound of distress put her hand to his cheek. "Jock—I didn't mean that nastily. You know it, don't you?"

Her hand was disregarded. "I know it," he said after a moment, "but it slipped out—out of a full heart the mouth speaketh. You can't forgive me, can you." It was a flat state-ment, not a question.

Anthea stared at him, puzzled. "But I have forgiven you! I told you—I've never felt any need to forgive you."

"Maybe," said Jock. "But what kind of forgiveness?"

"How many kinds are there? What *is* forgiveness anyway?"

"I can't tell you in one word. It's a big subject to put into words. But I can tell you this: if your forgiveness is a saintly smile, a condescending word and a closed door, you can keep it. I don't want it." He was still holding her—at arm's length—and he now gave her another shake. "The hell with it, Anthea! If you'd really forgiven me your hand would have been in mine that first day on the pier, and that's the truth." He dropped his hands from her shoulders and moved away.

"It is *not* the truth," snapped Anthea. She glared at his angry face and let her own temper fly. "I must say this is a bit much! It's nothing to do with forgiveness. Why the hell *should* I fall into your arms? What do you think I am? A piece of property to be shoved into a cupboard and taken out again at your convenience?"

"Ah!" Jock said nastily. "Now we're getting at it. Pride, of course. And cheap distortion of facts which you understand perfectly well—as well as I do." He put a hand to his head and pushed it impatiently through his hair. "Hell! I'm sorry. . . . But, Anthea—if any girl was ever capable of thinking straight you are. Why don't you do it? We're neither of us naive enough to believe that 'love conquers all': that everything—wisdom, integrity, expedience—must give way to it. But when people love each other as we do, it should surely conquer pride or—"

"It's *not* pride."

"Very well then. Silly scruples. Heroics."

There was a pause. Anthea turned away and began vaguely looking for her belongings—jacket, cigarettes, handbag—wondering how they had got like this: quarrelling with savage bitterness. She had behind her a kind of bank account, a balance of thought which had been accumulating since the time when she had been able to accept Jock's need to be free, to put his work first, as a good and valid reason for her heartbreak. Even before Randal's disgrace isolated her she had known that it was her misfortune to be the kind of girl who, having given her heart, never gets it back. The ideal of freedom, independence, had been forced upon her, so to speak, twice over. It was on independence that she had built her hopes and the events of yesterday had proved the soundness of the principle. Only by keeping herself to herself could the havoc left behind by Randal be contained. Already it had spread; merely by coming to Balgarvie, relaxing so far, she had involved the McNaughtons, Jock himself, Chet Hart—Morgan. . . .

Jock began to speak again. He had taken his pipe from his pocket and, after the customary sharp blast, was filling it with irritable stabbing fingers, hardly aware of what he did but driven to do something. "I know what's in your

257

mind," he said, "and I don't want it any more than I want your forgiveness. I can protect myself—and you—from the effects of Randal's piddling little crime a damn' sight better than you can. I don't deny your courage, but if you want to know I think you've been wrong from the start and William was right. You should have stayed where you were and gone on with your work. But you—and your mother—reacted as women do: emotionally. You can't be blamed, I suppose, being women. You let it engulf you, and it's that, not Randal, that's dangerous—damaging."

"I don't know what you—I don't understand," said Anthea.

She was staring blankly at the pipe, and as if he suddenly noticed its irrelevance he put it on the mantelpiece, turning away from her as he spoke. "Randal isn't responsible for Hart's career or that stupid clot Morgan slipping over the edge. . . . Nobody can be an island—that's a platitude. And you can't escape from your background, Anthea. If you try it you're as dangerous as hell to yourself and everybody who comes in contact with you. You've no stability."

She was silent. It was so utterly unexpected. Half stunned she made an involuntary gesture, pushing away a wriggling, worm-like doubt, and with fumbling hands put on her jacket. Jock made no move to help her. He faced her, one hand left on the mantelpiece.

"Well?" he said. "Look at it. Isn't it true?"

"No," said Anthea. "It isn't true. You don't know what you're talking about. You're looking at it from outside and making it up—like a writer—to suit yourself. You're just angry."

"That's true anyway," Jock said grimly. "I am angry. I wouldn't be if I didn't know that you could see it straight if you had tried. But I've carried the burden of my own sin for seven years—I shouldn't have let you love me. I'm damned if I'm going to carry your martyrdom."

"Nobody's asking you—" Anthea began hotly, but he shook his head and taking his hand from the mantelpiece walked past her, surprisingly, to the door.

"I'll tell you what I'm going to do," he said, "and it's final: not open to discussion. I'm leaving Balgarvie. I'll offer you two alternatives. You can buy the Tully at the price I paid for it— a hundred and thirty-five pounds: or I will make it over to you—legally, by deed of gift." He glanced briefly at her horrified face. "If your pride can't stomach either of these proposals the place can fall down. It's yours. I never want to see it again."

The door opened and shut. There was a scrabbling of claws as Dan gathered himself up from the floor. He hurried to the door, sniffing at it with small whining sounds, and then looked back at Anthea and broke into agitated barking.

From the Tully Anthea went to the hotel, from the hotel she returned to the Manse, and soon after supper she retired to her room carrying a hot-water bottle, a glass of milk and two aspirin tablets. "In case you don't get to sleep at once, dear," said Mrs. McNaughton, pressing these comforts upon her. "But I think you will," she added encouragingly, "and nobody will disturb you." She was glad of the promise but she had never felt less like sleep. Moreover she had no intention of going to bed, and she spent a few moments in repentance and mental apology to Cousin Maud whom she loved but so frequently found it necessary to deceive. But how could she tell that kind, anxious woman that she was going down to the harbour at midnight? And that the last thing she wanted was that Ness should put on a muffler and tramp down with her . . .?

She put the bottle in the bed, lost the aspirins and drank the milk in a fit of absent-mindedness: and as she moved about the room her thoughts moved too, in a kind of winding-up process. Already the last week had receded and became a dim, rather unreal memory. In this familiar spare-bedroom it was quite difficult to believe that Balgarvie House existed, and it had been evident when she went to collect her things that the House was finding it easy to forget her. The disturbance was over, nonsense had been eradicated, and the place was itself again. Even Chet, whom she saw for a moment, had been a little embarrassed: but if it was unflattering to have become the girl over whom he had once dangerously lost his head, it was a relief to know that, after all, his career was not seriously affected. The incident was over. Anthea sat down in the hard little armchair which the Manse provided for the comfort of its visitors and turned from the pink roses and blue ribbons of the wall-paper, the staring picture of Lake Geneva and the soggy one of highland cattle, to the garden, the huddle of roofs and the sea.

It was a few minutes before midnight when she crept out of the Manse and hurried down the Church Wynd. There was no sign of life about the harbour. Lights showed here and there, very subdued lights, but the Sabbath was being observed so rigorously that she almost believed it was all a mistake. The boats were not going out: everybody was asleep. She walked forward on to the quay very quietly, feeling that she was offending the Almighty just by being there, and saw Lawrence coming towards her.

"Hi," he said in a whisper which sounded as guilty as she felt. "I wondered if you might come down." And because he had not seen her since the solving of the mystery and remembered how weary—sad—she had looked last night, he slid his arm through hers and caught her hand.

Anthea returned the affectionate, eloquent squeeze. "Is this true?" she whispered.

He made a small sound of laughter. "It is, you know. I doubt it every time, but wait till the clock strikes. Where do you like to be?"

"I can never decide. From the high bit of the pier you get sea as well as harbour but not so much detail."

"Plenty of time," said Lawrence. "We can do everything."

As they turned to walk round to the pier the church clock cleared its throat with a portentous, self-important noise and the first stroke of twelve rang out. Anthea started and he pressed her arm reassuringly. She was fairly jittery, he thought. Not much wonder, really, and he began talking about the boats to take her mind off it; hoping a little anxiously that seeing them go—a sight which could bring a lump to the cheeriest throat—wouldn't make her emotional. . . . nine, ten, eleven, TWELVE, said the clock and it was Monday. As if the final stroke set some mechanism in motion, the harbour came to life. Lights appeared in the windows and one after another doors opened and men came out, still with something of the Sunday quiet about them or consideration for sleeping children.

The first engine spoke. Lights sprang up, brilliant in the dusk and reflected softly in the water, the red and green navigation lights and small yellow stars on the mastheads: and the air was full of the subdued, pulsing tonk-a-tonk-atonk with no other sound to rival or disturb it.

The two spectators reached the pier and paused. *Crimond* went out close under their feet, the crew glancing up at them incuriously. *Guiding Light* followed and they moved along to stand beside *Ocean Harvester* and *Embrace* as the men went aboard and made ready to go. But lovely as the scene of preparation and departure within the harbour was, the best thing to see was when the boats passed the point and took to the open sea: gathering speed and drawing away till only the triangle of lights, yellow, red and green, could be seen and then only the tiny masthead stars on the blackness of the water.

"Let's go on," said Lawrence, and as he spoke Anthea heard quick footsteps, not hushed like their own but confident of their right to be there. A hairy body came with a quiet patter of paws to brush against her leg and the footsteps stopped.

"Hallo," said Jock. "So here you both are."

Without a word Anthea turned and they walked slowly on along the pier, Lawrence looked after them and hung back, allowing himself to wallow for a little in a sense of ill-usage. He was not, he told himself, fool enough to be jealous. He knew his place and was, indeed, well content with it. But it would have been nice, on this occasion, not to be making a third. *Lea-Rig* just below him was beginning to move. He stood looking down at her, stirred as he always was by the small craft and the five men taking her away into the vast emptiness: wondering what they would see and do out there before they tied up again. Dan came and looked with him, keeping him company since neither of them was wanted elsewhere, and as *Lea-Rig* went through the gap Lawrence, restored to good humour, strolled on again and Dan made a cursory inspection of a heap of lobster pots which sometimes sheltered a rat.

"Anthea," Jock was saying, "I'm sorry. I was a savage. Can you possibly forg—"

"Sh!" said Anthea. "*Not that word.* But—did you mean it?"

He looked down at her. "What? The savagery? Yes—I'm afraid I did."

"It wasn't just a deliberate rocket?"

"Lord!" said Jock. "No! Far from it. I hardly remember—I hate to think what may have burst out—but I meant every word of it."

"That's all right, then," she said. "I thought so."

Jock held out his hand. She brought hers out of her coat pocket and gave it into a warm grasp, and they stood close together watching the boats go out. When the last had gone they walked to the point of the pier and round the railed cat-walk under the light where they were hidden from the land, and watched the last triangles diminish, become single pin-points and vanish. Neither of them said anything till Jock asked:

"Do you remember telling me that this was what you would like to see when you're dying? I've never seen the boats go out at night without hearing your voice saying it."

"Haven't you really?" said Anthea and silence fell again. "I wish," she said presently, "that I could think of something memorable to say now. Something that would express everything. All this and heaven too has been done, unfortunately. You'd think a couple of writers, one famous, might manage it."

Jock looked sympathetic. "No dice?" She shook her head. "Well—are you happy?"

"Yes, I'm happy. Are you?"

"Yes," said Jock. "And that really covers everything, I think. It'll do."

Also published by

Greyladies

THE GLENVARROCH GATHERING
by Susan Pleydell

The advertisement in *The Times*

> *"Glenvarroch. Scottish family with large house on West Highland sea loch welcomes paying guests for summer holidays"*

attracted an oddly assorted group: a schoolboy, an American couple, a schoolmistress from the Midlands, a young man writing a novel and an exotic brother and sister from London. But after a while the charm of the visitors begins to pall, and the C.I.D. warn Professor McKechnie that his daughter Fiona may be in danger.

Originally published in 1960

A YOUNG MAN'S FANCY
by Susan Pleydell

The spring term is always disaster-prone, but this one at Ledenham School surpasses itself. The Headmaster's invaluable secretary collapses with appendicitis and has to be replaced by Oonagh – 'Swooner' to the boys; a young master's fancy, lightly turning to thoughts of love, causes a major crisis at Governors' level; the Headmaster's daughter Alison's romance is all but blighted by avid public scrutiny and comment.

We meet several of the same characters from *Summer Term*, decent chaps and the right sort of girls, plus a few outright cads to give added spice.

Originally published in 1962

BRIGHOUSE HOTEL
by Susan Pleydell

When Clunie, homesick for the hills, returns to Glen Torran after four years in London, she finds a job as temporary receptionist at the Brighouse Hotel, the Mountain Rescue centre for the area and the meeting place, or 'howf', of the local and visiting climbing fraternity. She finds everyone exactly the same – only more so. No one has forgotten that both Keith Finlay and Malcolm Graham, now climbing partners planning an expedition to the Hindu Kush, had been her boyfriends, or that she had always fought with Pat McKechnie, and speculation is rife.

Originally published in 1977.